BLOOMING
INTO LIFE

BLOOMING INTO LIFE

Kristie Booker

to my dad

ACKNOWLEDGMENTS

Thank you to Rebecca Rosen for sharing your heavenly gift and connecting me with the messages I needed to hear.

My brilliant writing coach, Sara Connell, helped to make my dream of writing and publishing a book a reality. Thank you for your wisdom, encouragement and for guiding me through the final drafts.

Thank you to my editors Tricia Callahan and Elizabeth Wetmore for making every page of this book better, and to Elizabeth-Anne Stewart and Melanie Bishop for reading and commenting on my first drafts. Thanks to Melinda Martin for your quick turn around and for always being available to answer all of my questions, and to Mary Ann Smith for your patience.

I am grateful to the late Patricia Brooks whose generous and unexpected gift helped launch my writing career. I am grateful to my parents for always loving, supporting and believing in me.

Finally, and most importantly, all my love and thanks to my husband, Brant, and my children, Will and Cam for your absolute belief in me. This book would never have happened without the three of you cheering me on.

PROLOGUE

Colleen shivered as a gust of wind shot through her cashmere sweater. Her fingers froze against the cast aluminum lid on the mailbox. She was glad she had listened to Jay and selected the wall-mounted mailbox instead of the oversized staked type she had wanted along the walkway near her rosebushes. She gripped the bundle of mail and pushed the front door shut against another burst of bone-chilling wind.

A large, glossy square envelope decorated with delicate textured leaves stood out from the bills and catalogs of children's clothing. Two stamps with pictures of tulips were pressed against the top right corner. Her name and address had been carefully scripted in black calligraphy, taking up most of the front side of the envelope. Raised letters spelling Harborview Country Club and the return address filled the backside just above the seal. Finally, she had received her invitation to the Spring Fashion Show. For weeks, she'd worried that the invitation had been lost in the mail or even worse, not sent at all.

Colleen tossed the other pieces of mail on the kitchen island between her freshly opened can of Diet Coke and the white-lidded paper cup that had contained a large vanilla latte. She tore through the heavy cardstock. White roses swirled up each side of the invitation.

Harborview Country Club cordially invites you to attend the Forty-Fourth Annual Spring Fashion Show — featuring Raina Rose. The event will be held on Friday, the first of April at noon. RSVP by the eighteenth of March. Spots are limited!

Today was March 17. Colleen dialed the club and was put on hold. While she waited, she thought of her doctor's appointment scheduled on Friday, April 1. She would have to reschedule. She wasn't missing the fashion show for the second year in a row.

The club receptionist finally returned to the line. "I'm sorry, Mrs. Adler, but the event is full."

"Were the invitations mailed late?" Colleen said.

"I sent them three weeks ago," the woman said. "Would you like me to add you to the waiting list?"

"But I just got mine," Colleen said. "Who's in charge this year?" She already knew the answer to that question — her mother-in-law, Dinah, and her porcelain-faced lackeys, Ashley Barr and Victoria Heller.

The same thing had happened last year, and Colleen had given the three women the benefit of the doubt. She believed them when they blamed the post office for the delay. This year, however, Colleen knew her invitation was sent late on purpose. Dinah didn't want her there.

Two months earlier at the club's Winter Luncheon, Colleen's mother-in-law had stood before a dining room full of posh women, striking in her cream-colored Raina Rose tailored jacket with a matching wool box pleated skirt. Her glossy red lip color popped against the wavy silver hair she wore in a short bob. Just as the waitstaff began to serve the first course, an endive salad topped with blue cheese and walnuts, Dinah clinked her spoon against her martini glass. She enthusiastically announced that Raina Rose was the featured designer at this year's spring fashion show. The women at the luncheon were exhilarated to learn they would be getting a first look at the spring line. For the rest of the afternoon, pomegranate martinis flowed and the women gushed about wearing the designer's beautiful cocktail dresses to the club's annual Fourth of July Gala. It was an unspoken rule that the Harborview women wore a dress purchased from the spring show to the annual summer celebration. Dinah handled the problem of the women all wanting the same dress by holding an auction, with the money going to a charity of Dinah's choice.

Colleen's face flushed as she remembered that January luncheon. She had been the first of the eight women sitting around her table to receive a slice of flourless chocolate cake. The small salad, three scallops and small mound of green beans hadn't been enough. She realized only as she finished the last bite that not another woman had touched the cake. She ran her tongue around her lips. She was certain she had chocolate crumbs smeared somewhere. Their table was so far from the bathroom that Colleen feared she would trip if she tried to go check.

Except for the quick glances from the women, their heads were all turned away from Colleen. She turned to her right, making an effort to join in on Sloan and Claudia's conversation.

"I've got to lose at least five pounds before April. I refuse to go up to a size six," Sloan said.

"I hit six last year and it was awful," Claudia said with her eyes carefully fixed on Sloan. "Two workouts a day and a three-week juice cleanse finally got me back to normal." She lengthened all the words to emphasize the stress she had endured. When Claudia's eyes shifted briefly to Colleen, her face turned pink and she widened her eyes at Sloan. She brought her napkin up to her lips to hide her smirk. Colleen hadn't seen a size six since before she became pregnant with her oldest daughter eight years ago.

"I have to use the ladies' room," Claudia said.

"I'll join you." Sloan stood to follow Claudia.

The memory brought the same sick feeling to Colleen's stomach as it had that afternoon. She remembered wanting to run to the women's restroom to vomit up the cake. She stared at the beautiful invitation. What if the dresses only came in a size six or under? What would she wear to the club's Fourth of July Gala? Dinah had made the rules perfectly clear — you don't have a dress from the spring show, you don't exist at the gala.

ONE

April 8, 2011

Colleen couldn't believe it when she enlarged the picture on her phone. She wasn't even Jay's type. Then again, Colleen wasn't either when she and Jay Adler first met. The Harborview Country Club women all wore Loro Piana cashmere twin set cardigans and pearls. Farm girls from Brockville, Illinois, didn't marry wealthy lawyers from Chicago.

Colleen O'Brien Adler sat in her silver Range Rover as the Chicago spring rain pounded across the top of her car. The forecaster promised the series of rainy days would be over by tomorrow. Colleen hoped he was right about the sunny days ahead. She pressed her foot on the brake, keeping the car in drive as she waited her turn to pull up. Her two daughters, Mabel and Chloe, would be exiting the large wooden doors of Northside Day School any minute.

The Wyatt Art Gallery had posted a picture of Jay and a mysterious blonde. The woman looked like the type to be friends with Jay's sister-in-law, Alexis. She and Jay stood side by side, each holding a glass of champagne, with their heads tilted, looking at one another. They stood as though they were a couple, as if they were one, waiting for people to stop by to say hello. The woman was either tall or had on high heels; Colleen couldn't tell from the picture, but she was practically looking Jay in the eye. Her long, messy hair looked as though she had been at the beach all day. She probably had been, considering they were in Los Angeles. The gallery was actually in Beverly Hills, but the ripped skinny jeans, chunky cropped sweater hanging off her shoulder and rings covering her thumb, middle and ring fingers were proof that she was a product of LA, not Beverly Hills.

Jay reciprocated the woman's gaze with a charming smile that he hadn't shared with Colleen in a long time. Colleen always thought if Jay left her it would be for someone more attractive, but mostly, someone more refined. This woman was definitely attractive but there was nothing refined about her. Before Colleen, Jay had always dated elegant women. His brother Eli had been the one to fall in love with an artist. Jay may have followed Eli to law school and then joined his law firm, but to fall for an artsy woman would have been a stretch for Jay.

Colleen stared at the phone screen, twirling her hair around her fingers, as was her habit when she felt anxious about something. She had thought it was odd when Jay mentioned he was going to Alexis's gallery for a show. As far as she knew, he had never stepped foot in Wyatt Galleries. He had never shown any interest in art. Now, after seeing the picture, his current interest made sense.

THE ALARM TRILLED. SIX A.M. Colleen nudged Jay to hit "snooze." As if by instinct, he stretched out an arm from under the covers and groped for the alarm clock. Then, without so much as a groan, he was under the covers again, sleeping blissfully. She wasn't sure what time he had gotten in, but she was relieved to wake up at some wee hour of the night to see him lying next to her. For once, she was able to fall back to sleep. Most other nights she stared at the ceiling. The extra sleep made her eyes feel as though they had been wiped with honey. The need to see her husband in their bed forced her to pry the swollen skin open.

Colleen brought her arm up under her pillow and shifted to her side so she could stare at Jay's backside. She longed to be on the other side of him, nestled into his warm body. She wanted to feel his breath up against her, wanted to be close enough to sort through his stale deodorant and capture the hint of rosemary that maybe still lingered from his shampoo. She stared at the distinct tan line on his neck. The thought of all the beautiful women he was around in New York most weeks, and in LA this past week, made her stomach twist. The Facebook picture was now permanently engrained in her mind. Were there others? As much as she wanted to know who the woman from the art gallery was, Colleen couldn't bring herself to shake Jay awake and ask. She simply did not feel strong enough to handle the heartache of knowing the truth.

The salt-and-pepper curls that formed around the back of his head and flipped out over his ears were a sign of a busy week. Jay got a haircut every two weeks to prevent such a thing from happening. Colleen loved it when his hair was longer. She thought his curls made him look more youthful. He disagreed. He felt he was taken more seriously at his firm without the curls.

The alarm rang again and Jay tapped the top of the clock again, easily slipping back into a cozy slumber. He had not even noticed when Colleen began setting the alarm an hour earlier on January second, vowing to rise every day and run three miles, even though she was not a runner, never had been. But she'd been filled with hope that the early-morning exercise would help her lose some of the weight she had gained, or, at the very least, not gain any more. But her body wouldn't cooperate. She hadn't made it to the treadmill once.

The original twenty-five pounds had stuck around after she had Chloe. The additional thirty pounds snuck up out of nowhere. Dr. Bradley said her sluggish thyroid was to blame, but Colleen was still waiting for the newly prescribed Levothyroxine to do its magic and solve things. She had a "condition." Taking medicine was a forward step. Every day, she told herself she was trying.

A new sound emerged from the kitchen. The house alarm chirped. Their housekeeper, Maria, wasn't supposed to start until eight a.m. Colleen flung her side of the comforter on top of Jay. He didn't budge. The late-night flight home from Los Angeles left him exhausted. Colleen still needed time to hide the laundry from Maria. Clothes littered the floor. With Jay's middle of the night arrival, she could only imagine the condition of his closet.

Pulling a pair of black control pants from her shelf, she prepared for the battle between her growing thighs and the waistband of the pants. A deep breath was required before finishing the processes of squeezing the remaining flesh into her matching black body-shaping shirt. The desired slimming effect far outweighed the discomfort, but the energy it took to squish her body into a social safety zone felt like a workout. The required long, dark cardigan would have to wait until the sweating subsided.

She glanced up at the Raina Rose dress she had purchased last week after her appointment with Dr. Bradley. According to the sales associate at Neiman Marcus, the navy-blue silk dress with hand-embroidered silvery-white stars hadn't arrived in time for Harborview's Spring Fashion Show. Neither Dinah nor her minions would have seen it. The glistening stars sparkled against the reflection of the lights overhead. It was the perfect dress for the club's Fourth of July Gala. The dress would draw the kind of attention she needed to regain the social approval of the club. The women at Harborview believed they had seen the entire Raina Rose spring cocktail dress collection. Everyone would wonder where she got it. And how. She felt sorry for the fury that Dinah would deliver to Neiman Marcus's sales department for excluding this particular dress from the show. She didn't even want to think about how many pounds she needed to lose before the zipper would close.

Feeling like an overfed turtle with her head, feet and arms popped out from its shell, Colleen quickly gathered the dirty clothes that littered the floor from one closet to the next.

Regardless of how often she told Maria not to do the laundry, if Maria saw dirty clothes, she would wash them. Colleen had done her best to learn a little Spanish so she could communicate with Maria, but it wasn't enough. She never had the right words. One of the few phrases that she learned was "*No lava ropa, por favor*" but it was of no use. Maria would press her thick eyebrows together and shake her head before responding with a chuckle, "*Ropa sucia, Señora.*"

Once she caught Maria putting the dry cleaning pile into the washing machine. Several of Jay's custom-made suits narrowly escaped being ruined. Maria collected whatever she saw on the floor and put it in the washer, along with the bedding and towels.

Despite these communication challenges, the Gonzalez family had become part of the Adler family and Colleen could not imagine life without them. She kept Maria's favorite butterscotch candies in a bowl on the entry table and her Guatemalan black SerendipiTea in an airtight opaque ceramic container in the pantry. She admired Maria's courage in packing up her pregnant daughter Mia and moving to the United States in search of a better life. Maria kept their house cleaned. Mia and Mia's teenage daughter Gabby babysat anytime the Adlers called.

Colleen was running later than usual and frustrated for letting her schedule get out of hand again, especially with Jay being home to witness. She took a quick glance at her reflection in the full-length mirror. She did her best to look beyond her growing body, swollen eyes and puffy face and, instead, focused on her hair. These days, her hair was the only thing she could count on looking good. Her life had changed the day her hairdresser, Sandy, introduced her to the Keratin Treatment. Her wild, frizzy curls had seen their last day. Now she spent every Tuesday and Friday morning at the SS Beauty Bar getting her hair professionally washed, dried and styled. Her long, smooth locks were, she thought some days, the only thing she did not hate about herself.

"Can you lock the door behind you?" Jay mumbled as Colleen walked out. "Tell Maria to skip our room today."

Like speaking to Maria would result in anything, Colleen thought. Colleen stared down at the nickel grey geometric patterned runner that stretched the full distance of the long narrow hallway as she made her way toward Mabel and Chloe's bedroom. Her mind raced through her growing to-do list. She still needed to make a list for Al, the handyman who was scheduled to come that afternoon. She also needed to return Pedro's call. He had left two voicemails trying to schedule the spring yard work and her container plantings. She had noticed yesterday that she was the only one on their street who didn't have any spring flowers planted. The windows needed to be cleaned, too. They looked terrible but Colleen kept forgetting to call the window cleaning company.

"Mabel, wake up! Chloe, wake up! It's Friday, last day of school for the week. We're already behind." Colleen noticed the sweetness of the little girls' sleepiness as they buried under their pink cherry blossom duvet comforters. Her accusatory tone left her chest heavy. After all, it wasn't their fault that she was just now waking them up.

Heading back down the hall toward the spiral staircase that led to the kitchen, Colleen found Maria in the upstairs laundry room, putting clothes that had been sitting in the washer for two days into the dryer. "No Maria," Colleen yelled.

Maria looked to Colleen for more direction. "Señora?"

Colleen tugged open the dryer door, pulling out the various leggings, panties and baby doll dresses. She stuffed them back in the washing machine.

Maria shook her head in confusion. Putting wet clothes from the washer into the dryer was a perfectly logical thing to do, but the communication barrier was a complication Colleen didn't have time for. She still needed to pack lunches and make breakfast for the girls.

"Mommy!" Chloe's muffled voice came from downstairs.

Colleen walked into the kitchen to find Chloe's voice coming from inside the pantry. She stood engulfed by the empty pantry holding her opened Hello Kitty lunch box. Five-year-old Chloe gave Colleen a glimpse of Jay as a child. She envied her daughter's soft smooth curls.

As was to be expected, Chloe stood with her pigtails lopsided and was wearing her "Chloe-fit," as Mabel called her outfits. She wore a different variation of the same outfit every day— a baby doll dress covered in a floral pattern, with striped or polka-dot leggings underneath and shiny, hot-pink Mary Jane shoes. Since turning three, Chloe had insisted on doing her own hair into pigtails and wearing that particular outfit, which drove Dinah crazy.

Dinah was appalled that Colleen let the girls wear what they wanted. And Colleen did her best to ignore Dinah. Pleasing her was difficult. The girls had a great eye for color and putting outfits together. Everyone but Dinah commented on how cute they looked, and Colleen found relief in the girls' ability to get dressed without any help.

She crossed the kitchen and opened the large built-in Sub-Zero refrigerator. Condiments were scattered across the two top shelves, an expired gallon of whole milk sat next to a Ziploc bag containing two slices of four-day-old pizza and a moldy bowl of macaroni and cheese sat alone on the bottom shelf. Colleen realized that she had forgotten to go to the grocery store.

"Today's lunch will be chips, Oreos and a juice box," Colleen said as she bent down to Chloe's soft, round face and forced a smile for her daughter's benefit.

Chloe looked up at her mother with the corners of her lips turned down.

Colleen let out a breath as Chloe put the chips, cookies and drink into her Hello Kitty lunch box and then into her Hello Kitty backpack.

Colleen wondered where Mabel was. She still needed to figure something out for breakfast. Back to the pantry, she was relieved to find two Pop-Tart boxes shoved to the back of the bottom shelf. One box was empty but the other one had a package left. There was no time for the toaster; the girls would have to eat them cold. Thankfully, there were still two unopened chocolate milk boxed drinks on the kitchen table from the night before. She bagged the Pop-Tarts and chocolate milks so that the girls could eat in the car.

"Mabel!" Colleen climbed back up spiral staircase. She felt the sweat streaming down the skin tunnels created by her tight top and pooling in the areas where skin was pushed together too tightly for the liquid to escape. She took several deep breaths and fought the urge to scream. Finding Mabel half-dressed, sitting on the large flower-shaped pink rug covering the girls' wooden bedroom floor and playing with a Barbie doll, caused the fury to become so intense that she couldn't control her explosive outburst. "Why aren't you dressed?"

Lower lip quivering, Mabel half directed her tearful eyes up at her mother. "Can't find any underwear in my drawer."

Looking down into Mabel's eyes was like looking into a mirror. Colleen couldn't remember if her eyes were ever as big or as blue as Mabel's, but her ginger-colored frizzy hair and fair, freckled skin were exactly like Colleen's. The two of them were a stark contrast to Jay and Chloe.

Colleen's heart sank as she realized that Mabel's underwear was in the load that she had instructed Maria to re-wash. From the sound of it, the laundry was mid-cycle. A desperate search through Mabel's underwear drawer proved useless. Opening Chloe's drawer, she was relieved to find one pair left. They were a little small but they would do.

Mabel's eyes pleaded with her mother. She bit her lip as she shook her head no.

"You have two choices," said Colleen grimly. "Wear a pair of sopping wet underwear out of the washing machine, or wear a pair of your sister's clean, dry underwear."

Tears ran down Mabel's cheeks as she looked down at the floor.

Colleen's waistband cut into her stomach as she squatted down next to Mabel. "I'm sorry, honey," Colleen whispered. "Mommy promises this won't happen again."

Mabel pushed the attempted hug away. "You always say that!"

Colleen stood outside of the bedroom, out of Mabel's sight. She hoped Jay hadn't heard Mabel yelling. She was grateful for the long hallway between their rooms.

Colleen got her own tears under control and stepped back in. "We need to hurry, sweetheart."

English wasn't necessary for Maria to understand what was

going on. She shook her head at Colleen in a scolding manner as she passed by in the hallway.

Colleen knew she was heading for the girls' bedroom to comfort Mabel. More and more, Maria was the one able to comfort her daughters. Between the small amount of Spanish the girls had at school and the time they spent with the Gonzalez family, they seemed to understand quite a bit of what Maria said.

"I hate my mom," Mabel said.

Hearing those words pierced Colleen's heart. Even her eight-year-old daughter hated the lazy, forgetful person she had become. Colleen would never have been permitted to speak this way. No matter what Mary Ann looked like, did or didn't do, if Colleen had said she hated her own mother she would have been sent out to clean the chicken coop, turn the compost pile, and pull weeds from the fence line. She stood in the hallway listening to Maria's soothing voice, the rolling r's and the cha-cha sounds she did not know but Mabel would understand.

The girls munched the dry Pop-Tarts without speaking. After the yelling and racing around, Colleen felt lucky that they were only a few minutes late for school.

As they clambered out of the car, she did her best to be loving and cheerful. "Have a great day. Mommy loves you."

Chloe gave her a little wave, but Mabel pursed her lips and ignored her.

Colleen watched them run up the stone staircase and disappear through the main entrance. She regretted not getting out of bed earlier. She thought of the disgusted look Maria had given her in the hallway. Maria was right. Her girls deserved better. She had promised them, promised herself things would be different, but they hadn't. They just seemed to be getting worse.

THE CHICKADEES AND BLACKBIRDS TWEETED in harmony as they celebrated the blue sky that finally banished the grey of winter. The recent warm temperatures had brought out the green shadows surrounding the edges of bare branches and the sharp green tips cutting their way through the thawing ground.

Pink hydrangeas appeared to be the trend this year. Their magnificence sat in the center of the deeply colored pansies. The pussy willow branches brought the eye up while the English ivy gave balance by vining over the edges of the various rectangular window boxes and round urns. The price of a Chicago spring frost ruining the beautiful early blooms was a price worth paying in order to get some color after a long and dreary winter. The abundance of container gardens and densely planted tulips and daffodils made spring one of the most beautiful times in Chicago. All around Colleen, Chicagoans flocked to outdoor cafes, meandered down the sidewalks with babies in strollers and went running along the lake. Colleen's own breath felt discordant. She felt only the slightest uplift from the sunshine and trappings of the new season.

When Colleen had first moved to Chicago, she found the planting of spring flowers a new concept. Outside of the changing weather, the only signs of spring in Brockville had been the absence of the farmers hanging around town drinking coffee, seeing the fields full of tractors and combines and getting stuck behind those same tractors and combines on the country roads and adjacent highways. Manure was the scent of spring in Brockville, a far cry from the sweet-smelling blooms in the city. Although Colleen's family had their share of lilac bushes and peony bushes growing in their yards, they went unnoticed during planting season. They were busy getting the crops planted in the fields, managing the birthing of farm animals, and getting the gardens tilled and planted with fruits and vegetables for the summer ahead.

Colleen knew she should take advantage of the unusual weather and go for a long walk, but that was the last thing she wanted to do. Her stomach was grumbling, she felt pressure building in her lower intestine and her head was aching. Constipation was one of the problems that Dr. Bradley said would go away. Having been constipated on a regular basis since having Chloe, Colleen accepted this as normal. Drinking the miracle potion Smooth and EZ every night before bed combined with a Diet Coke first thing in the morning usually did the trick. She had been out of both for the past couple of days, so a strong cup or two of coffee on an empty stomach was her only hope. She didn't have the energy for any more judgment from Maria and she was not prepared for a conversation with Jay. A restaurant bathroom was her only option.

Molly's Café always lifted Colleen's spirit. She couldn't help but indulge in one of Molly's buttery scones. The roughly square-cut scones reminded Colleen of her mother's handmade biscuits but were even more delicious with Molly's addition of sweet fruits, lemon zest and some with cinnamon, nutmeg and cloves. They were the best in Chicago. Molly's was also casual, much too casual and ordinary to interest the likes of the ladies from Harborview Country Club. Colleen felt safe there, no showering or makeup required. Even better, Molly's was right next to the grocery store.

"Sit down over there by the window, doll, I'll get you a coffee," Brenda yelled across the small room.

Colleen took the only table available. She loved the lacy curtains that hung on the bottom half of all the windows. They reminded her of her parents' old farmhouse.

Brenda brought over the promised cup of coffee. "How are those precious little girls? Bet they're ready for summer, aren't they?" Her raspy voice sounded as though she had been smoking her entire life. Not giving Colleen a chance to answer, she yelled at a man across the room, "Hold your horses, Phil!" She pulled a pen out of the dark part of her otherwise yellow hair. "What are you having this morning, sweetie?"

Brenda's rush flustered Colleen. She had planned to say "Yogurt Parfait" but instead she said, "Pancakes and bacon."

"I'll sneak you a scone while you wait," Brenda said.

Sipping her coffee, Colleen thought about how much energy she used to have before she became a mother, before her thyroid malfunctioned. She used to be eager to do whatever was necessary to fill the role of becoming Mrs. Jay Adler. She volunteered to help with charity luncheons, helped plan the club's New Year's Eve celebration and played paddle tennis on Sunday afternoons with other couples at the club. She had all the energy in the world to devote to her mission of being accepted by Dinah and her entourage, and of being the complete wife Jay deserved. She used to look forward to sex on the weekend.

She thought about the lunch her mother-in-law had scheduled for the two of them right after she and Jay became engaged. "If there is any chance that you are going to fit in at Harborview Country Club, you are going to have to make some changes," Dinah said over lunch. "To begin with, you need a stylist. I already spoke to Lyla. She's been my stylist for years. She said she would squeeze you in. As a favor to me, of course."

Colleen did everything she could think of to win Dinah's approval. She patiently went along with what she was told to wear, how to style her hair and makeup, and what color she should be painting her fingernails and toenails. According to Lyla (Dinah), a respectable woman should wear sheer pink on her fingers for everyday and bright red on her toes. Color could be worn on the fingers, but it must be a classic color and must match the toes.

"And for God's sake," Lyla told her, "if any nail becomes chipped, do not walk around with it like that, go into the salon and get it fixed!"

Jay had told her on more than one occasion to ignore his mother. "Stay true to who you are," he said. "If I wanted a standard country club wife, I would have married one of them." He didn't care if his mother was happy and he wished Colleen didn't care either. Colleen felt different. She wanted to fit in. She got frustrated with Jay for not understanding. He had always been rich, handsome and connected. He had never been in a situation where he was the one left out.

Colleen had thought things would be different after she

changed her hair, clothes and choice of fingernail polish. But Dinah was only friendly when Jay was by Colleen's side. Only when the girls were born did Dinah nod to Colleen. She wasn't warm, but being visibly recognized made Colleen warm in her gaze. The other women at the club followed along with the club queen and began to say hello to Colleen. But as Colleen's weight went up, Dinah began making comments.

"Victoria and Ashley have been doing cardio workouts with the new tennis pro. If I were younger, I would be right there beside them. Their arms and legs look amazing," Dinah had said.

More recently, she said, "Well, maybe if you exercised more, you'd look better."

Other women snickered or ignored Colleen. Lyla had lost faith in her too.

"Your size is out of control. You are going to have to go into Neiman's and buy black control pants with matching control tops. Get a handful of cashmere cardigans that are long enough to cover most of you," Lyla had said, speaking so fast Colleen could barely keep up. "I call it outfit UMWIG, which stands for Until My Weight Is Gone," she said. "Don't call me until you get yourself back to at least a size 12."

Colleen hadn't spoken to Lyla for two years. She hoped Lyla would be there to see her at the Fourth of July Gala. Lyla would wonder who helped Colleen get the Raina Rose dress. She would assume Colleen hired a new stylist.

Smells of maple syrup and bacon curled under Colleen's nose. Her stomach grumbled as she looked down at the stack of three pancakes covering the oval plate that sat before her. "Thanks, Brenda," Colleen said. She took a bite of a meaty strip of bacon while she waited for the maple syrup to soak into the spongy pancakes. She thought about how she got out of bed in the morning counting the hours until she could get back in. She always felt better once she filled up on sugar and caffeine. By the time lunch rolled around, she was exhausted again. Without a latte in the afternoon she would not have the energy to get through the evening. Once she got the girls home from school, she watched the clock until it struck a reasonable time for a glass of wine. Dr. Bradley had suggested anti-depressants. For now, she held out hope that the Levothyroxine would eventually help.

Savoring her last bite of the salty bacon mixed with the sweet maple and notes of vanilla in the pancakes, she felt a wave of sadness wash over her. She found herself, once again, missing her mom. Their relationship had changed after she left Brockville.

TWO

1986
Brockville, IL

Colleen woke to the sound of a fly buzzing in her ear and a trickle of sweat running down her neck. She flipped over to give her backside a turn with the summer sun coming in through her bedroom window. The pillow she placed over her head gave her darkness and protection from the persistent insect. The screeching and shuddering sound of her dad's gas-powered lawn mower ended her moment of peace. Whether she liked it or not, the first of many hot and sticky days had begun.

The family's best fan was mounted in the kitchen window, humming along and doing its best to deliver a breeze over the kitchen table. Like her bedroom, the kitchen was drenched in sunlight. Despite the fan's best efforts, the heat lingered.

Stepping over the missing floorboards of her old farmhouse's wraparound porch, Colleen plopped her tired, thirteen-year-old body onto the porch swing. Giving a strong push with her legs, she leaned her head against the wooden back and enjoyed the temporary breeze. She did her best to drown out the noise of the mower by shifting her focus on the moaning sound of the old rusted chains above her.

Colleen hated the old farmhouse she lived in with her parents and little brother, Johnny. She wanted to live in town like her friends. They had air-conditioning and cable television, and they got to see each other all summer. She felt trapped out at her family's legendary farm.

Begging to move was of no use. Her dad was locked into the family promise of keeping the house and his portion of the farm in the O'Brien family. His grandfather, the original John Robert O'Brien, built the house after he inherited the farmland and married her great-grandmother, Mabel.

Everyone in Brockville knew the story of the lucky Irishman who climbed off a boat from the Atlantic and found his way to the barn of an aging, childless couple in Brockville, Illinois. The Irish teenager accepted the work, shelter and, ultimately, the gift of the couple's farm when they passed away.

Just when he thought he couldn't get any luckier, the neighbor's only child blossomed into the most beautiful young lady he had ever seen. John Robert O'Brien began courting Mabel Bower and they quickly fell in love. He married the most sought-after girl in the area who just happened to come with a large chunk of land. The union of John and Mabel made the O'Brien farm the largest in the area.

On Herbert Hoover's urging, Colleen's great-grandfather gladly increased his wheat production. He was happy to do anything he could to help his beloved new country in the war effort. With the price of wheat rising, John did the American thing; he borrowed money to buy more land and new farm machinery. He embraced his new mortgage with pride.

The war ended. The European battleground turned back into the agriculture-producing land it once was. With Europe and Russia no longer needing America's help to eat, the price of wheat dropped drastically. The world had an over-production problem. John, along with most other American farmers, did everything he could to keep up with the bank payments. He continued to plant wheat across his doubled acreage, praying every year to make just enough. Year after year, "just enough" didn't happen. With easy credit from the bank, John hobbled through the rest of the 1920s growing deeper and deeper in debt.

With many farmers forced to sell and either become tenant farmers or find work in town, John O'Brien was one of the few farmers in Brockville to survive, at least until the stock market crash in October 1929. The collapse of the economy created panic among Americans, and the people living in Brockville were no different. Lines of people formed outside of Brockville Farmer's Bank demanding their money. The bank had no choice but to call in their loans from the farmers. The farmers, including John, had no money. He was forced into foreclosure. He watched his hard work and luck vanish underneath him. The devastation turned into depression. His farm would be auctioned to the highest bidder and he was powerless to stop it. The once lucky Irishman now thought of himself as an Irish idiot.

When the day of the auction came, John watched both friends and strangers line up as the auctioneer began the bidding. Thinking they were there to buy his farm left him feeling betrayed. These same people had told him how much they valued his hard work when they awarded him Brockville's Farmer of the Year for the past three years. He was always quick with a joke and a helping hand when needed. But then the men he'd worked with, helped and served over the years began blocking the bidders so no one could bid on the farm. He watched in dismay at what seemed like a cruel joke until he saw the president of Brockville Farmer's Bank motion him over to the bidding table. They remained a blockade against any other bidders. He bought his farm back at the opening bid of $5.35.

The O'Brien Farm became known as Farm Five-Thirty-Five. Colleen's grandpa, dad and uncles vowed to never forget how privileged they were to have the land. The four of them vowed to do everything in their power to keep it in their family.

Despite hearing the tale more times than Colleen could count, it wasn't until she saw a picture of her late great-grandmother Mabel as a young woman that the story took on a whole new meaning. She finally understood what everyone meant when they said she was a carbon copy of Mabel. Hours of quiet contemplation followed that discovery. Colleen struggled to understand how she could look identical to someone who lived through so much suffering.

The black-and-white photo didn't reveal her grandmother's hair and eye color, but there was no denying that Colleen got her mass of curly hair, as well as her big, almond-shaped eyes and turned-up nose, from Mabel O'Brien. This woman may have been considered beautiful back in the early 1900s, but those same looks weren't as kind to Colleen in the 1980s. Kids at school often made fun of her orange-colored hair that was usually big and frizzy. "Hey, big red, why don't you take your finger out of the light socket?" was a common taunt. If her looks weren't embarrassing enough, living in an old, out-of-date, falling-down farmhouse was. Colleen might be stuck looking like her great-grandmother, but she didn't want to live like her.

She did not hide her feelings about her looks; she did, however, hide the fact that she felt a special connection to the woman she had never met. She secretly wondered if she was a reincarnated version of Mabel. And if so, was she destined to have a life full of hardship? She prayed to God every day not to have the same destiny. She did not want to live on the farm her whole life.

Colleen felt guilty for having such bad thoughts about the house she lived in. She often felt sorry for the house. Unlike her deceased grandparents, the house had to continue to endure the misery of those living inside, often cussing its very existence. The house held a lot of heartache from the very beginning. In the early days, when it was newly built, looking the best it probably ever looked, it was filled with her great-grandparents' grief from losing their babies, one after the other. Her grandpa John had been born just in time for the Great Depression to begin. She supposed the house must have begun to deteriorate during the Depression the same way the people did.

After hearing her parents discuss whether or not they should rip up the worn linoleum floors in the kitchen, Colleen asked why linoleum had been laid over the hardwood floors in the first place. She learned that her grandparents were trying to modernize the house and came to realize that her house was 1950 modern. She found it interesting that the wood floors that were put in more than eighty years ago were able to outlast the modern enhancements.

She began to investigate what was original and what was "modern." She knew the bathroom was a modern addition. The fact that no one seemed to know for sure when it was added blew her mind. How could the day indoor plumbing came into their lives not be a momentous occasion, one that was celebrated and remembered? Colleen was certain that she would always remember the day she finally got cable television.

She was not the least bit surprised that their porch, porch swing and the old barn, which was basically falling down, were originals. She wondered why her dad told her that with so much pride. Those things along with their pea green "upgraded" kitchen were the very things Colleen was least proud of, and suffered the most embarrassment about. She grew tired of the kids on the school bus asking her if she ever thought the old barn might collapse on her when she walked in, or if anyone ever broke their ankle walking up and down the crumbling front steps. She was grateful that those kids never came inside to see her hideous kitchen; otherwise, they would probably ask her if the color of her kitchen ever made her throw up.

Colleen had been surprised to find out that the massive dining table was original to the house. It made her sad to think of her grandfather building the table with the intention of filling it with food for the large family he planned. Little did he know that he would barely be able to feed his one and only child in the coming years. The large brass chandelier that hung over the table wasn't original because there wasn't electricity when the house was built. Colleen couldn't get a straight answer on when it was added, but most of the family assumed her grandparents added it during the modernization period in the 1950s. Although it was tarnished and no longer worked, it was the nicest thing in their home. The lacey curtains that hung in the dining room made the room feel fancy and special. At one time, she knew, the room must have been really beautiful.

Colleen concluded that her grandpa and grandma O'Brien received the best the farm had to offer. The acres of debt-free, rich Midwestern soil had easily supported their three growing boys. Despite a flooding problem that began in the late 1960s, they made a nice living. Her grandma grew a garden, fed the farmhands and raised their boys.

By the time it came for Colleen's grandpa to hand down the farm to her dad and uncles, the flooding problem had extended over more acres. The reduction in acreage divided by the boys wasn't large enough to support any of the families on a single-income basis. Her grandpa felt as though he let his sons down by not being able to hand down a better piece of land. He remained hopeful that someday the area would stop flooding but, in the meantime, the farm wives would have to go to work outside of their homes.

Farm life had changed. It had become rare to find a farm wife at home, cooking for the men and raising the children. Colleen's mom found a job as a teller at The Brockville State Bank. Uncle Pat's wife, Linda, was a manager at Brockville Grain Store and her uncle Jimmy's wife, Susie, was an English teacher at Brockville High School. Times had changed and the younger generation accepted what had to be done to keep the farm going.

IT WAS THE FIRST DAY of summer. Colleen wished she could sleep in past eight a.m. Sleeping in would surely make her day go by faster. She wouldn't have to wait so long to call her best friend, Tara. Last summer, the girls began the routine of Colleen calling Tara every weekday at ten a.m. to wake her up in time to watch *The Price Is Right* followed by *The Young and the Restless*. They would then spend the next two hours on the phone together while they watched the two shows, making fun of the silly contestants on *The Price Is Right* and gossiping about the characters on *The Young and the Restless*. Colleen didn't love the shows quite as much as Tara, but she pretended to because that was the only thing they had to do together over the summer. She was grateful that her shows were on the same channel as her dad's beloved mid-day farm report. Otherwise, she would have been in trouble for moving the perfectly positioned rabbit ears on the TV that her dad had fixed to CBS.

Colleen sat in a wooden chair that she had pulled far enough away from the kitchen table that the stretched-out phone cord would reach. The phone's location wasn't ideal for talking and watching television, but with some maneuvering she was able to see the TV and feel a small breeze from the fan in the window. She rested her head against the phone as she waited for Tara to pick up. Finally, a groggy voice on the other end said, "Hello."

Colleen was thrilled to hear Tara's voice. She had been Colleen's best friend since first grade.

"Can you come over today?" Tara asked while they waited for *The Price Is Right* to start.

"I'll ask, but I doubt my dad will drive me in to town."

Colleen knew her dad would say no. They couldn't afford to waste gas on a trip to town.

After months of begging to go to town last summer, Colleen's parents finally gave in and allowed Colleen to spend the night with Tara. Colleen was beyond excited for the twenty-four-hour trip to town. Her dad pulled his dusty Chevy pickup truck up to the house for the three o'clock departure time. Colleen stood at the edge of their yard with her small overnight bag sitting on the ground next to her old bicycle, all cleaned up for the special occasion.

"You've got to make sure you pay attention," Colleen's father said. He shifted his focus away from the country road and toward his daughter. After riding in silence for most of the thirty-minute trip to town, her father decided to deliver a lecture. "You need to be careful on your bike. There're a lot of cars in town."

Colleen pressed her thumbnail into the quarter-sized mosquito bite on her thigh. "Okay." She didn't know why her dad always worried so much.

"I don't want you going all over town. You listen to Mrs. Meyers and be respectful of her rules," John said.

Colleen couldn't wait to get her bike out of the back and escape any more lectures.

John placed her bike in the yard next to Tara's. For the first time, Colleen realized how childish and old-fashioned her pink bike with cruiser type of handle bars and a long banana seat looked compared to Tara's shiny sky-blue ten-speed with the dropped handlebars wrapped in blue-and-white-striped tape.

"Bye, Daddy," Colleen said.

Mrs. Meyers answered the door appearing fresh and tan with her wet hair cut short, curly from a recent perm. The short shorts exposed her tan legs, something Colleen's mom would never wear. No sooner did Colleen say hello to Mrs. Meyers than Tara came around the corner. She was dressed much like her mom with short shorts, a matching tank top and tanned body. The two girls set off on their bikes the minute John pulled out of the driveway. Colleen looked down at her pale legs under the cut-off jean shorts as she pedaled. There was nothing about her as perfect or as pretty as Tara. Colleen's hair was in the usual tangled mess while Tara's blond ponytail lay in a silky mass behind her as she sped up ahead.

Tara sped forward, past the crosswalk. Colleen cranked her legs hard, pressing her flip-flops into the metal pads. Her old bike required double the strokes as Tara's ten-speed.

Colleen followed Tara as she zigzagged through the leisurely traffic on the town square and expertly popped her bike up over the curb at the edge of the park. Colleen wondered why Tara didn't ride over to the sidewalk without a curb but she followed along doing her best to keep up. Tara rode her bike full speed toward the basketball court where Wes Fischer and Tony Lang were playing against two boys Colleen didn't know. They were a year older than Colleen and Tara; they would be freshmen in high school in the fall. Wes dribbled the ball past the other boys for a scoring lay-up. Tara screeched to a stop just under the basket. Colleen trailed behind her a little slower. She wasn't prepared for a bold entrance and definitely didn't want to draw attention to her pink, little girl bike.

The boys stopped their game when Tara jumped off her seat. Tony set the ball down as he took a big slug from his water bottle. The two unknown boys sunk down against a huge oak tree that provided a break from the late-afternoon sun. By the time Colleen caught up to Tara, Wes and Tony, they were well into a conversation.

"Hey, Big Red, night out in the big city, huh?" Wes joked as he picked up his T-shirt from the ground and wiped the sweat dripping off his face.

"I guess," Colleen said. She felt her face flush. She hated when people called her that but couldn't help smiling at Wes.

"So what's on the agenda for your crazy night in good old Brockville?" Tony said.

Colleen felt lost for words around these two boys. They were both really cute and she didn't want to say something that sounded stupid.

"We're just going to ride around and maybe hang out with Paula later," Tara said.

Colleen stared at Tara as she spoke so easily and naturally around the boys.

"Okay, we'll probably be up here playing ball all night, so come back later if you want," Wes said. "See you, Big Red."

MRS. MEYERS MADE HAMBURGERS AND macaroni and cheese for supper. Colleen quickly devoured the macaroni and cheese.

"Colleen, do you want more?" Mrs. Meyers asked.

"Yes, please." It was the best macaroni and cheese Colleen had ever tasted. "Can you give the recipe to my mom?" Colleen asked.

"Oh, honey," Mrs. Meyers laughed. "It's just a box of Kraft."

"Oh." Colleen's cheeks flushed a bit of color as she took a

drink of Dr Pepper to hide her embarrassment. She should have known that it was something from a box. Her mom wouldn't spend extra money on packaged food or canned soda.

After supper, Tara was eager to take off toward the park to see the boys. Colleen would have rather stayed at Tara's house to watch cable TV and drink more Dr Pepper. Also, she was desperate to watch some of the shows that her friends always discussed. She was left silent when the girls talked about *Gilligan's Island*, *The Brady Bunch*, and *My Three Sons*. And the boys didn't talk to her the way they talked to Tara.

WHEN HER DAD DROVE HER back to the farm after her sleepover with Tara, Colleen felt even more out of touch with her friends and their conversations. She hated her hand-me-down wardrobe. Tara had whole sets of tops and shorts that were made to go together. She envied Tara's freedom of getting around town on her bike. She dreamed of being able to go over to a friend's house on a whim, or to ride her bike to the Brockville town square, where she could congregate with whoever happened to be around.

Colleen's mom lived by the motto "There's no time or money for beauty and fashion on a farm." Mary Ann O'Brien got her hair cut straight across her neck every Good Friday. She had it cut as short as possible, but not so short to require layers or a neck shaving. By Colleen's birthday on August 1, it was usually long enough for a low ponytail. Once it became long enough to pull back into a bun, which was usually around Christmastime, Mary Ann would wear it that way until the next Good Friday, when it would be cut again. After Johnny was born, her blond hair began turning white. Colleen wished she would do something about her hair color, but when she asked, Mary Ann said, "There are far more important things to be concerned with than the color of my hair."

Colleen loved looking at pictures of her mom when she was younger. Her mom's senior picture and the few pictures from her parents' wedding were among Colleen's favorites. In those pictures, it appeared that her mom was wearing eye makeup and lipstick, something she had never seen her mother do.

Occasionally, Colleen complained about not having the right kinds of clothes or being able to wear makeup, and Mary Ann would curtly tell her, "You have plenty, more than most." She wanted to ask her mom who the "most" were that she was referring to, but she didn't.

COLLEEN HUNG UP THE PHONE just as *The Young and the Restless* ended. The *Mid-Day Farm Report* was on and her dad still hadn't come in for lunch. She didn't have much time. She needed to let Tara know whether or not she would be coming to town.

"Ask him now," she had said before they hung up. "I'll wait thirty minutes before I head down to the park."

When Colleen saw her dad's truck parked down at the machine shed, she knew something must have broken down. She laid two slices of bread on a plate and smeared mayonnaise on each slice. She opened several Country Crock Butter containers that her mom used to store leftovers in until she found last night's roast. Her mom had carefully cut it into thin slices for sandwiches. She laid four of the slices across the top of the mayonnaise, closed the sandwich and cut it in half.

Her dad was always in a bad mood when something broke down, especially when it interfered with his lunch break.

"That should just about do it," John said over the blaring farm report coming through the static of the old radio he had perched in the windowsill. He wiped the grease from his hands with an old towel as he stepped away from the faded red Massey Ferguson tractor.

Colleen tried to breathe through her mouth to avoid sneezing from the dust-covered shed. She handed her dad the plate she made for him. "Thank you, honey," John said over the shaky commentary of the dropping price of grain.

She began sneezing as she switched her breathing back to her nose. The taste of oil lingered in her mouth. The fumes held on tight to the stagnant air. She sat on the riding lawn mower and watched her dad eat his sandwich. He leaned against the tool table doing his best to make out the broken words of the radio hosts. She picked at the peeling vinyl seat cover that exposed the foam padding underneath her while she waited for a commercial to come on. Interrupting his show would most definitely be met with a "not today" response.

Finally, the show broke to commercial. "Can you drive me over to Tara's? I can ride home with Mom when she's finished at the bank."

John chewed his sandwich. He walked over to the spigot outside of the shed and filled his plastic cup with water. Colleen wished she had thought to bring him an iced tea. "No time for that today. Got to make sure I got the PTO working right. Hay's dry and ready to mow. Rain predicted tomorrow night. Got to get the hay cut by this evening."

Colleen knew she wasn't going to get to town any day soon.

"Why can't we sell this farm? Tara's family sold their farm. So did Paula's," Colleen said.

"You get all those weeds pulled?" John shot back.

"I was waiting for the rain so they'd be easier to pull," Colleen said. "You could get a job at Metal Works Factory like Paula's and Tara's dads did."

Colleen remembered the pride that radiated off her father last week when the cashier at Brockville Grain Store commented on how fascinating he found the history of Farm Five-Thirty-Five. Her father beamed when the cashier said, "Your great-granddad must have been quite a guy."

"Let's stop talking nonsense and get our work done," John said as he climbed up the tractor.

Colleen knew the conversation was over even before her dad started the tractor. She tried not to think about the long summer ahead, all by herself out in the country.

COLLEEN HAD JUST FINISHED PULLING the last of the radishes from the garden when she heard the gravel crumbling and knew her mom and Johnny were home. She set her basket down on the porch before racing over to take Johnny from her mother's arms. He giggled as Colleen buried her nose into the crook of his neck. She inhaled his baby scent and brushed her face into the softness of his fleshy skin. The timing of her mother's pregnancy and the discovery of how babies were made felt like a cruel joke to Colleen. The mortification of her mother's swelling belly was compounded by her parents' plan to call him J.R., short for John Robert. It was worse that her parents wouldn't even know that everyone would assume they'd named him after the unsavory character in the popular television series *Dallas*. Colleen was relieved when she was able to get them to agree to call him Johnny.

"I'm going to change his diaper," Colleen told her mom.

"Let's try to get that diaper to last until after supper," Mary Ann said. They had a hard time getting bills paid before little Johnny came into their lives but, after he was born, their financial difficulties intensified. Between the low price of grain, old farm equipment breaking and the extra cost of childcare, there just wasn't enough money to pay for everything. Talk of Colleen babysitting during the summer months ended when the woman who cared for Johnny threatened to give his spot away.

The diaper was just beginning to droop. Colleen had seen it look worse. Never did she imagine poop came out in nine different colors or seep into the elastic around his legs. Johnny stood, holding on to Colleen's shoulder while she sat down on the ground next to him. He didn't seem to care about his diaper as he plopped down and helped Colleen line his blocks up. He loved to scoot his toy Massey Ferguson tractor across the floor and load the trailer with the blocks. At one year old, he was already pretending to bail hay. The farming gene seemed to have skipped Colleen and gone straight to Johnny.

COLLEEN WASN'T HAPPY ABOUT GETTING up at dawn on Saturday morning to work at the farmer's market. Her dad gave a questionable look when she walked out of the house after he and Aunt Susie had most of the truck loaded. She had been in the bathroom trying to get her hair to lay down. For a change, she wanted to not wear it pulled back into a rubber band, but it wouldn't lay right. Regardless of how many times she squeezed water from the washcloth over the taller side, her hair remained uneven. The only way it was going to cooperate was if she washed it and there wasn't time for that. She finally gave up and pulled it back into her standard ponytail.

Colleen carried the last remaining basket of onions and radishes over to the bed of the pickup truck. They were loaded and ready to go. Her dad shut the door after she climbed into the truck with Aunt Susie. She expected a lecture about her tardiness as he leaned in through the rolled-down window. "Good luck, girls," was all he said. Colleen knew the lecture would be waiting for her when she got home.

To raise more money, the O'Brien brothers planted a massive garden in the spring. In addition to masses of tomatoes, zucchini, yellow squash, green beans, potatoes, onions, peppers, beets and radishes, the chickens began producing more eggs than the family could ever eat.

"Why don't you find us some good music?" Aunt Susie said.

Colleen's youngest uncle, Jimmy, had married Susie when Colleen was barely five years old. After marrying Jimmy, Susie finished her college degree and became a high school English teacher. The excitement of being the first O'Brien to receive a college degree quickly faded upon learning she wasn't able to have children. She quickly became the favorite aunt among the cousins. Colleen, being the only girl in the clan, had developed a special bond with her aunt Susie.

Colleen turned the dial to 100.3, one of the few stations to play popular music. She looked up for her aunt's approval when she finally got the dial just right and Cyndi Lauper sang

"Girls Just Wanna Have Fun" with very little static. Aunt Susie's head shifted slightly from side to side as she sang along with the lyrics. Colleen loved spending time with her pretty young aunt. Unlike Mary Ann, Susie wore her hair long, wore makeup, and always dressed in stylish clothing.

Colleen and Susie had almost sold everything. The eggs were gone within the first two hours. Their checked-covered tablecloth had a few bundles of beets and a small collection of potted herbs left. Colleen smacked another biting fly off her leg as she heard a familiar voice call out her name. She was surprised to look up and see Tara standing in front of her. She would have been embarrassed to be seen working at the farmer's market with anyone except Aunt Susie. She sat up with pride as she greeted Tara with her beautiful aunt by her side. Her hair and old clothes didn't matter when she was in her aunt's company.

"Can you stay in town after the market?" Tara asked.

Colleen knew better than to even ask after her tardiness getting to the truck this morning. "I have chores waiting for me at home," she said.

"Oh, come on, you can do them tomorrow. I'm going swimming at Noel's house. You'll die when you see her pool," Tara said.

Colleen looked up at Aunt Susie. She was busying herself stacking the empty baskets. Her silence confirmed Colleen's answer. "I can't," she said as she rested her chin down on her hands that were propped up on the table.

"When can you come back to town?" Tara asked.

"I'll ask my mom, maybe next weekend." Colleen was hopeful. She had never been in a real swimming pool. The only swimming she got to do was down in the creek on the other side of the pasture. If there was a lot of rain, the water would come up to her waist, but usually she was lucky if the water hit her knees.

"Maybe you can spend the night, too." Tara's eyes lit up like they always did when she talked about something she worshipped. "She's having a pool party later this summer. You have to come!" she said.

Tara seemed to be spending more and more time over at Noel's. In addition to swimming in a real pool, Tara was hanging out with Noel's older brother Ronnie and his friends. They were the cutest and most popular boys at Brockville High School.

"She's only inviting town kids," Tara said, "but I'm going to tell her that she has to invite you. I know she will." Tara sped off on her bike.

Colleen could tell Tara was on a mission, a mission to convince Noel Bellman, the coolest girl in their class, to invite her, the least cool girl in their class.

COLLEEN HAD JUST FINISHED COLLECTING the last of the eggs and was beginning to load them in their cartons in the barn refrigerator for Saturday's market when she saw the mail truck come down the lane. She hopped on her bike and rode down to the mailbox as she did every day to collect the mail. Colleen couldn't believe it! There was a large purple envelope addressed to her with Noel Bellman's name as the sender. She got invited!

Tara called. "Steven, Peter, Wes and some of Noel's

brother's friends like Tony, Brian and Jason are going to be there," she said.

Colleen was overtaken by anxiety. What was she going to wear? Just as quickly as her emotions hit an all-time high, she began to panic.

The thought of those boys, especially Wes Fischer, seeing her wear the aqua-blue, one-piece hand-me-down swimsuit with snags all over the bottom made her want to run and hide. She wanted a bikini, like the one Tara told her about a few weeks ago.

If there was one thing that would sway her mother's practical nature, it was chores. Colleen did her best to make the house look perfect. She dusted the living room and swept the floors, then filled the old yellow bucket with vinegar and water and mopped the entire first floor of the farmhouse. After she finished with the inside, she went outside to clean all the windows along the wraparound porch. She had just finished mopping the front porch for the second time when she heard the crunching of gravel approaching the house. Colleen took the last bucket of dirty water over to the garden to show her mom how resourceful she had been with all the water she used to clean. She rested the mop in the empty bucket before rushing over to help her mom with Johnny.

"What do you want?" Mary Ann asked. She held her hands on her hips and looked at Colleen skeptically.

There was no point in lying. "Noel Bellman's having a pool party and I want to go."

"Of course you can go, why would you think you couldn't?" Mary Ann said.

"I know how tight money is and I might need to take a gift

or something." Colleen stood looking at her mother's worn-out chinos and tired-looking shirt.

"I think we can manage a small gift if you want to go to the party," Mary Ann said.

Colleen knew she had one opportunity and if she blew it, all hope would be lost. Once her mom made her mind up about something, it was set. She fell silent thinking about what to do.

"Sweetheart, if you want to go to the party, we'll make sure you can go and that you have a gift. Now let's get supper started," Mary Ann said.

Colleen sat on the floor with Johnny while her mother diced an onion and added it to the sizzling ground beef on the stovetop next to the giant pot of water. Colleen lined up the blocks as though they were bails of hay in the field for Johnny to collect with his tractor. As Johnny carefully stacked each block on the bed of his tractor trailer, she thought about asking her mom for the new swimsuit. Colleen watched as her mom added spaghetti noodles to the boiling water.

"Colleen, would you go down to the cellar and get a jar of tomatoes? There should be a couple left," Mary Ann said as she stirred the noodles.

Colleen saw that there were only three jars of tomatoes. She dreaded the canning season that was fast approaching. Peeling bushels of tomatoes for hours on end while the pressure cooker hissed steam into an already hot kitchen was enough to cause a heat stroke. Colleen handed her mother the tomatoes. Once she poured those into the meat mixture, supper would almost be ready. "Can I please get a new swimsuit to wear to the party?"

Mary Ann's chest rose as she inhaled. She popped the lid off the jar and stood back as she poured last season's plump tomatoes into the skillet. "Pam was just telling me today that Janet had another growth spurt and she has a bag of clothes for you," Mary Ann said.

There was no way Colleen was wearing an old, hand-me-down suit to Noel Bellman's party. Colleen wished her mother had just said no. Now, if she pressed the issue, she would seem spoiled. Colleen's mom had said over and over "money is only to be spent on necessary purchases."

COLLEEN HELPED HER AUNT SUSIE pull the coolers of eggs down from the bed of the pickup truck. The checkered tablecloth was barely visible with baskets of zucchinis, yellow squash, tomatoes, green beans, potatoes, broccoli, cauliflower and multicolored peppers. Colleen flicked a green tomato worm off the table as she took a seat next to Aunt Susie.

"Colleen, how about after we pack up today, we go to Charlestown and find you something to wear to Noel's pool party?" Susie said. As a high school teacher, she knew how the girls dressed.

"But I don't have any money," Colleen said.

Susie gently lifted Colleen's chin so she could look at her in the eye. "It's going to be my treat. You've worked hard helping me all summer and I still need to buy you a birthday present."

Before Colleen knew it, they were heading to the shopping mall in Charlestown, an hour's drive from Brockville.

Back home, Colleen raced inside to show her mom and dad her new hot pink bikini with white ruffles across the top and the pink and white cover-up dress.

"Where's the rest of it?" her father said.

"It's a little skimpy, Colleen," Mary Ann said.

Colleen's excitement faded. She stuffed her new clothing back into the shopping bag. "It's what everyone wears."

"I know you're proud of your new things, but I want you to be yourself and stop trying to keep up with what all the other girls are doing and wearing," Mary Ann yelled up to Colleen as she stomped up the stairs toward her bedroom.

After slamming her bedroom door, she sat and looked at her new bikini. She was glad she didn't model it for her parents, since the ruffles around the top gave the illusion that she was more developed than she actually was. She hoped to be able to wear the cover-up as a dress to school for at least a couple weeks before the weather got cold. Colleen couldn't wait for the party to come.

AFTER MUCH DISCUSSION, COLLEEN AND Tara decided they would get ready for the party together at Tara's house. It would save Colleen from having to listen to her parents lecture her about how inappropriate they thought her new swimming suit was, or her mom's comment about how long she was taking in the bathroom.

As the girls got ready, Colleen stared at Tara's perfectly golden tan compared to her freckled pink skin. Tara's mom agreed to let them use some of her makeup, as long as they let her approve of their faces before they left. She warned them that mascara would create raccoon eyes once they got wet.

Colleen did her best to follow Tara's instructions for applying the makeup. After several mistakes, Tara took over. Colleen didn't recognize herself when she looked in the mirror.

"Do you think it's too much?" Colleen asked.

"I barely put any on," Tara said. "You look great!"

Mrs. Meyers gave Colleen mousse that tamed her wild curls. For once, her hair wasn't frizzy. Mrs. Meyers taught her how to run a comb through it when it was wet, apply the foamy mousse and let it dry naturally.

Full of nervous energy and a lot of giggles, the girls set off for the party. Thumping sounds of Bon Jovi singing "You Give Love a Bad Name" greeted them at the driveway. A large bouquet of balloons was attached to the mailbox. Colleen couldn't believe she was finally going to get to swim in Noel Bellman's underground swimming pool, and maybe if she was lucky, she would get to see the inside of her beautiful, red-brick house.

The three-car garage was larger and cleaner than any garage Colleen had ever been in. She'd never been in a garage that was attached to a house. The floors were spotless, without any dirt or dust. The cars parked to the far side of the garage looked brand-new, as if they had never been driven. So different from Colleen's dad's filthy Chevy pickup truck and her mom's rusted-out Ford Granada. She followed Tara through the garage that led them into the backyard.

The pool was bigger and more beautiful than she had imagined. Even with Noel's brother and his friends splashing the water up over the edges in their intense volleyball game, the blue water was mesmerizing as it sparkled under the sunshine. The patio was covered in cobblestone pavement with moss growing in between the stones. Rosebushes with hot pink blooms lined the fence and various-sized containers sat in groups around the pool, each filled with exotic-looking flowers, not the typical petunias, marigold, geranium and impatiens that Colleen was used to. The side of the pool by the house had a large, iron table with matching chairs and six lounge chairs covered in marine blue cushions and orange and pink floral throw pillows. The outdoor furniture was nicer than Colleen's home furniture.

Tara led the way toward Mrs. Bellman, who was carrying a white wicker basket full of plush orange towels. Tara politely introduced her. Mrs. Bellman's hair was also permed, but it was long and blond. She wore a green short jumpsuit with blue high heels, a look that Colleen hadn't seen around Brockville. She led them over to the table where they could wait for Noel to come out. Colleen and Tara began to wish that they waited a little longer to walk over, since they were the first girls there.

"My mom said that Mrs. Bellman spends a fortune on her flowers every year," Tara whispered to Colleen. "Can you imagine?"

Colleen's eyes widened. Her parents would never spend money on flowers. The only flowers they had growing were from the free seeds the grain store gave them every spring.

"My mom said that they hire someone to do everything and Mrs. Bellman just sits around telling people what to do," Tara whispered.

Colleen knew the Bellmans were rich, but she had never thought about how different their lives were compared to everyone else's in Brockville. She knew Noel's dad was a doctor because everyone referred to him as Dr. Bellman. Until then, Colleen didn't realize how much money doctors made.

Just when she was getting ready to whisper back to Tara that she was going to grow up to marry a doctor, Noel came out.

She looked a lot different than she had at the end of May when school ended. Like Mrs. Meyers, she wore her hair in a curly permanent. Unlike Mrs. Meyers, she had cut her long hair short, making it stand out in a straight line from her face. Her now shoulder-length hair was curly and decorated with a huge bow on the side of her head. She wore blue mascara, white eyeliner, and frosted pink lip-gloss that matched her pink-stained cheeks. She'd also gotten her ears pierced, not once, but twice in both ears. She had big hoop earrings hanging out of the four new holes in her ears and both arms were covered in bracelets that stopped over the edge of her lacey gloves with cutoff fingers. Colleen was shocked at how short Noel's skirt was, and how her cutoff shirt exposed so much of her stomach. As she walked toward Colleen and Tara, she flashed a big smile to show off her new braces. She was obviously very proud of her new look.

Colleen quickly went from feeling great about her own new outfit to feeling completely out of style and, yet again, ashamed of what she was wearing.

Noel walked over with a smirk on her face. "You guys look so cute." She batted her eyes at them.

Colleen tried to think of something nice to say, which was hard after Noel's phony compliment. "Thank you for having us."

Attempting to be polite and to change the subject, Tara said, "Who else is coming?" She crossed her arms awkwardly and looked down at the rock she had been moving around with her foot.

Colleen wished her parents could see the way Noel was dressed and how much makeup she was wearing. They would no longer think Colleen's outfit was inappropriate and may not even notice the tiny bit of makeup she had on.

"Just some kids from our class, some girls from my dance class, and a few of my brother's annoying friends," Noel said. "Look, there's Winnie, she is one of the girls from my dance class. Winnie, come over here!"

Colleen and Tara stood gawking at the two girls as they embraced each other. Noel's reaction to her "new" friend was a lot different than the greeting she gave them. Winnie looked just like Noel. She had her hair styled the same way and was wearing the same kind of makeup, accessories and outfit. Colleen realized Noel had another life that she and Tara weren't part of.

"Winnie, this is Colleen and Tara, they go to school with me." Noel rolled her eyes at Winnie, making it apparent she found Colleen and Tara embarrassing. "Look, Monica is here! Come on, Winnie!" Winnie squealed in delight. She and Noel raced off, leaving Colleen and Tara standing alone.

"She really seems to like her dance friends," Colleen said after a few moments of silence.

Colleen followed Tara over to the pool steps. "I hope no more show up," Tara said as she stood with her feet in the three inches of water on the first step.

Noel and her new friends never got close to the pool. Tara and Colleen were thrilled when Paula, Daisy and Emily arrived. They were there dressed to swim like Tara and Colleen. The girls sat and stared at Noel and her dance friends, who seemed oblivious to the fact that anyone else was at the party.

Colleen and Tara watched them from across the pool, envious. Realizing they'd be ignored anyway, they eventually got into the pool. Tara stayed upset but the clear blue water in the swimming pool captivated Colleen. She had never seen something so alluring or felt something as invigorating. The rainbow of colorful blooms that danced around the pool seemed magical.

THREE

2003
Chicago

Colleen felt the crinkle of exam paper under her back. Her legs were up in stirrups. She and Jay had celebrated their one-year wedding anniversary with a positive pregnancy test. When she had stopped taking birth control the month before, Colleen envisioned months of anxious waiting, taking her temperature and urinating on ovulation sticks. She had even wondered if she would have to do IVF like so many of her coworkers had. Colleen was beginning to feel nervous.

"Am I going to be okay for my trip to LA this weekend?" Colleen asked Dr. Kerr. Jay was already there and expecting Colleen to join him. Dr. Kerr was the third doctor called in that morning. Colleen knew something was wrong.

"You're not going anywhere for a while," Dr. Kerr said.

Colleen wondered what he meant by a while. She still wasn't sure what the exact problem was, but knew something was wrong. "What about work? I'm on my lunch break," Colleen said. She had barely gotten away to begin with. She had come in to see her ob-gyn, Dr. Anderson, for what was supposed to be a routine ten-minute check.

Dr. Anderson was now standing up by Colleen's head in

order to give the current examining doctor space. "You're not going to go back to work today," Dr. Anderson said. "We'll have one of the nurses call your office."

Colleen was glad one of the nurses was calling and not her. Larry was going to be irate. He was already mad about her taking Friday and Monday off. As a human resources assistant at JJ Consulting, she was responsible for processing new-employee paperwork. The recent acquisition of Tech Solutions created a pile of paperwork for the fifty new employees. Larry had approved her two vacation days on the condition that all paperwork was completed before she left.

"Colleen had a LEEP done six years ago," Dr. Anderson said to Dr. Kerr.

"Current gestation?" Dr. Kerr asked.

"Nineteen weeks. Due to the LEEP, we decided to start the internal examinations early," Dr. Anderson said. "We were going to start next week but because of Colleen's travel plans, we started today."

"Any other complications?" Dr. Kerr asked.

"No," Colleen jumped in. Besides being a little tired, she felt great.

"Her weight's good. Baby's heartbeat has been strong from the beginning," Dr. Anderson said.

Dr. Anderson took off her rubber gloves. She brought up the head of the bed and helped cover Colleen's legs with the flimsy gown she was wearing for the exam. "Colleen, you have what's called an incompetent cervix," she said. "This is when your cervix weakens and starts to open prematurely. Your cervix has thinned and is just beginning to open. At this point, the only way to save your pregnancy is to stitch your cervix closed." Dr. Anderson paused a few seconds while Colleen processed what she was hearing. "The procedure's called a cerclage. We need to do this as soon as possible." Dr. Anderson stood from her chair and sat on the edge of the examination table. She took hold of Colleen's hand. "You need to understand that there's some risk involved. While I'm optimistic everything will go smoothly, there's a chance of puncturing your amniotic sac."

Colleen's palms were wet up against Dr. Anderson's hand. She couldn't believe what she was being told. She felt fine. Her nausea had ended right at twelve weeks, just like the book said. She was hungry all the time and her belly was growing. She had even felt the first tiny kicks a couple of days ago.

"If that happens, the baby won't live," Dr. Anderson said. "It will be considered a late-term miscarriage."

Colleen sat in disbelief. She wanted Jay. He had his last day of orientation for his new job at Beck and Larson on Saturday. Colleen was looking forward to spending time in Los Angeles with her sister-in-law, Alexis, while Eli introduced Jay to all of the other partners at the firm. Eli had organized a dinner to celebrate Jay joining Beck and Larson on Saturday night. Colleen was no longer going to be part of the celebration. "When can we do it?" Colleen's voice shook.

"This afternoon," Dr. Anderson said. "Jay needs to be here with you. Would it be okay for one of the nurses to call him?"

There was no way he could get there in time. "He is in LA for his new job. I'm not sure he'll be able to answer his phone."

"Is there anyone else we can call?" Dr. Anderson asked.

Colleen had lost touch with most of her friends after she and Jay got married. Everything in her life had become about

Jay and his friends and family. Colleen didn't feel close enough to any of them to call.

The only person Colleen really wanted there was her mom, but she hadn't spoken to her since she called to announce her pregnancy. She was hopeful the new baby would bring them closer, close the chasm that cracked between them when Colleen left for Chicago. At this moment, though, she couldn't bring herself to call and ask for help, especially in the heart of planting season.

"We don't want you walking. An ambulance will be here soon," Dr. Anderson said. "Once you're prepped and ready, I'll head over."

No, Colleen thought. *No, this can't be happening. An ambulance? Surgery? What if the surgery doesn't go well and I lose my baby?*

She had gotten up early to pack for her trip. With the help of Dinah's stylist, Lyla, she had spent a small fortune on maternity clothes at Belly Time Maternity Boutique. She had been looking forward to wearing a few of the smallest outfits, since they actually fit her almost-pregnant-looking belly.

There was a knock on the door. "An ambulance should be here in just a few minutes."

More than anything she wanted to talk to Jay. She began to wonder if the nurses had gotten hold of him. If not, what kind of message did they leave for him? She had lost the battle with her tears, which were now streaming down her face.

THE NEXT THING COLLEEN KNEW, she was waking up in the recovery room. Her eyes remained closed but she could hear the commotion of the nurses moving around her as she lay under the weight of the warm blankets covering her.

"Colleen. Your surgery was a success. Your baby is doing great. Can you hear the heartbeat?"

Colleen squinted at the blurry face in front of her. She tuned in to the drumming of her baby's heart coming from the monitor next to her bed.

"In just a few minutes, you'll be taken down to your room. Your mom and aunt are waiting for you."

Colleen thought the nurse must be confused with another patient. Too tired to clear up the confusion, she didn't say anything.

Upon being wheeled into her hospital room, she discovered the nurses weren't confused. Her mom and Aunt Susie stood waiting for her. She started to cry.

Rushing to her daughter, Mary Ann reached down with a hug and then Aunt Susie followed. "Of course we came," Mary Ann said. "We're family." Colleen could sense the tension even through the loving tone.

Aunt Susie said, "We're just so relieved everything went smoothly."

"I was just as shocked as you'd imagine when I picked up the phone at the bank and Jay was on the other end. He's one resourceful fellow, being able to track me down at work," Mary Ann said. "I couldn't believe it when he told me he was all the way out in California. I can't believe you didn't call us."

Colleen could see the hurt in her mom's eyes. "I didn't want to bother you. I know what a busy time of the year this is," Colleen said.

Mary Ann gently stroked Colleen's hair away from her face.

"Jay called while you were in recovery. I filled him in on everything the doctor said. He wanted to board the next flight home, but I told him to wait," Mary Ann said. "Colleen, it's important that you listen to your doctors and do exactly as they say."

Susie brought a chair over by Colleen's bed for Mary Ann to sit on.

"Right now they want you in bed and you're not to do anything but go to the bathroom and take a quick shower," she said as she sat down. "We plan to stay for the weekend and get you set up at home."

Colleen was pleased her mom had spent some time speaking with Jay.

"Jay needs to stay in LA and finish the meetings. I don't want to do anything to jeopardize his new job," Colleen said. "If you guys stay with me, I'll be fine." She felt a rush of relief go through her body. Aunt Susie's empathic nature and her mom's practicality were a perfect combination for her current situation.

Mary Ann straightened the covers around Colleen before leaning down to kiss the top of her head.

Colleen hadn't realized how much she missed her mother's touch. She didn't think her mom would ever forgive her for going along with Dinah Adler and moving her wedding to Chicago. Dating back to her grandparents, the O'Briens always got married on the farm. Too much time had passed since she felt the closeness of her mom. As terrible as the day had been, it suddenly seemed a lot brighter. She was now glad she wasn't going to Los Angeles.

Aunt Susie drove while Colleen did her best to give the

tired women the easiest route to her house. Her parents had visited the first year she moved and sworn to never drive in the city again. Her mom referred to the expressway as "nightmare alley." The few times since then that they had come to visit they took the Amtrak.

Finally, after what seemed like a long time, the phone rang. Her composure was lost the minute she heard Jay's voice.

"I'm good. Really tired but relieved this is over and our baby is okay," Colleen said. "I can't believe my mom and Aunt Susie are here."

"I feel terrible that I am not there with you. I'll get on the next flight out if you want," Jay said.

"My mom and Aunt Susie will take good care of me," she said. Regardless of how much she wanted Jay with her, she didn't want to jeopardize his new job.

"Please don't be mad, but I called my mother to let her know what was going on. You know how she gets if she thinks she's been left out of something," Jay said. "Don't worry, though, I told her to leave you alone until after your mom and aunt leave."

Dinah had met Colleen's family only once, at their wedding. Her hardworking family appalled Dinah. There wasn't a chance Dinah would visit knowing she would have to socialize with Mary Ann and Susie. Besides, she would never go out of her way to help Colleen, especially without Jay there to witness.

Colleen stared down at the spiral phone cord as she wrapped and unwrapped it around her finger. She struggled to sound cheerful and suddenly felt very alone. She wondered if Jay had any idea how close they had come to losing the baby.

"Looks like I'm going to be spending quite a bit of time in New York. I'm going to be handling all of Eli's referrals out east. This is going to be life changing for us," Jay said.

The lump in her throat ached. She closed her eyes. They burned as the overflow of hot tears ran down her face. The thought of the next several weeks with him traveling created more worry than she had the strength to handle. She dreaded Dinah. Somehow, she would make Colleen feel at fault for her situation.

After sleeping for a few hours, Mary Ann and Susie followed Jay's instructions to get money from his desk drawer and go to Juliette's Grocery.

"I feel bad that we spent so much of Jay's money," Mary Ann said.

"I couldn't believe the cheapest eggs there were $4.99 a dozen! They even had some that were almost $7. Can you imagine if I tried to sell our eggs for that much?" Susie said.

The three women laughed.

Mary Ann and Susie had bought dozens of eggs, ground beef, whole chickens, loaves of bread, blocks of cheese, flour, sugar, baking powder, baking soda, spices, apples, bananas, onions, celery and carrots. The essentials were in place to begin the cooking production line. Colleen had enough egg sandwiches, mini quiches, muffins, meat loaves, soups and countless casseroles in the freezer to last for the next several weeks.

She wished her mom could stay with her, but Mary Ann had obligations at home. In addition to the usual spring work at the farm, Johnny was finishing up his senior year in high school. He had become quite a local track star in the past few years. Unlike Colleen, he included his parents in every aspect of his life. He was proud of his family and their farm life. From the time he could walk, he begged to work alongside John. He was able to drive the combine and tractors long before he got his driver's license. The countless hours he worked with his dad prepared him to take over the farm one day. Not only did Johnny look just like his father, he seemed to love the farm just as much.

When the women finished cooking, they moved on to cleaning. On one of her precious trips to the bathroom, Colleen walked into the bedroom to find Mary Ann digging in between the mattress and the headboard.

"Colleen, look at all the dust down here," Mary Ann said. "Honey, I know you like having a cleaning lady, but no one cleans a house better than the people living in it." Her ear touched the mattress as she reached her arm down the crack as far as she could. Mary Ann lifted her head and checked the clock. Her dad said he would call the women with Johnny's race results.

The phone jingled. Her mom's smile told Colleen all she needed to know. Johnny had broken the state record. She couldn't recall ever earning such an expression from her mom. "Oh, I knew he could do it!" Mary Ann said. "First place in both events and state record!" She looked away as tears began to roll down her cheeks.

Colleen couldn't help but feel envious of the pride and happiness Johnny created for their parents. She vowed she would be a better daughter and sister right after the baby was born.

A year earlier, when Colleen had announced that Dinah

offered to pay for their wedding at her "amazing" country club, her family had fallen silent. Colleen thought her mom and dad would be relieved that they didn't have to incur any costs for her wedding. She became frustrated with everyone, but especially her mother for not understanding her predicament with Dinah. She was going to be living in Chicago and around her on a regular basis. She felt it was more important to keep Dinah happy than to appease her family.

"She's fine. We have her all fixed up with plenty to eat and a clean house," Mary Ann said. "Yes, she is being a good girl and staying in bed like the doctor said."

Susie must have heard the commotion up in the bedroom. She came in just as Mary Ann hung up the phone. "I take it we have good news!" she said.

Colleen couldn't believe it had been over a year since she last saw Johnny. She wished they were all home together celebrating his success.

Mary Ann and Susie left late on Sunday morning. Colleen worked hard to hold back her tears until the car turned off her street. Before Mary Ann left her pregnant daughter, she made Colleen get dressed and make her bed. She told Colleen being bedridden didn't mean she should stay in pajamas all day under the covers. "Get dressed and make your bed. Lying on top of a made bed will be less depressing," she said. For once, Colleen intended to follow her mom's advice. She would create a daily routine to follow. After she dressed and had her breakfast, she would re-read *What to Expect When You're Expecting, On Becoming Baby Wise*, or *Ina May's Guide to Childbirth* until she had a mid-morning snack. Then, if Larry allowed her to work from home, she would do some work until lunch, have a nap, do more work, have an afternoon snack and watch TV until dinnertime. She would save movies for the evening. Colleen hoped a daily schedule would help the days pass more quickly. Since she had already dressed and had her breakfast, it was time to read, but, instead, she lay on the bed and cried.

THE SUN SHINING THROUGH THE wood blinds cast rectangular shadows across the ceiling. While Colleen stared at the horizontal stripes, she noticed a dull place on the crown molding that the painter had missed. The six hours since her mother and aunt drove away stretched into an abyss of time that had dropped her firmly into melancholy. She broke the hours down into twelve thirty-minute increments, then increments of fifteen, then five. The first five minutes felt like an hour. She made a list of the movies she wanted to watch. The list had two columns, one with Jay and one without. Under with Jay, she wrote *The Godfather* (I, II and III), *Schindler's List* and *Silence of the Lambs*. She would let him add to the list later. She would watch *Gone with the Wind*, *Casablanca*, *The Graduate* and *The Grapes of Wrath*. The shades of blue gingham on the duvet below her flashed in her peripheral vision and made her feel dizzy. Colleen spread the solid blue knit blanket that her mom laid across the bed underneath her, across the duvet. She added *Pretty Woman*, *Steel Magnolias* and her favorite old Doris Day movies to her list. She stared out the window in search of the squawking blue jay that was drowning out the other bird's flute-like sounds. There was a crack above the windowsill that she hadn't noticed before. Another thing Jay would want to fix.

In the midst of one of these interminable intervals, she counted the weeks until her baby was considered viable; twenty-four weeks was five weeks away. Dr. Anderson said after twenty-seven weeks, the baby had a 90 percent chance of survival, but would face a mountain of challenges. Every week after that, chances of survival increased and chances of complications decreased. Thirty-six weeks was the goal. She only had to get through one hundred and nineteen more days. If she were able to sleep twelve hours a day, she could divide the two thousand eight hundred fifty-six hours in half and only have one thousand four hundred twenty-eight hours to get through.

A car door slammed somewhere outside the townhouse. The rustling at the door below her bedroom window confirmed that Jay was finally home. Colleen stared at the doorframe waiting for Jay's body to fill the empty space. After a thunderous ascent up the wood stairs, Jay dropped his bags in the doorway. He launched himself onto the bed next to Colleen and wrapped his arms and legs around her entire body. He smelled of Creed Green Irish Tweed Cologne. Colleen was dominated by the woodsy scent as she buried her face into Jay's shoulder. Her tears dampened his shirt as she sobbed.

He kissed Colleen's forehead and wiped tears from her face. "We're going to get through this. Let's find a way to make the best of this crummy situation," Jay said. He sat up and began appraising the space. His eyes darted around the square bedroom. Colleen had seen that look on his face before. He furrowed his eyebrows and chewed on the side of his cheek, considering.

"If this is going to be the main room in the house, we'd better get it fixed up," Jay said. "Maybe a small refrigerator? A microwave?"

Colleen wanted him to lie back down. She wanted him to stay in bed with her; they could watch a movie, play cards, talk about the tightrope they were now walking every day until the baby was viable.

She knew what came next once he started down this path. Calls from a general contractor would begin. Which from a choice of one thousand microwaves would she like? Did she want a 52-inch or 72-inch TV screen? She imagined the doorbell ringing on Maria's day off. She would have to throw her keys down from her bedroom on the second floor and hope the person locked up when they left. She'd better get some extra keys made.

If she voiced these objections, Jay would think her ungrateful. Or he'd install one of those mechanized seats to go up and down the stairs. She'd seen one of those at a stroke victim's house. The smell of urine soured the air.

"A microwave sounds nice." Colleen sat up in bed and ran her finger around the section of hair she had been twisting all day, did her best to smile and tried to lighten up.

"All I could think about the entire plane ride home was you stuck in this room. If anyone can handle this, it's you," Jay said.

Colleen couldn't help but to smile through her trembling lips. Jay was the first and only person to say how much he admired where she came from. He said he had never seen anyone work harder than the O'Brien family. "Not like my family," he'd said once after they were married. "A bunch of lawyers and entitled wives."

"God, I love you so much." He hugged her again.

His smell alone was enough to make her feel better. Her heart beat in a different way when he was next to her. Colleen remembered the day her roommate's boyfriend, Ryan, brought Jay over to their apartment. She blushed later when her roommate, Harper, told her that Jay had said she was beautiful. He'd actually used that word. She hadn't believed Harper, whom she'd awkwardly asked to repeat the conversation. She must have misheard. Colleen had been told she was attractive before, nice-looking, and the worst — once "hearty." Beautiful was for women like Tara; long straight blond hair, flawless skin, hips that ran straight up and down, so slender you could see their ribs in a bikini.

Jay told Colleen he loved her for the first time after he woke one morning to find her making him pumpkin pancakes from scratch. "I mentioned it one time to Ryan, not even to her, over a month ago," she heard him on the phone to Eli. "She filed it away and then, the next thing I know, the smell of pumpkin pancakes wafted through the house."

He seemed shocked each time Colleen offered some tiny gesture. She filled a bowl on the kitchen counter with salted cashews (his favorite), downloaded his favorite songs onto a CD and cut out articles about golfing and legal cases she thought he would find interesting. When he'd come back from a run to find her folding his laundry, he proposed to her. No one, except for hired help, had ever folded his boxers.

"These are normal things you do for someone you love,"

she said as he sat wide-eyed on the bed watching her fold his shirts into thirds.

He bragged to a colleague that Colleen was a revelation. She didn't understand until she met Dinah how unusual her behavior would be to him. Someone who put his needs first, someone who wanted to know what they were, instead of using him as a chess piece to win her latest social campaign.

She grew used to his gratitude, which he extended with every small offering she made, but she still contracted when he used the word "beautiful." Mary Ann's presence seemed to float into the room. Scowling. "There are far more important things to worry about than the way you look," Mary Ann said time and again. Accepting Jay's adoration felt like a betrayal.

Jay stood next to the bed looking down at his BlackBerry. "I've postponed my first day with Beck and Larson. I'm not going to New York until Wednesday." He shifted his eyes to Colleen. "Also, I think you need to quit your job. The last thing you need is more stress right now. We don't need the money."

Colleen looked out the window, continuing her search for the annoying bluejay and wondering what she would do all day once Jay went to New York. Had Jay seen daytime TV?

Jay was outside the bedroom now, banging around in the closet in the hallway. He returned with a tape measure.

"I wish Larry would let me work from home," she said.

Jay scribbled down the measurement between the wall and the doorway.

"Why don't you ask? One of my law professors said, 'You don't get what you think about, you get what you ask for.'" Jay measured the wall from the floor up to the windowsill.

"Don't let them pay you less. You're too nice. If they want to pay you less, say no."

"I'm sure he'll say no," Colleen said.

"What if he does? It's just a few months. You don't want to work after the baby is born anyway," Jay said as he wrote down more measurements.

She had never envisioned herself at home all day cooking, cleaning, doing laundry and changing diapers. She had taken the job at JJ Consulting instead of continuing on with the secondary school counseling program that she had been accepted into. She had dreamed of having her own office in a high school where young girls stopped in every day to discuss their problems. There would be kids like herself who didn't have the right clothes or the right hairstyle, who had a thermos filled with leftovers and another filled with milk in their bagged lunch instead of deli sandwiches, individual mini chip bags and cans of soda. She would help those unfortunate kids navigate their way through their self-doubt and zone in on their interests. She would encourage them to work hard in school and guide them through the financial aid paperwork for college.

"I'm sorry but you don't qualify for any more financial aid," the financial aid officer had told her and handed her an application for a student loan. Colleen had been afraid she wouldn't be able to pay back the loan. She thought of her family's history with farm debt and decided to move to Chicago with her college roommate, Harper, and get a job instead.

"I guess so," she told Jay.

"We'll get through this together and when it gets tough,

we'll focus on the beautiful healthy baby that comes at the end," he said.

Her husband disappeared downstairs into the kitchen, and Colleen heard the cabinet doors close and the microwave beep. He returned to the bedroom carrying a tray with two plates of chicken and broccoli casserole, a Granny Smith apple cut into chunks and a large bowl of purple grapes. He set the tray down on the bed and placed a votive candle on each of the bedside tables.

Colleen noticed the white envelope that the ultrasound technician had given her sitting on her bedside table. She had forgotten about it. "Do you want to know the sex?" Colleen said. She smiled through her tears.

"Are you kidding?" Jay said. His eyes sparkled as he looked at Colleen. "Do you know?"

"No, I waited for you. We can wait if you want to be surprised," Colleen said. Her eyes blurred as they filled with water again. Her hands shook as she picked up the envelope.

"I think we've had enough surprises," Jay said. "Open it."

The seal on the envelope wouldn't budge. She forced her index finger in the small space in the top corner. Her tears dripped and dampened the paper, making it harder to rip open. Inch by inch, her finger tore at the top until the paper inside was exposed. Colleen's eyes widened. She turned the paper toward Jay, revealing little pink hearts covering the page. The rest of the night was spent marveling at the thought of having a little girl.

"What should we name her?" Colleen said. She couldn't wait to create a pink shabby chic nursery, buy frilly dresses and hair bows. Her little girl would never see a hand-me-down piece of clothing.

"Abigail Adler? Adeline Adler? Too many As." Jay laughed.

"I hope she has your hair and complexion," Colleen said.

"Our little girl is going to steal my heart with these beautiful eyes…" Jay paused as he kissed Colleen's eyes, "and these wild curls…." He gently moved Colleen's curls away from her face. "Just as her beautiful mommy has."

Colleen felt tired when they turned off the lights at eleven, but now her mind raced. Jay's breathing became louder as Colleen lay next to him in their dark bedroom. She wanted a special name for their baby girl, one with meaning. She wanted her daughter to be strong. She thought of the women who were responsible for her place in the world. The only one she really knew was her mother. Her maternal grandmother died before she was born and her paternal grandmother died shortly after. She never met her great-grandmother Mabel, but she felt as though she knew her. She had imagined the hardship her great-grandmother endured and survived. She had lost three babies before she finally gave birth to Colleen's grandfather. Filled with grief, she still managed to fight her way through the Great Depression. Every time Colleen looked in the mirror she saw her great-grandmother's picture staring back. The connection had always been there. Now, it seemed, her body was handling pregnancy the same way Mabel's had. Thank God for modern science. Colleen used to resent inheriting Mabel's thick, coarse spiral curls and her turned-up nose, but now she was grateful; those looks had brought Jay to her. She hoped her baby girl was as strong as her great-grandmother was.

Colleen rolled from her back to her left side; she had read it was better for the baby. She watched the red digital numbers on the clock turn to 1:30. Lying in bed all day made it difficult to sleep at night. *Mabel*, she thought. Colleen's middle name was Ann after her mom. *Mabel Ann. Mabel Ann Adler.*

She flipped over to face Jay. "Jay," Colleen whispered.

He didn't move. His chest rose and fell.

Colleen leaned up and shook his shoulder. "Jay," she said louder.

Jay's body jerked as he woke.

"Mabel Ann. I want to name our baby Mabel Ann, after my great-grandma and my mom," Colleen whispered.

Jay rubbed his eyes. His eyes were dewy as he gazed at Colleen. "Mabel Ann Adler." He pulled Colleen into his arms, nestled his chin over her head and let his body fold into hers.

LARRY CALLED COLLEEN BACK ON Monday afternoon to inform her that working from home was not an option. Since she didn't plan to go back to work after the baby was born, her days working for JJ Consulting appeared to be over. Colleen pinched the bridge of her nose between her thumb and forefinger after she hung up the phone. She needed to stop the tears before they surfaced. She didn't want Jay to witness more weakness. Jay smiled when he realized her job was over. He had never liked Larry anyway.

Before Jay left for New York on Wednesday, he saw to it that their bedroom was set up as a small studio apartment. A new 72-inch television had been placed in the new entertainment center that was installed the day before. Colleen could watch the TV in comfort from her bed or the new reclining chair that sat on the opposite side of her bedside table. Jay filled the new mini fridge with Aunt Susie's famous crunchy chicken casserole, mini meatloaf, lasagna, three-egg sandwiches and a container of chicken salad. A microwave, coffee maker and toaster were placed on top of the shelving unit next to the tiny refrigerator. Paper plates, napkins, crackers, chips, ground coffee, homemade muffins, a loaf of bread and jugs of filtered water were stored on the lower shelves. Colleen did her best to follow her routine after getting dressed and eating an egg sandwich, but couldn't wait for the designated mid-morning snack time to munch on her mom's banana walnut muffins.

The highlight of Colleen's day became the six o'clock call with her parents. They hadn't missed a day since her mom left. The night before Jay left for New York, she put the phone on speaker after her parents shared the news that Johnny had been ranked the highest in his class and would be the class valedictorian. She and Jay enthusiastically congratulated Johnny and spent the next thirty minutes offering him tips on his speech. Colleen couldn't wait to hear the final speech. John and Mary Ann promised Colleen they would have Uncle Jimmy record the entire graduation and the graduation party so Colleen could be part of it. Aunt Susie said she would have everyone over to their house when Colleen came to Brockville with the baby for a graduation-viewing party. Jay promised Colleen that he would drive her and the baby to Brockville for a long weekend as soon as she felt ready for the trip. Colleen couldn't wait to have little Mabel in her arms and be in Brockville with her entire family celebrating Johnny's success and Mabel's arrival into the world.

She waited for the bonus round on *Wheel of Fortune* to end

before she tried calling the farmhouse again. After five rings, Johnny's recorded voice instructed her to leave a message. She smiled at the thought of Johnny persuading them to get an answering machine. Once Johnny moved out, the answering machine would most likely go with him. She sat back in her recliner and admired her newly decorated bedroom. She wondered how much longer until the walls began to close in on her.

The phone rang. She knew it was her mom or dad or maybe even Johnny calling back. Hopefully, he had his valedictorian speech ready for her to hear. "Hi, Colleen, it's Lulu from Belly Time Maternity. I wanted to let you know that we got a new shipment in today. The summer dresses are simply stunning!"

Colleen didn't want to hear about all the beautiful clothes that no longer made sense to wear. She didn't plan on getting dressed up to lie on top of her bed. She wasn't in the mood to explain her situation to Lulu.

She dialed her aunt Susie's number. Her machine picked up also. "Where is everyone?" Colleen said out loud as she set her phone down.

She thought about the graduation party her family was planning for Johnny. It was going to be held in the restored barn she was supposed to get married in. She imagined the string lights draped across the rafters inside the barn and a big bonfire outside. Her dad and uncles would get a pig from a local farmer and spend the twenty-four hours before the party roasting it in the large cast iron roaster they bought years ago. Colleen craved the smoky flavor of the tender pieces of pork that fell off the pig after being roasted for so many hours.

Finally, the phone rang. Colleen answered before a second

ring came through. Her body softened as she heard her mom's voice on the other end. "A letter from the U of I School of Agriculture came today confirming Johnny's four-year scholarship and his place on the school's track team," Mary Ann said. "We were at the high school watching him get his picture taken by the Brockville Press. Don't worry, I'll be sure to get an extra copy for you when it comes out next week."

"Where's Johnny?" Colleen asked.

"He stayed in town with his buddies. It's senior prank night," Mary Ann said.

"The water tower," Colleen said. She remembered the group of boys from her class who climbed up Brockville's water tower and spray-painted "Class of 1991." She remembered standing below, keeping watch with Tara and Paula.

"Does he have his speech ready for me yet?" Colleen asked.

"He wanted me to tell you that he'll call you tomorrow with it. He wants to make sure Jay is there to hear it."

"Jay gets home later tonight. Tell Johnny we will be waiting for his call tomorrow," Colleen said.

COLLEEN WOKE TO THE PHONE ringing. She looked at the clock. It was only 6:30 a.m. She quickly picked up the receiver, hoping not to wake Jay. Her dad's tone told her something was wrong. Perhaps something had happened to one of her uncles in a farming accident. "Where's Jay?" he said.

"He's right here." Colleen's heart raced. "Dad, what's wrong?"

Jay sat up in bed.

"Honey." He did his best to compose himself. "Johnny had an accident."

Colleen couldn't believe what she was hearing. "Is he okay?" she said, but she knew by the way he spoke that he wasn't.

"No, sweetheart." His voice broke up. "We lost him."

"What....No, no!" Her head shook.

"He slipped on his way down from the water tower." John choked over the words and started sobbing so uncontrollably that Colleen couldn't understand anything he said.

Colleen's uncle Jimmy came on the phone. "He fell about a hundred feet, honey. He died before he got to the hospital," Jimmy said.

Jay held her as he began to put together what was being said on the other end of the line. She handed the phone to Jay. She was too numb to hear more. When Jay hung up with Jimmy, he lay by Colleen's side, holding her as she wept, her body wracked with sobs. Time stood still.

"I have to go home," Colleen said as she walked out of the bathroom. Her eyes were swollen and her nose was red. Her chin quivered and tears ran down her cheeks as she pulled her bag from her closet.

"You need to lie down. Let's talk with Dr. Anderson and see what she has to say," Jay said.

Colleen's body crumbled to the floor. Crying into her hands, "Why? Why did he have to be taken?"

Jay sat on the floor beside her, doing his best to scoop her into his arms. "We need to get you back into bed." He gently guided her up and back under the covers. Returning from the bathroom, he gently wiped Colleen's swollen face with a cool washcloth.

"You don't understand." Colleen's eyes were pleading in desperation. "I have to go home. I have to see my parents."

Jay called Dr. Anderson. Colleen wept as she listened to Jay explain her situation. Jay put the phone on speaker so Colleen could hear Dr. Anderson. "Colleen, I am so sorry, but you need to stay put," Dr. Anderson said. "Traveling poses too much risk."

Jay made Colleen some tea. He guided her up from the fetal position she had been lying in and wiped her face again with the cool washcloth.

"How do you still want to be here? With all my problems?" Colleen said.

Jay leaned against Colleen's pillow and brought her head down to his chest. "When my dad died, I came down to the kitchen like I always did on a school morning. I was so excited to see my mother instead of the nanny sitting at the kitchen table. She didn't show any emotion when she told me that my dad had died in a car accident the night before. She told me I could stay home and mope alone or go to school and try to forget about it. I was only twelve. I didn't know what to do. I didn't want to go to school but I didn't want to sit alone all day either. I would have given anything for someone to sit with me, hold me and let me cry."

"I'm so sorry. I didn't know that's how your mother told you," Colleen said.

"I want you take the time you need. Cry as much as you need to. I'm not going anywhere," Jay said as she stroked her hair.

Aunt Susie's call couldn't have come at a better time. Colleen had struggled to follow Jay's logic to stay in bed as Dr. Anderson had ordered.

"Driving to Brockville isn't worth risking the life of your

precious baby," Aunt Susie told Colleen. "Things are so hectic here — half the town's out here working. We've got people mowing, cleaning out the chicken coop, washing cars, cleaning the house, hosing down the front porch and cleaning out the freezer and fridge for all the food people started dropping off. Honey, your parents are in no state to worry about you and the baby," Aunt Susie said.

Colleen wanted to be there helping. She wanted to be the one accepting the food and loading the roasted chickens, scalloped potatoes, chicken and rice casseroles, turkey potpies, lasagnas and meat loaves into the refrigerator and freezer. She wanted to be the one to place the platters of sandwiches on the table for all the people coming in and out of the house. She should be the one who answered the questions about how her parents were doing. She would collect the eggs, wash the clothes, wipe down the counters and wash the dishes. She imagined standing in her parents' kitchen and going back into labor. She would be rushed to Central Community Hospital, forty-five minutes away, where she would see a general doctor who may not even know how to handle a high-risk pregnancy. Assuming the doctors there did know how to treat pre-term labor, the chances of her getting to the hospital in time were slim. Her baby girl would be born and most likely die in the same hospital as her brother.

"I'll stay in bed," she finally agreed with Aunt Susie. She looked down at the calendar she had been holding. By the time the funeral was planned she would be twenty weeks. The baby still wouldn't be viable. She could ride in the car with the seat reclined, get a wheelchair for the funeral and go straight home after.

Every time Colleen closed her eyes, she saw Johnny fall from the water tower. So many unanswered questions filled her mind. Why him, why was he the one who fell? How were her parents going to get through this? How was she? She kept imagining the fear he felt as he slipped. Unable to contain her weeping, she went into the bathroom to cry in peace without worrying Jay, who after a long day was finally sleeping. She felt a sudden tightness come across her stomach, followed by cramping. She sat on the toilet thinking maybe emptying her bladder would help.

"Jay," Colleen screamed. She sobbed as she tore away her blood-soaked underwear.

Words were not necessary for Jay to know what was going on. He helped his defeated and exhausted wife down the stairs and to the car. Colleen's face was stripped of color as Jay raced her to the hospital.

The doctors in the Emergency Room confirmed that Colleen had gone back into premature labor. She was given Magnesium Sulfate through an IV as well as a low dose of an antidepressant to help her relax. A few hours later, Dr. Anderson believed the labor had stopped. She declared it was best for Colleen to stay in the hospital for a few days, possibly longer. The doctors were empathetic, but there was no way she could attend the funeral.

FOUR

April 15, 2011
Chicago

Colleen was startled by the sharp honk from the Range Rover behind her. She jumped and smudged her freshly manicured left index finger on the steering wheel. A text notification interrupted her preoccupation of comparing herself to the women who chose to park a few blocks away and walk to pick up their children. The women walked by in pairs. The few times Colleen had experimented with walking versus the carpool line, she had never managed to pair up with anyone. She walked up alone and she waited alone. Now she carefully placed her middle finger and thumb around the edge of her phone.

> Jay: *Flight delayed due to storms. Not sure when I'll get out. Hoping it's tonight and not in the morning.* ☹
>
> Colleen: *Ok, be safe. Keep me posted.*

Not that long ago a text like that from Jay on a Friday afternoon would have made her mad and frustrated. Usually by the week's end, she was counting down the minutes for Jay's help with the girls. Recently, however, things had changed. She had another night without worrying about how she looked or pretending to be in a good mood. She was grateful for one more night where she didn't have to hold back her questions about the pretty California woman in the picture drinking champagne with him. She didn't know how much longer she could go on pretending he wasn't having an affair.

Just as she sat her phone back in its place on the center console, it rang. Dinah.

"Colleen, Dinah Adler." Colleen was barely able to say hello before Dinah started talking. "We missed you at the fashion show. I had the most marvelous time with Ashley and Victoria. Two of the classiest women of your generation, that's for sure." Dinah worshipped these two women as much they did her. They followed in Dinah's footsteps as the up-and-coming leaders of Harborview Country Club. Deciding on whom and whom not to speak to, based on Dinah's body language and comments, was a medium in which they flourished, like corn growing in rich Midwestern soil under the hot summer sun.

Colleen struggled to keep her voice steady. "I had a doctor's appointment." She lost her nerve to confront Dinah about the late invitation. The urge to tell her about the Raina Rose dress that didn't find its way to the Harborview Spring Fashion Show was so forceful she had to squeeze her teeth together to keep quiet.

"I found the most adorable matching Dolce & Gabbana dresses for the girls. They've got the most exquisite blue floral pattern. They're perfect for our Mother's Day dinner." Dinah was always buying her granddaughters new clothes. She spent a fortune at various children's boutiques. Prada, Gucci, D&G. Colleen had not even been aware high-end designers made children's clothing. Dinah didn't blink an eye at buying the girls each a one-thousand-dollar wool coat with matching boots or a five-hundred-dollar cross-body bag (which they would never carry) when they already had several coats and boots that were perfectly fine. She said nothing was too expensive for her son's little girls, but she really meant there wasn't a price tag too large for her reputation.

"Feel free to drop them by anytime that works for you," Colleen said. Her lip became a victim of her frustration. She bit down hard in an effort to maintain her polite tone.

"I'm too busy this week. I'm going to leave the dresses with Harrold," Dinah said. Harrold was the doorman in Dinah's condo building. She spoke of him as though he worked for her personally.

At least her building is on the way to the girls' school, Colleen thought as she went along with Dinah.

"Make sure the girls try them on right away and let me know if they don't fit. I want to be sure they look nice for pictures." Dinah said.

Colleen's phone went silent. Dinah always controlled the conversation, never giving Colleen the chance to even say "good-bye." Colleen wondered if she treated everyone that way or if it was just her. Was Dinah even aware that she hurt Colleen's feelings multiple times in that short conversation? Colleen wished she had said that she was too busy to pick the dresses up. She yanked her hair and fumed as she sat in her idling car.

The school pickup attendant motioned for Colleen to pull forward. She was now the first in line. Why weren't the girls out yet? Other cars were pulling around her. She felt foolish sitting in the front of the line waiting for her tardy children. She watched the skinny women swoon around Ashley Barr and Victoria Heller. Those two were enough of a reason to stay in her car. They probably thought she was stupid and lazy for choosing to sit in the carpool line.

Finally, Colleen thought as she saw Chloe's pigtails bouncing through the stack of moms lingering outside the school entrance. Her face beamed as she skipped up to the car. Colleen envied her confidence and zest for life. She wondered if she had ever been that way. She certainly couldn't remember it, if she had.

"Hi, Mommy!! How was your day?" Chloe asked.

Chloe's cheerfulness brightened Colleen's mood. She took a deep breath before answering her sweet daughter. "My day was good," she lied.

"My day was sooooo good, Mommy. Mrs. Everly gave us Jolly Ranchers today! I got watermelon. That's my favorite. What's your favorite, Mommy?" Chloe said.

Colleen hadn't thought of Jolly Ranchers in a long time. Lacking the energy to really think about her favorite flavor, she went along with Chloe. "Definitely watermelon," she said.

"Sara wants me and Mabel to come over when we get home. They just got a brand-new playhouse in their backyard. It's got a kitchen and everything! Can we go?" Chloe said. She sang more than spoke her words when she wanted something.

Before Colleen could answer, Mabel opened the door. She didn't look as though she had quite as good of a day as her little sister. There was no skipping to the car. She got in the car quietly. Before she could even fasten her seat belt, Chloe started telling her about their plans to see the playhouse.

"How was your day, Mabel?" Colleen said.

"Fine." Her tone said the opposite.

"What's wrong, honey?"

"I don't want to talk about it." She ignored Chloe and stared out the window in silence.

Colleen imagined from Mabel's sour face that the trouble was with Rebecca. Rebecca Barr was just like her mom, Ashley. She bossed the girls around, telling them whom they could and couldn't be friends with that day. Some days Mabel fell into the friend category and some days she didn't. As often as Colleen found herself in the same situation, she knew Mabel had it worse. The younger girls were a lot more brazen with their attacks on each other. Grown women had learned to project meanness with such finesse that those being spared didn't notice.

Colleen wished she had encouraging words to offer Mabel. Unfortunately, she was at a loss. Unable to get herself through similar situations, she felt helpless in guiding her daughter. Colleen moved on to something she was better equipped to handle. "Sounds like you guys are going to have fun over at the Wilsons'," Colleen said.

"Yesssss!" Chloe sounded as if she'd just won the lottery.

The girls raced out of the car. No sooner had their backpacks hit the floor than Chloe grabbed Mabel's hand, pulling her along as she skipped down the long hallway to the front door.

"Bye, Mom!!" Chloe yelled out as they set out across the front lawn toward the Wilsons' house.

Colleen struggled to catch up to them. She wanted to make sure they rang the doorbell and didn't barrel into the Wilsons' house.

"Stella and Sara are out back anxiously waiting for you girls!" Stephanie Wilson stood up from the crouched position she had been in. Her gardening gloves were covered in dirt.

"Are you sure you don't mind having them over?" Colleen asked.

"Finishing this last pot and I'm done for the day. They can stay as long as they want," Stephanie said. She wasn't like Colleen. She seemed to genuinely like being at home with the kids all day. She didn't outsource, hire a staff. Homemaking was her profession, and she was good at it.

Colleen looked at the sad state of her yard as she made her way back inside. She wished she could be more like Stephanie. She wished she had the energy and desire to do her own yard work. She couldn't even muster up the motivation to return Pedro's call. One phone call and her yard would be beautiful. Speaking to anyone right now felt like a chore. She would text him later.

Colleen admired her freshly painted red toes as she removed her shoes. At least her toenails looked good. The cold hardwood felt good on her bare feet as she walked through the house. She paused as she saw Stephanie out of her kitchen window. She walked closer to the window and watched Stephanie hose off her back patio. After giving a quick shot of water to her newly planted containers, she wrapped the hose around the iron holder that was neatly attached to the back of her house. Ashley Barr wouldn't have invited Stephanie to a single gala. Colleen was sure Stephanie didn't care. She didn't care about having the biggest diamond or the latest and most expensive purse on the market. She kept her distance from the Ashleys and Victorias. She didn't care about not being part of "the group."

Lance Wilson emerged from the garage door leading to the backyard. Colleen stood back toward the corner of the window where she couldn't be seen. She watched as Stephanie greeted her husband with a loving kiss. Stephanie stood with her fingers interlaced behind Lance's head. Her head was tilted as she looked up at his doting face. Colleen knew from watching on other evenings that Lance and Stephanie would soon have a glass of wine in their hand. They would sit on their back deck talking and laughing as the girls played around them. Seeing the happiness of the couple in front of her made her wonder what it would be like to have Jay home every night. She couldn't decide if his daily presence would help, or if it would leave her more exhausted.

Having the house to herself was glorious. Colleen went against her general rule of waiting until five o'clock to have a glass of wine. With Jay coming home late and the girl's guaranteed exhaustion, tonight's bedtime was going to be an early one. A four o'clock glass of wine was acceptable. Her enthusiasm vanished momentarily when she was faced with a nearly empty bottle sitting on the counter. She had just opened the bottle last night. Begrudgingly, she made her way down to the wine cellar to get a new bottle.

Jay's wine enthusiasm developed during their honeymoon in Napa Valley. Colleen was thrilled when Jay wanted to plan the honeymoon. At the time, the notion of being surprised on the way to the airport seemed romantic. The instructions to bring dresses, lightweight sweaters and a swimsuit left her guessing. Deep down Colleen had hoped for a relaxing beach getaway but when Jay surprised her, she went along with his excitement about Napa Valley.

Colleen began to like wine when she and Jay started dating but didn't really have an interest in learning about it. Even after all the tastings and tours, she still couldn't tell the difference between pinot noir and merlot. She eventually came to know she liked cabernet better than most other reds, oaky chardonnays over non-oaky ones. She liked sauvignon blancs. But she couldn't tell the difference between the type of soil, the region, what made one wine gain a score of 93 in *Wine Spectator*, and another sell for five dollars at Trader Joe's.

The wine cellar smelled like leather. The two walls of unfinished mahogany shelving could hold more than four thousand bottles of wine, which was a nice idea but most of the shelves sat empty. Neither Colleen nor Jay ever got around to putting away the cases of wine Jay had delivered every month. The wine boxes littered the antique terra cotta floor tiles — some were empty, some picked through and several sat unopened.

According to Dinah, you were supposed to switch over to white and rosé wines in the spring. Colleen wasn't in the mood for those wines, and she certainly wasn't in the mood for Dinah's rules. Red had been the flavor of last month's box, so cabernet would be the choice for the evening. As she reached down into the dwindling bottles of the boxed case, Colleen saw a white envelope lying on the ground next to the special case that had been delivered to Jay last week. The top was torn. Her heart pounded as she gently pulled out the note.

The name Chad Chenick was engraved on the top of the stationary. Colleen took a seat at the large oak table that sat in the center of the wine cellar where the light was strong enough to read.

> *Can't thank you enough for all of your help. Your strategic maneuvering still has me scratching my head. The beautiful women and martinis didn't help my state of confusion! This vintage is a real beauty. I remembered your fondness for oaky, smoky reds and this has got plenty. Looking forward to another night lighting up the West Coast with you! Chad*

Jay had never mentioned that he was spending time with Chad Chenick, the star of the popular TV series *Daring Greatness*. He used to tell her about all of the famous clients he worked with. Was Jay's pretty blond friend one of the beautiful women Chad Chenick was referring to? For all Colleen knew, the woman might have spent the entire night "lighting up" the West Coast with Jay and his celebrity clients.

Looking past the letter on the table, Colleen remembered when Eli sent this table to Jay as a housewarming gift when they first moved in. He had it made out of old oak wine barrels. Colleen felt bad for going along with Arthur, the designer Dinah recommended, in telling Jay that the table wasn't appropriate for the dining room. The various colors that had been naturally stained into the wood as it held wine over the years was beautiful. For some reason, Colleen could only see that now. When she and Arthur were designing the house, she had been caught up with creating a picture-perfect home; one that didn't include stains.

Colleen remembered vividly one Monday after her weekly checkup, during the tense days of bed rest when she was pregnant with Mabel. Instead of taking her straight back to the house as their doctor insisted, Jay drove her around the quaint Southport Corridor neighborhood. He pointed out the variety of restaurants and cute shops lining Southport Street. Turning right on Cornelia Street, he drove Colleen to the house he had just made an offer on. He parked in front of the grey-shingle-style home stretched across two city lots and pulled out a folder with floor plans and pictures of the interior. Although the exterior was complete, the interior of the newly constructed home was an open maze of wood beams and wires. Jay did his best to describe the interior's dramatic high ceilings, massive room sizes, four fireplaces and seven bedrooms. The traditional layout of the eight-thousand-square-foot home was finished with a front porch extending the width of the house with a door off to the south side leading to an expansive backyard that included an outdoor fireplace in the center of the raised terrace.

Colleen's excitement grew as he pored over the plans. The new home helped bring her back to life. He had already told Dinah, who had paid Arthur a retainer to help them decorate. Unlike Dinah, Arthur became a confidant, and a friend. He provided Colleen with the company she so desperately needed during that difficult time when she spent ten hours a day languishing in their bed, allowed to rise only to go to the bathroom. He helped direct her mind away from her anxiety and, instead, focus on designing the home of her dreams.

Colleen poured what was left from last night's cabernet bottle. The wine filled barely half a glass. Tonight, she vowed to pay more attention. She would stop when she reached the label. She topped her glass off with the new bottle, took her wine and iPad to the back living room where she could have the windows open and enjoy the breeze. She put her freshly manicured feet up on the leather ottoman, settled into her favorite blue chair and prepared to do some online shopping.

She could hear the girls playing outside in the Wilsons yard from the open windows. She leaned her head closer to the screen. High-pitched giggles echoed across the backyard. Besides her daughter's laughter, Colleen's joy came now from coffee and wine. She was grateful for anything that would help her fight off the emotional heaviness she felt as she embarked on getting through another May. Her brother Johnny had died on May 18 seven years ago. The date glared at her on the calendar like a dark hole.

The thought of the warm summer days ahead had helped get her through the past seven Mays. This year was different. Besides her new Fourth of July dress (that didn't even come close to fitting), she didn't have new summer outfits to look forward to wearing. She wasn't going to buy new clothes at her current size — she weighed as much now as she had at the end of her first pregnancy. Before having kids, she had always been a size six. She hovered at a size eight after having Mabel and settled into a size ten after Chloe was born. However, for the past two years, her weight had gradually been going up until she was out of regular sizes. Her plus-sized pants had even grown tight. She refused to go any higher.

Colleen didn't want to have hypothyroidism, but she was glad for a diagnosis where her lack of willpower was not to blame. She expected the doctor to scan her pityingly with his eyes and tell her to exercise more and eat less.

"After several weeks on the medication, some weight loss is expected," Dr. Bradley had assured her. She had weighed herself that morning. After she removed all of her clothing, emptied her bladder, removed her ponytail holder, blew her nose, emptied her bladder again, spit until she had nothing left to spit, she finally stepped on her brand-new Weight Gurus smart body fat scale. The digital number was as hateful as it had been a week earlier. Dr. Bradley told her to be patient. Colleen felt she was running out of time.

She unzipped the beige garment bag that held her social future. The hand-stitched embroidered silver stars exploded against the dark silk fabric. The two-toned navy silk gave the illusion of wide stripes draping down the skirt of the dress.

"The A-line cut and the tonal stripes create a wonderful slimming effect," the sales associate had told her. If Colleen could jam herself into the reserve Raina Rose, she was going to stand out. For once, she would be better dressed than Ashley Barr and Victoria Heller. That night, Fouth of July, would be the day of reckoning. She would let Jay and Dinah and the entire club see how beautiful she looked. She would finally be socially accepted within the country club circle, and then she would confront Jay about the woman in Los Angeles. Dinah would think twice about sending Colleen's invitation late next year. But all this was still a fantasy. If she didn't fit into the dress, none of this could happen. Her phone reminded her it was already April 15. The date was getting closer and her weight was going up.

She pulled up Facebook and typed in Alexis Wyatt Adler. Sifting through the recent posts, she finally came to the picture of Jay and that woman. She snapped a screenshot. Now, she could look at the picture whenever she wanted. Taking a long drink of wine, she clicked the forward at the bottom of the screen. Staring at the blinking cursor in the recipient space, she thought about sending the photo to Jay. "Who is this woman?" she wanted to write in the subject line.

Colleen glanced at the clock in the top corner of her screen. Almost 6:00. The girls would need dinner. "Pie in the Sky, can you please hold?" a woman chirped. Colleen hoped they weren't as busy as they sounded. She wanted a quick delivery. The woman's voice returned to the line.

"Oh, hi, Mrs. Adler, you want the usual? Medium, half veggie, half cheese?"

She winced at being recognized by the pizza delivery shop. She scrolled back through the past few days. She had ordered pizza three times that week. Tomorrow she would install Pie in the Sky's app and order online in the future.

Her phone blinked with another call — the Wilsons' number.

"The girls are having a blast in the playhouse. Do you mind if they stay and eat with us? I'm grilling kebabs. I made some zucchini chocolate chip cookies to use as a bribe to get them to eat the mushrooms, broccoli and cauliflower I skewered with the chicken. Is it all right with you if they have dessert?" Stephanie said.

Colleen couldn't remember the last time her girls were fed something so healthy. She tried to match Stephanie's cheery tone. "Sure! That's so nice of you. What time should I get them?"

"Lance can walk them over. Have them home by 8:30, if that's not too late?" Stephanie said.

Colleen looked at her almost empty glass of wine and thought she had better slow down or she wouldn't be able to stay awake that late. It was nice, the Wilsons' walking the girls home. It meant she wouldn't have to go back out.

She looked out the window and saw the Baldwins and the Spencers congregating on the sidewalk in front of the Frosts'. By seven, there would be a group of ten or more, regular couples whose husbands lived at home during the week. Husbands who were not in LA having affairs.

The neighbor discussion tonight would be the beautiful work their landscapers had done on their yards and flower boxes. Colleen looked out over the dead leaves and other remnants of winter that still loitered their yard. The brown evergreens and winterberry branches that had been plucked bare by hungry birds still filled her flower boxes.

She remembered their yard the first spring they lived there. Pedro carefully arranged the bulbs of purple alliums, pink tulips, crocuses, grape hyacinth and snowdrops deep in the soil the fall before, right after they moved in. He showed up after the last of the snow melted to replace the wintery evergreen that filled the ornate urns on each side of their front door and all the window boxes lining their front porch. The front of their house had looked like a Monet painting. The Adlers' yard was the first one done in their neighborhood that spring and was by far the most beautiful. Noel Bellman and her mom would have been jealous.

Colleen poured another glass of wine. Tomorrow, she would call Pedro back and do something about the yard. She pulled her iPad to her lap and returned to the girls' summer wardrobe. They still needed dresses for the Fourth of July party, and she wanted to be the one to take credit for their attire, instead of Dinah. When Dinah called to say she got them dresses, she could tell her to return them. Colleen filled her Neiman Marcus cart with a sleeveless pleated blue-and-white-striped floral jacquard dress for Mabel, a matching dress but red-and-white-striped instead of blue for Chloe, two embellished star rhinestone headbands, one in blue and one in red and two pair of white Aquazzura wild fringe suede sandals. If Colleen could fit in the navy dress, the three of them were going to look like perfection.

AN EMAIL FROM HER CHIROPRACTOR, Dr. Metzger, sat at the top of her unread mail. The subject line read, *Spring Cleanse: Letting go of what no longer serves you.*

Colleen opened the message. It was from some wellness coach Dr. Metzger had just brought into her practice. Dr. Metzger had been encouraging Colleen to meet with this woman. "Just meet with her. The medication is going to take a while and it's not going to magically take away the amount of weight you want to lose."

Dr. Metzger had been Colleen's chiropractor since the end of her pregnancy with Mabel. Spending the majority of her time lying on her back as her body grew resulted in back pain. One session with Dr. Metzger and the pain was gone. Colleen had continued to see her after the pregnancy. Colleen gave Dr. Metzger's daughter, who also went to Northside Day School, an occasional ride from school to her office when her nanny canceled. Colleen shared her mother's banana walnut muffin recipe — the one Mary Ann had said must stay in the family — with Dr. Metzger, printing it out on a card and decorated it with scrolls made using the girls' markers. In the seven years, the women had become friends.

The email finally loaded.

> *I am pleased to announce the addition of Kory Stone to my practice. Kory comes to us after running her own personal coaching practice for the past eight years. After seeing the great results so many of my patients have had with her over the years, I began my quest of getting her to join my practice...*

Colleen clicked on the tab linking her to Kory's website. The pages of testimonials were impressive. One after the other they read the same way. Kory changed lives. According to the testimonials, she had helped women lose ten, twenty, and thirty pounds. She helped some with depression, or find the right therapist. Even find their life's purpose, one testimonial said. The list continued.

Colleen clicked around the website. The amount of work required for all of those transformations sounded exhausting. Kory wrote, "I'm not any different than a midwife. Just as a midwife helps a mother give birth, I help my clients give birth to their very own life."

Colleen kept thinking about the testimonial that said,

"Kory helped me find the courage to follow my dream in becoming a photographer. I finally feel alive." Colleen didn't know the last time she'd felt alive; she didn't even know what her dreams were anymore. She didn't seem to have any. Colleen knew she needed more than a diet. She thought of the testimonial about the woman who had gained and lost the same twenty pounds over and over. She said Kory helped her learn how to keep those twenty pounds off for good.

Colleen navigated through the packages Kory provided. She offered private, one-on-one sessions as well as group sessions. Colleen paused when she read the nonrefundable first month commitment — sixteen hundred dollars. *That's definitely a commitment*, Colleen thought. Clicking back to Dr. Metzger's email, Colleen read about the wellness meeting Kory was hosting tomorrow morning at 9:30.

She clicked on the meeting registration button. Her screen was directed to an online registration site. She filled in the blanks before she chickened out or changed her mind. A credit card number was required at the bottom of the form. Her card was in her wallet in the kitchen. She had been meaning to tape her credit card number to her iPad so she wouldn't have to constantly get up every time she wanted to buy something. Her wine glass was full and she was comfortable. She contemplated waiting for the next coaching session to come around. She would have to get a sitter, Jay may not be home from New York, and if he was, he would be exhausted from a late night of travel. The medication prescribed from an actual doctor hadn't helped, so how could talking to someone?

Colleen's bladder throbbed. She had no choice but to get up. She stared at the popped stitches around the waistband as she sat on the toilet. One woman said Kory had helped her lose thirty pounds. Thirty. Kory could help her give birth to her own life, the one that had gotten lost in all of her fat. She pulled her credit card from her wallet on her way back through the kitchen. If Jay couldn't watch the girls in the morning, maybe the Wilsons would take them. She could offer to have Stella and Sara come over tomorrow night for dinner while Gabby was babysitting.

The girls were delivered at 8:30 as promised. Colleen kicked the empty pizza box under the couch before Lance Wilson could see it. Colleen and the girls left Jay a voicemail. She got them through their baths and the girls were in Mabel's bed reading stories by nine. Regardless of how much wine she drank, Colleen made sure to read to the girls every night.

"Mommy, wake up," Chloe said. "It's time to go to your bed."

She didn't want to think about how often this happened, the three of them falling asleep in a tangled heap on Mabel's comforter. Colleen kissed each girl on the head, turned off the lights in the girls' room and stumbled down the hall to her own bed.

FIVE

Gertrude's mouth dropped open when Colleen walked into the office. "Please tell me you are here for the wellness meeting and not the doctor," Gertrude said.

Colleen guessed Gertrude to be about seventy years old. She had been Dr. Metzger's receptionist as long as Colleen had been a patient. Colleen had a standing appointment every other Monday at eleven a.m. She had never come on a Saturday.

Colleen smiled at Gertrude. "Don't worry, I'm here for the meeting."

Gertrude stood to come out from behind her desk. She wasn't much taller than she had been sitting in her chair. Her hair was cut in a short pixie and was so thin and white that you could see through it, especially with the sun shining in through the window. "Oh, you are going to love Kory. She's just the sweetest thing," Gertrude said.

Colleen hesitated to follow Gertrude back to the meeting room. She contemplated an excuse so she could bolt out of there. Maybe she could say she forgot something in the car? She could say she needed to make a quick call and then not come back.

There were at least ten other women sitting around a long rectangular table. The women sat in threes and in pairs chatting with one another. Colleen quickly scanned the room looking for an empty seat. Unfortunately, the only seat not sandwiched between groups of women was at the opposite end of the table. She hooked her fingers around the straps of her purse, trying not to bump into any of the women as she walked past.

"This seat is open," an older woman said. She gave Colleen a warm smile exposing her straight Chiclet-square teeth. The tomato red lipstick made her teeth appear more yellow than they would have if she'd selected a different lip color. "Have you ever worked with Kory?" she said. She handed Colleen a name tag from the center of the table.

Colleen rested her purse down on the ground next to the chair and sat down. She shook her head. "Have you?" she said. She searched for a pen to write her name. She noticed the nice woman had *Fran* written on her nametag.

"No, but I met Kory through a friend at a party a few months ago," Fran said as she passed a pen to Colleen. "My friend has been working with her for a while and I've seen her change before my eyes."

Colleen wanted to ask what kind of change but Kory arrived. The women's chatter quieted as they shifted their attention to the woman of the hour. Kory walked into the room as though she knew everyone there personally. The fact that she was ten minutes late for her own meeting didn't seem to faze her. Her slightly disheveled sandy-blond hair was damp and pulled back into a ponytail, she had two distinct pink patches right in the middle of each cheek and her eyes were bright and so blue that the white part seemed to disappear. The evidence of sweat dotting the front and back of her shirt was further proof that she had just come from some kind of workout. Colleen wondered how she was capable of looking so fabulous in sweaty workout clothes and no makeup?

The other women must have been thinking the same thing because the room fell silent as they all stared at her. A woman, almost as heavy as Colleen, with thick dark hair pulled back in a sloppy bun wasn't able to contain her wonder. "You must be a runner," she said. Her tone begged for more details about what kind of workout Kory had been doing.

Colleen strained her eyes to see that the stout woman's name tag read *Beth*.

The women waited for the details of Kory's secret to looking beautiful. Maybe, they all hoped, if they did exactly what she did, they could look like her. Besides the older woman sitting next to Colleen, Kory was just as old or older than most of the women in the room.

"I don't think I can fairly call myself a runner these days," Kory laughed. "I used to be a runner but as I've gotten older, running has become too hard on my body. I ran today for the first time in a long time. My sixteen-year-old son didn't think I could keep up with him. I proved him right!" Kory laughed again. "I need to take advice out of my own playbook, don't do things to impress others."

"I don't know what's worse, that you look that good and have a sixteen-year-old or that you're able to keep up with one," Beth said.

"Believe me, I didn't keep up with him!" Kory laughed.

Colleen enjoyed being part of the collective laughter. It helped her begin to relax.

"I've never been one to run," Fran whispered to Colleen.

"Me either," Colleen mouthed back.

After giving a brief introduction, Kory said, "Place both feet on the ground and your hands on your lap, one hand on each leg. Nothing crossed." She turned off the lights. "We're going to get started with some deep breaths. Close your eyes. Breathe in and out." Kory let out a deep breath.

Colleen uncrossed her legs and slid back in her chair to comfortably rest her hands on her legs. Doing her best to follow along, she closed her eyes. She inhaled as Kory counted to eight and then slowly exhaled as Kory counted to ten. She was out of breath before Kory got to nine. Exhaling slower the next round, she made it to ten. She tried to soften her belly as Kory instructed but found herself at a loss when told to feel the breath come up through her spine. Her breath was coming up through her nose. There was nothing in her spine. She had never heard of such a thing.

"We're going to do this three more times," Kory said.

Colleen struggled to keep her mind from wandering. She was glad when Kory said they were on the last breath.

"With this last breath, let go of any lingering frustrations," Kory said softly.

Colleen thought about her weight, Dinah, Victoria Heller, Ashley Barr, Rebecca Barr, *the woman in the picture*. She didn't have much air left, but she pushed out the little bit that was there and hoped those frustrations went along with it.

"Keep your eyes closed and sit with that bit of peace that you created for yourself." Kory paused for a few seconds and turned the lights back on. "Now slowly open your eyes. Write down the first thing that comes to mind on the paper in front of you and fold it in half."

Colleen was surprised by how relaxed the breathing left her. The softness of her neck and shoulders made her realize how tense she had been. The first thing she thought was "peaceful." Was that really something to write down? She thought it should be something else, something more concrete. Colleen didn't know what else to write so she picked up her pen and wrote down "peaceful." She hoped she didn't have to share it with the group.

Looking around, Colleen realized she was the first one finished. People were writing a lot. Colleen had just written one word. She wondered if she should pick her pen up and write more? She didn't know what else to write.

Just as Colleen picked up her pen, Beth asked, "What if our mind's blank?"

Good, nothing came to her either, thought Colleen.

"All of the answers we need are inside of us," Kory said. "The first thing that comes to mind after a meditation is usually what your soul most desires. When we quiet our mind, we open ourselves up to our internal voice." She walked around to the opposite side of the table. "Sometimes a thought will come out of nowhere, other times, nothing comes and that's okay. Your message will come when the time is right. Don't judge what happens."

Colleen prayed they wouldn't have to share what they wrote.

"Was that really a meditation?" a woman named Angela from the opposite side of the table asked. She had smooth brown hair with matching brown eyes. Her light brown skin was flawless and her straight teeth were unnaturally white. She didn't seem to have any extra weight to lose.

Colleen was wondering the same thing. She had never meditated before. She didn't imagine meditation being anything like that. It felt like she was just breathing.

"It's a good beginning meditation. Quieting the mind and focusing on your breath is a great exercise to lead yourself into a meditative place," Kory said.

Doing exactly as Kory instructed, Colleen took a deep breath into her chest while holding her paper with the word "peaceful" written on it close to her heart. Maybe she should have left the paper blank? What if her message hadn't come yet and her mind was just peaceful? How was she supposed to know the difference?

"How many of you are here to lose weight?" Kory asked.

Colleen raised her hand along with every other woman in the room. Noticing how skinny over half the room was, Colleen wondered why they were raising their hand.

"While your goal is weight loss, my goal is to help you find yourself, your true self," Kory said.

"What if our true self just needs to lose weight?" Beth said.

The women around the table laughed. Kory smiled at her. "I want to help you see beyond your physical body and dig deep into what makes your heart happy."

Beth's smile faded as she considered Kory's words. Colleen had no idea what made her heart happy. She loved the girls and Jay. They made her happy. They also made her exhausted. Besides her bed, a vanilla latte and a bottle of wine, she couldn't put her finger on anything that truly made her happy.

"The hardest part about finding out what makes you happy is being truthful about what isn't making you happy," Kory said. "In order to lose weight and keep it off, you have to commit to working hard to overcome the things that are holding you back."

Colleen wasn't sure she could commit to doing whatever work Kory was talking about. Some things in her life were too difficult to overcome. She did want what this woman was offering if it meant she could age as gracefully as she had. There was a unique quality to Kory's beauty that wasn't defined by the latest social standards. She didn't have a perfect face or perfect hair. Her body was very fit but not perfect. Unlike most of the woman Colleen was around, she had a very natural look to her. She didn't appear to have had any plastic surgery or Botox. She looked real. She had crow's feet at the corners of her eyes and a frown line between her eyebrows. Her lips were natural-looking and had small lines around them. Somehow she looked more beautiful and younger than so many women who have spent thousands on plastic surgery.

Kory handed a clipboard to Beth to sign and pass around. "Next to your name write what type of program you're interested in."

The clipboard finally made its way around to Colleen. Most of the women had written "small group." The thought of sharing her issues in a group setting was not appealing. Remembering what Kory said earlier about trusting your instincts, she wrote "one-on-one sessions" next to her name.

Kory walked over to the corner of the room and picked up a box full of books. She began handing them to the women to pass around. "I have so many favorite books that I like to share with my clients but this book seems to be the most appropriate for those just getting started with making changes in their life." Kory held up the book, *You Can Heal Your*

Life, by Louise Hay. "This is a book everyone should read. It contains great exercises to get you thinking and discovering the things that are holding you back from making positive changes in your life."

Colleen pretended to look through the book while Kory handed out a daily exercise plan. She invited everyone to join her in a group wellness walk after class. Colleen didn't want to socialize, she wanted to go home and read her new book and look over the meal plan. Having a meal plan might be just what she needed. She couldn't ever think of healthy things to make. There was so much conflicting information about what was healthy and what was not. She'd read that there were good carbs and bad carbs, but she couldn't remember what distinguished one from the other. She'd seen a pamphlet in Dr. Bradley's office that suggested processed meats like hot dogs, ham, bacon, sausage and some deli meat could cause cancer. The girls' pediatrician told her to choose organic meat and dairy for kids to limit their exposure to pesticides, hormones and antibiotics. Everything, it seemed, was toxic.

Colleen shifted her weight from one leg to the other while she waited for the other women to exit. She wanted to get to her car and away from everyone.

Fran didn't seem to mind the standstill in the doorway. She turned to Colleen. "Are you going to join us on the walk?"

Colleen looked down at her loafers and said, "I didn't wear my walking shoes and I need to get home to my girls." Colleen regretted saying so much. A simple "no" would have ended the conversation.

"Oh, how old are your girls?" Fran said.

Colleen's mind raced. She needed to be alone to process

what she had just experienced. She didn't want to talk to this woman. "Seven and five," she said.

Fran had the look of nostalgia, unique to mothers of older children. "Oh, how I miss those days and how I miss being missed."

Hoping to end the conversation, Colleen gave her a guarded closed-lip smile.

"You probably hear this all the time: enjoy every minute. It goes by so fast." Fran closed her eyes as if she were fondly remembering times of the past. "I remember wishing the time away. I was exhausted." She smiled as she looked Colleen in the eye. "Now I realize those days were some of the best of my life. Live and learn, right!" she laughed.

"Thank you, I needed to hear that." Colleen appreciated hearing that she wasn't the only one exhausted.

"Are you going to try the program?" Fran asked.

"I'm going to try the one-on-one sessions," she said. "The group sessions are all at night. Days are better for me while my girls are at school."

Fran's understanding smile put Colleen at ease. "You're a good mommy, I can tell. I do anything I can to fill my evenings," she laughed.

Colleen needed someone like Fran in her life. Too much time had passed since she felt the security of an older woman's love and support.

SIX

Colleen had expected to find Jay and the girls waiting for her, but she walked into a quiet house. Weekends were Jay's time. Trips to Lincoln Park Zoo, the Aquarium, the Field Museum, swimming at the country club and Cubs games were his favorite things to do with Mabel and Chloe. His car was still in the garage. They were probably at the park.

Colleen sat at the edge of the kitchen table and pulled out her new book. She slid out the thick pages of meal plans and recipes that she had placed in the front cover.

Upon waking: 8 oz. warm or room temperature lemon water. Breakfast: Very Berry Smoothie. Lunch: Mexican Chicken Salad. Dinner: Fish Stew with Brown Rice. Drink: water (enough ounces to equal half of your body weight), green tea (before 2 pm) and herbal tea.

The plan didn't look complicated. What about coffee, she wondered? Was the green tea supposed to replace it? That would never work. Colleen needed coffee. And the water, Dr. Bradley nagged her about it. She needed a calculator to do the math on the number of ounces. She hated drinking water. It made her go to the bathroom all day.

Begrudgingly, Colleen filled a water bottle before taking her new reading materials to the front of the house where she could enjoy the sunlight spilling through the windows.

Unable to resist the warm spring air, she opened the front door. She leaned up against the doorframe as she stared at the sprays of decaying spruce branches, the drooping brown foliage of the cedar tree in her window boxes hanging from the porch railing and the dead evergreen-decorated containers on each side of her. She walked back to the kitchen to get her phone.

> Colleen: Pedro, sorry I haven't returned your call. Come ASAP. Thanks!

She wished she hadn't waited so long to respond. It would be nice to have the porch full of pansies, tulips and hydrangeas. At least the porch floor was clean, Maria saw to that. She set her phone down by her book and water bottle on the entry table. It was too nice of a day to sit inside. She tugged at the cover draped over her outdoor couch and realized it was fastened down. She slid the dusty covers off the couch, chair and ottoman. She wasn't even sure where Maria stored the furniture covers. She kicked the canvas covers under the furniture. She would search out Maria's storage area later.

Colleen wiped the sweat that had accumulated above her lip. Her body sunk into the sharp blue fabric covered cushions. Flipping through the pages of pictures and recipes, Colleen noticed there were a lot of salads. Not her favorite. Big bowls of porous vegetables. She always felt unsatisfied. These salads were decorated with fruits and nuts. The colors of the blueberries, purple grapes, red apples and oranges were vibrant against the green leaves. The salads looked good, but they also looked like a lot of work. She hated cleaning and cutting all the vegetables. She'd heard Dinah rave about her personal chef. "She measures everything out to ensure that I don't go over twelve hundred calories a day," Dinah had said. A personal chef would take away one hurdle. Jay wouldn't mind. He supported anything she wanted. But personal chefs were for women like Ashley Barr who was Northside Day School's PTA president, drove down to Michigan Avenue for duties as chairwoman of the Women's Athletic Society, and was constantly going to Harborview Country Club for committee meetings. Colleen couldn't justify one more employee when she didn't do anything all day.

Colleen turned to the fish stew recipe — carrots, celery, onion, garlic, tomatoes, salmon and saffron; dice the onion, mince the garlic and chop the other vegetables... Colleen wasn't interested in spending that much time in the kitchen cooking or in the grocery store searching for the ingredients. She wondered if there was a place to order healthy prepared food. She was pathetic, she knew, but getting the girls to and from school and feeding them with as little effort as possible was all she could manage.

Colleen picked up her phone, clicked on the Facebook app and scanned through Alexis's posts until she came to that picture again. She zoomed in on the woman. Buttery-blond hair enhanced her sun-kissed face. Her square jawline was softened by her small nose, pretty eyelashes, perfectly shaped eyebrows and light-colored eyes — maybe green, but Colleen couldn't tell from the picture. Jay deserved much more than she was giving him, but she wasn't ready to let this woman have him. She clicked on Alexis's "friends." Alexis had almost two thousand Facebook friends. She was going to have to go through all of those in order to discover who this woman was, assuming she was one of the two thousand.

Her body jolted when her phone pinged.

Jay: We're at the park. Girls having blast…lots of friends here. What a gorgeous day! Think about what you want to do for date night. Let's do something special. Maybe Spiaggia?

Colleen wondered why he wanted to do something special. Was he feeling guilty? She wasn't in the mood for refined Italian cuisine. She would look like a bloated whale in any of her dresses (assuming one would even fit). Jay would see her and begin to fantasize about being with the buttery-blond woman in LA, or one of the trim women dressed in haute couture who would be at the restaurant. How could she possibly get through the three-hour tasting menu that Jay loved to order without confronting him about the photo? She'd read in *Oprah Magazine* that if a marriage was in trouble, the couple should focus on what made them fall in love in the beginning. Re-create the first date, the article had said.

One week after Colleen met Jay, he invited her to go to a Saturday-afternoon Cubs game. The date was July 10. The air temperature was eighty-nine degrees but the humidity made it feel closer to one hundred. Halfway into the fifth inning, dark clouds gathered overhead and the wind picked up. "Let's get out of here," Jay said. He grabbed Colleen's hand and led her out of the stadium. They weren't the only ones wanting out of the ballpark before the storm broke out. The way he took charge, protecting her against the herd of people filing out, made Colleen's heart swell. Just as they crossed Clark Street, the sky opened up with a crack of thunder and a sensational bolt of lightning flashed. "Hope you can run in those shoes," he said, looking down at Colleen's flip-flop sandals. Colleen had never been much of a runner, but she didn't have a choice. He grabbed her hand and pulled her along as they ran down Addison Street. The rain felt refreshing at first, then it became cold. They both laughed and then yelled as marble-sized hail poured from the sky, stinging their skin. Jay pulled Colleen under an empty awning. He wrapped his soaked arm around her shivering shoulder then turned his body to face her. He wiped away a stray clump of hair that had become glued to her cheek. "So beautiful," he said as leaned down to kiss her. His lips were wet and cold, but the inside of his mouth was warm. Colleen's body was no longer shivering. Their first kiss had been one of the most romantic moments of her life.

Colleen hadn't been to a Cubs game in two years. Now Jay took the girls alone or with Eli when he came to town. A baseball game was something she could add to her list of special things to do with Jay. She would work through the list until she looked great in her new dress and found the confidence to confront him. Colleen made a note in her phone to look at the Cubs schedule and find a game for the two of them to go to. She would buy tickets and surprise Jay with a Saturday-afternoon game.

> Colleen: *Just got home. Glad girls are having fun. See you soon!*

Colleen ignored the part about tonight. She would rather stay home, order in, and drink wine with Jay. *Tonight*, she thought, *would be a perfect night for a fire in the outdoor fireplace on the back deck*, but, unfortunately, they had a standing arrangement with Gabby to babysit every Saturday night.

The girls got themselves bathed and in pajamas themselves on Saturday nights. They argued over who got to choose the movie on Netflix, but they almost never watched a movie. Instead, they spent time in the art room in the basement that Gabby helped Colleen design.

Gabby was an extraordinary artist with incredible patience when it came to teaching the Adler girls how to paint. Jay and Colleen were astonished when they saw one of her paintings. She had perfectly captured Mabel working hard to clean paintbrushes at the sink while Chloe stood next to her, hands on hips, eyebrows together, mouth open bossing her sister.

A text notification beeped on her phone.

> Gertrude: Hi Colleen! I'm helping Kory follow up from the meeting. Do you still want to meet with her? She's free Monday right after your appointment at 11.

Colleen hesitated to respond. She didn't know if she was ready to start this process. She worried she wouldn't be able to do what Kory asked. Looking down at her bulging stomach, she noticed the fabric of the control top was spreading beyond where it had ever gone before.

> Gertrude: I emailed you a Health History Form to fill out. Please send back before your meeting on Monday. Thanks Colleen!

Colleen hoisted her heavy body up. If she was going to get the form filled out, she knew now was the time. Once Jay and the girls got home, she wouldn't do a thing. She sat down at her desk and clicked open her email.

The Word document appeared. It wouldn't allow her to fill it out electronically. Colleen wondered how Gertrude expected her to send it back. Knowing Gertrude's lack of technology skills, she probably didn't have a clue. Colleen had no choice but to print it, fill it out, and scan it back. This process was already taking longer than she wanted.

As the third page began to print, Colleen began to wonder how long the form was. Finally, the fifth page printed and that, thankfully, seemed to be the end. Colleen gathered the form and a clipboard and headed back to the front porch. She filled in the name, address and phone number.

Current Weight? Colleen paused. She had stopped weighing herself at home after she had moved up to her latest pant size, which was now too tight. She'd had no idea of the number until she went to the doctor a couple of weeks ago. The shock of seeing 185 still stung. She left this question blank.

Weight six months ago? Skip. Weight one year ago? Skip. Would you like your weight to be different? Yes. Occupation? Stay-at-home mom. How many hours do you work per week? Skip. What are your primary health goals?

She took a deep breath. It didn't help. She closed her eyes and attempted the breathing and counting exercise they did at the meeting. The first thing that came to her mind when she stopped was: lose weight and have more energy. So, she wrote that down.

Next were all the health history questions. She had gone through all of these questions with Dr. Bradley, Dr. Metzger, Dr. Anderson and her whole team during the pregnancy with

Mabel. How many hours of her life had she spent filling out forms?

She turned to the last page.

What do you typically eat for the following meals: Breakfast: pancakes, scones, muffins, bagels, coffee. Lunch: sandwich, pizza. Dinner: pizza, hamburgers, pasta. Snacks: popcorn, frozen yogurt. Alcohol: wine. Drinks: diet soda, coffee, latte.

She tried to be as honest as possible but she couldn't bring herself to write down Dino Buddies Chicken Nuggets, boxed Kraft macaroni and cheese, or monster cookies and vanilla-frosted chocolate cupcakes from Southport Grocery & Cafe that she and the girls often indulged in.

Now she had to go back and deal with those weight questions. As she put down the dreaded 185, her eyes burned with tears.

Weight six months ago? 165. One year ago? 150.

Could her thyroid really be the reason she gained thirty-five pounds in one year?

What do you want your weight to be?

Tears streamed down her face. Getting back to one hundred and thirty pounds felt impossible. Kory would laugh if she read such a lofty goal. She walked back inside before any of the neighbors caught her crying.

Colleen was proud of herself for finishing the form. She scanned the pages, willing the printer to move quickly. Jay would be back with the girls any minute. She didn't want him to see what she had written. She had an image of Gertrude reading the form as it came over the email. Colleen had never felt judged by Gertrude. Her cheeks burned imagining her reading the weight numbers.

The screen door slammed. She heard Chloe's shrill giggle, the signature one she only used around Jay.

Colleen met them in the kitchen. Her heart skipped a beat as Jay locked his eyes with hers. The whites of his eyes were as bright as the brown was dark and his black lashes framed his eyes in a way that Colleen found irresistible. His hair was pushed away from his face. Curls flipped out over his ears and along his neck. He still hadn't gotten a haircut. Her mind flashed to the picture of the woman. Was she the reason he was growing his hair out? Did she gaze into his eyes? She brushed the image aside. One look into his eyes used to leave Colleen filled with everything she needed in life. These days, however, she did her best to avoid making eye contact with him. Somehow, it helped to hide from him.

Jay unloaded the armful of bags containing their lunch on the kitchen counter. He looked buoyant, energized by the outing instead of dragging and drained like Colleen would be. He leaned over the counter and kissed Colleen's forehead. "How was your morning?"

"Good," she said. She hoped there weren't any signs on her face from her tearful outburst earlier. "Better feed the girls before they kill one another," Colleen said, steering the discussion away from anything to do with her, or them.

Colleen set the table and carefully placed the sandwiches on plates. Disposing of any evidence of takeout, she threw out all the bags, containers, condiments, napkins and plastic utensils that came along with the food. By the time everyone was at the table, it appeared as though Colleen had made everything herself.

Jay promised the girls that if they ate all of their lunch, they could spend a few hours watching TV. If Colleen had said this, they would have argued that they weren't that hungry and wanted to watch TV first. The girls went along with anything Jay said. When he was home, it was all about him. The girls barely gave Colleen a second glance. She wondered if they recognized how much weight she had gained or how tired she always was. She worried that they didn't know her to be any different. She knew she had been setting a terrible example for them. She wanted to play with them and make them laugh the way Jay did.

The girls obediently finished their lunch, even cleared their plates and stacked them in the dishwasher. They ran to the back living room to settle into their favorite TV shows that were recorded on the DVR. Jay followed them. Colleen cleaned up the rest of the dishes. She heard the girls screaming and giggling and knew Jay must be playing "tickle monster." They couldn't get enough of him.

"I'm heading down to Southport Grocery for a latte, do you want anything?"

"I'm good. Just going to gobble up some little girls!" Jay growled and the girls started shrieking again.

Colleen waited until she walked out of Southport Grocery & Cafe before taking the first sip. The first drink from a latte was her favorite. She loved the contrast of the warm frothy milk on top of the hot smooth liquid underneath. She closed her eyes for a brief moment while exhaling through her nose, lips closed savoring the nutty vanilla aftertaste. With each sip the lingering fatigue slowly melted away, her heart beat a little faster, her thinking became a little more clear and each step was met with less resistance. As she approached the front of her house, she saw Jay sitting on their porch surrounded by dead plants. Her face flushed red as she stared at her neglected yard. Jay seemed undisturbed. He was sprawled across the couch intensely typing on his phone.

He saw her and slid his phone back into his pocket.

"Something wrong?" Colleen asked.

"Just giving Eli a little insight into a contract I renegotiated last week." Jay scooted over to make room for Colleen to sit next to him. "That smells good."

"Vanilla," she said. She became even more self-conscious about her size as she sat next to him. Even though he was six inches taller, she felt gigantic. "Pedro's coming next week." She crossed her legs in an effort to camouflage their growing size.

"I've always loved this front porch," Jay said.

"It's the first thing I fell in love with when you brought me here," Colleen said.

"Did I ever tell you how many houses I looked at before this one? They all looked the same," Jay said. "At the time, I wanted something special for you. This porch reminded me of the old porch at Farm Five-Thirty-Five."

Colleen wondered what her parents were doing. They were definitely not relaxing on the front porch. She remembered how ashamed she was when she first brought Jay there. She'd waited over a year after they started dating before finally agreeing to take Jay to meet her family. She could barely swallow when they reached the gravel road leading to the house. What first appeared to be a dust storm ended up being ten-year-old Johnny barreling down the lane on the old red Massey Ferguson tractor going much faster than Colleen's dad would have approved. He came to a stop as he approached Jay's car. Jay rolled down the window.

"What kind of car is that?" Johnny said. *Oh God*, thought Colleen. She knew that was the first of many embarrassing questions over the next couple days.

"It's a BMW," Jay said. "I'll let you drive it later if you want."

Johnny's eyes lit up. He shifted gears and did a U-turn, dipping down into the ditch and up into the recently plowed cornfield. His dog Leo had finally caught up to him and proceeded to chase him back up the lane toward the house.

It was the middle of October, the orange, red and brown leaves hung loosely to the branches with some losing their grip and dancing through the plowed fields. Jay drove slowly, staying a safe distance behind Johnny. Colleen dreaded the moments in front of her, Jay's first impression of the old farmhouse, her parents' basic life, the awkward moments around the kitchen table.

Johnny jumped off the tractor and ran up the front porch steps, two at a time. "Colleen's home, she's here! Her boyfriend said I could drive his car!" Leo trailed behind barking before making himself comfortable on the mismatched floorboards on the front porch.

Jay went out of his way to find things he loved about the old house on that first visit. "Are these the original floors?" he'd asked. "This house has so much character," he'd said. Colleen worried that his interest was an effort to hide his repulsion. But he kept asking questions. His cheeks took on a rosy glow — the way they did when he spoke to a sommelier at the wine store about a rare vintage of cabernet. "I think it's cool that you do your own dishes," he'd said, before taking over the task himself. Colleen thought he did a pretty good job considering he had never hand washed dishes before, which made Colleen love him even more.

"This one's nicer," Colleen said, looking around the home they'd built together.

Jay leaned closer to Colleen and put his arm around the back of her neck. "How was your meeting?"

Colleen's body tightened. She thought he'd forgotten about it. "Good." She leaned her head back against Jay's arm and twirled her hair around her fingers.

"What was it about?"

Colleen wasn't sure how much to share. She had to be careful not to build this up like she had with some of the other programs. She wanted the freedom to change her mind without an explanation. "Dr. Metzger wanted me to meet the new wellness coach who joined her practice. Kory. She was nice. She explained her program, gave out a book and led a short meditation," Colleen tried to sound casual. She took a long, slow drink of her latte.

Jay brought his hand up to smooth the mass of hair Colleen had been assaulting with her fingers. "Everyone seems to be meditating these days. Eli says he's been doing it every morning. What did you think?" he asked.

Colleen shrugged. "How was your week?" she said, desperate to change the subject.

Jay sat up straight and turned to look at Colleen. "Good. What's the program about?"

Colleen was always at a dialogue disadvantage with Jay. She remained reclined against the back of the sofa. She couldn't bring herself to face him. "She helps people lose weight; she helps identify what's holding you back."

"Why don't you try it?" Jay said.

Tears flooded her eyes and she wanted to hide her face. She hated crying in front of him.

Jay's eyes were intent on Colleen. He pulled her close and leaned his head over hers. She was afraid to say maybe the program would help her. She was afraid to give either of them hope.

Jay held her tight. "It's worth a try, right?"

She nodded. The latte napkin stuck to her shirt. She pulled it off the Lycra fabric. She thought of the woman in the photo with her bare sculpted shoulder brushing up against Jay. And Colleen sat like a blob of flesh, sweating on the porch, dripping nose and teary wet face.

SEVEN

After Jay left for the airport on Monday morning, Colleen couldn't go back to sleep. She went down to the kitchen for a Diet Coke. Retreating back to the comfort of her bed, she sipped the cold bubbles and watched the morning news — rainy weather every day until Friday.

Within a few minutes, the soda had mingled with last night's laxative drink, creating a sudden urge. She tried to straighten the sheet and duvet around her body before carefully slipping out of her almost-made bed. She had a successful trip to the bathroom. By seven, she had managed to squeeze into her clothing, run a comb through her hair and brush her teeth. So far, the day was off to a good start.

The morning's grey cloud cover gave the perception of an earlier hour. The soothing sound of rain outside wasn't going to make it easy to get the girls out of bed. Colleen opened the bedroom door to find both girls tangled in Mabel's twin bed sound asleep. Chloe was on her back, arm hanging off the side and mouth wide open. Mabel was on her side with her arm draped across her sister.

Colleen wished it were Maria's day to clean. It would be nice for her to see Colleen up and ready for once. She could see Colleen calmly toast the Pop-Tarts and pack the lunch boxes. She would have finally seen Colleen on a good day, a day where she didn't oversleep and wasn't constipated. No yelling, or tantrums. It was the kind of day she hoped to have more of.

The girls nibbled their Pop-Tarts as they rode to school in silence. Colleen's mind drifted to her time with Jay on Saturday. Her physical appearance was enough of a reason for him to leave, but her depression and lack of ambition made things worse. And yet Jay hadn't turned away. The man he was to her on Saturday wasn't a man who would have an affair. Maybe Alexis asked him to talk to the woman in the picture. Maybe they'd only spoken for a moment, just when the photographer sauntered by. Or maybe he just felt a duty to stick with Colleen as a husband, but not a lover. Maybe the unconditional support he offered her was pity.

She dropped the girls at school, on time for once. Colleen steered her car into the right lane. Burt's Pastry Shop was just around the corner. The rainy morning put her in the mood for a coffee and a scone. At the counter, she looked for the healthiest scone available. Sitting next to the chocolate chip scones, which were her favorite, was a vegan trail mix scone. She ordered it.

She unwrapped the scone in the car. She hoped it tasted better than it looked. The first bite filled her lap with crumbs. She immediately regretted her choice and wished she had gotten the chocolate chip scone instead. She was too ashamed to go back inside Burt's. She shoved a huge bite into her mouth. Her phone rang. The sharp edges of the dry scone scraped the roof of her mouth as she tried to chew. She didn't recognize the number, but the teachers were now using their personal cell phones to call parents. Chewing and swallowing as quickly as possible, she picked up the phone. "Hello." Her voice was strained as she struggled to recover from the scone's assault to her mouth and throat.

"This is Kory Stone." Colleen's stomach clinched. She felt as though she had been caught breaking rules.

"Something's come up that I need to take care of. Would you be able to come in at 9 instead of 11:30?" she asked.

Colleen didn't want to go earlier. She wanted to go home first. "Sure," she said. If she didn't take the appointment today, she might not go at all.

Colleen brushed the crumbs from her lap and the seat. She wasn't quite sure what was in store with Kory, but she doubted scones were included. She took one more huge bite of that awful scone, then she put the car in drive and headed to Dr. Metzger's office.

"You're early," Gertrude said.

Colleen felt sorry for Gertrude. She seemed to be in a constant state of confusion. The skin on her shaky hands seemed translucent, as blue veins protruded between her bones and saggy skin. Despite her aging body, her eyes continued to shine through the wrinkles. Her husband had passed away shortly before Colleen became a patient of Dr. Metzger's. Colleen couldn't ever bring herself to tell Gertrude that her brother died the same year as her husband, but she always wanted to. Never able to have children, Gertrude was alone in her old age. Dr. Metzger took her in as family and always made sure she had a place to go over the holidays. Colleen was glad Gertrude worked for someone as kind as Dr. Metzger. "Kory changed my appointment." Colleen was glad she arrived a few minutes earlier than Kory rescheduled her for. She enjoyed being able to sit and chat with Gertrude as she finished what was left of her coffee.

"Hi, Colleen," Kory said. She extended her hand.

Colleen looked over to the opposite direction. Her body began to tingle with nerves as she stood to greet the tall, slender woman. Kory had her hair pulled back in a ponytail like she had on Saturday but she wasn't sweaty. Her hair was blonder when it wasn't wet. She wore a loose-fitting white cotton top with faded blue jeans and Birkenstock sandals.

Kory's hand felt warm and her grip was strong and firm.

"Colleen's one of our favorites." Gertrude gave Colleen an encouraging smile.

Colleen gripped the straps of her purse as she trailed behind Kory. Regardless of how she positioned her legs, her thighs rubbed together as she walked. Trailing behind this perfectly poised woman with her sandy blond ponytail swaying behind her made the *swish-swish* sound of Colleen's thighs grow louder.

"Thanks so much for coming in early. I'm trying to get as many folks in from Saturday's meeting as I can today," Kory said.

Colleen smelled something sweet and earthy. *Lavender*, she thought as she entered Kory's office. The small room was cozy and comfortable. There were matching sage green velvet chairs sitting across from one another with a small table off to the side that held a small Buddha statue surrounded by different-shaped crystals. The room's only window was centered above the table between the two chairs. Crystals hung from the ceiling in front of the window caught the reflection of the sun to provide the little light that filled the room. On a small side table, a votive candle burned. The space was so different from the rest of the Dr. Metzger's office that Colleen felt as though she had stepped into a fantasy world. The tranquility of the room wasn't enough to tame her anxiety. It would take more than a peaceful room with a burning candle to crack her open.

"Sit wherever you're comfortable, I'm going to grab some tea. Would you like some? Or, maybe water?"

"No, no thank you, I'm fine." Colleen was too nervous to drink anything. She sat in the chair closest to her. Changing her mind, she quickly moved over to the other chair. She placed her purse on her lap. Being so big, it looked silly on her lap. She moved it to her feet. She moved it off to the side of her chair and kneaded her thumbs. She listened to Kory pouring the water and heard the clink of a spoon. Coming here had been a mistake.

Kory returned with a large stone tray that held a beautiful teapot that looked handmade and appeared to be very old. The tray also carried two small handmade-looking teacups.

"Would you mind pulling the small table out from underneath this one?" Kory said.

Colleen looked at the table to her side, searching for the table Kory was referring to. Beneath the Buddha statue, crystals and the candles, she finally saw the table stacked underneath. Colleen was impressed with the cleverness of Kory's utilization of the small space.

"I know you said you didn't want tea, but I have yet to meet someone who didn't want to try tea out of this teapot," Kory said as she set the tray down.

Colleen was taken with the teapot and the efficiency of the

stacking tables. "I have never seen a teapot like that before. Where'd you get it?"

"I bought it from a craftsman in India years ago. I gave it to my mom as a gift, but she never used it. She said it looked too old. She didn't like how the lid didn't fit properly. She claimed to be afraid of 'ruining it.'" Kory brought her fingers up to form quotation marks. "My mom didn't like anything that was different and certainly couldn't appreciate that the lid was part of the charm. Instead of putting it to use, she let it sit on a shelf collecting dust." Kory shook her head. "My mom was a very hard lady to please and an impossible person to buy for. After she passed away, the table and the teapot found its way back to me."

Colleen thought Kory's mother sounded like Dinah. "You're right," Colleen said. She loved the table and the teapot. "I think I will have a cup."

Kory smiled as though she knew something that Colleen didn't. "Congratulations, you just passed the first test."

Colleen's blank look gave away her confusion. Kory reached over and gave her hand a squeeze. Her whole face smiled. "I'll explain."

The meeting had barely begun and Colleen already felt lost. She ran her left thumbnail over the dry cuticle of her right thumb. After successfully creating a painful hangnail, she stopped. Kory poured the tea at an excruciatingly slow pace. Colleen clasped her hands together as her nerves festered.

Kory slipped her shoes off and sat back in her chair, bringing both of her legs up to sit, as Mabel and Chloe would say, in a "crisscross, applesauce" position. She was settling in for what Colleen suspected was going to be a long talk. Kory took slow sips of her tea with her eyes closed as if savoring every ounce. Colleen felt like she was back in town as a teenager and those awkward visits with friends. Everyone but Colleen knowing the words to some song on MTV.

Kory opened her eyes and looked at Colleen with the pride of a mother. "The test you passed was your ability to see the beauty in something as imperfect as this teapot. It's not a typical teapot that you'd see in a store." She raised the teapot. "It's old, it's misshapen and the lid doesn't fit. Somehow you were able to see something special." She paused and smiled at Colleen. "A simple object made out of clay from the earth, by an average man with the two ordinary hands that God gave him. What's so beautiful to you about this teapot?"

Colleen's face softened. She unclasped her hands as she considered why she thought the pot was beautiful. "It's so different and unique-looking. It looks like it has a long history and lots of stories to tell," she said.

"People aren't any different, Colleen." Kory's voice was quiet. "We all look different and we're all unique for a reason. If God wanted us all to be the same, he would've made us all the same."

Colleen nodded. She had never been religious and had become more conflicted about God after Johnny died. How could God allow someone to die who had so much potential? Why would God allow something to happen that hurt so many people? She liked what Kory was saying, but she didn't want to hear about God. She didn't want to be different. She wanted to fit in.

"So many, like my mom, just see an old teapot that doesn't

look the way a teapot is 'supposed' to look and those are the ones I have a hard time helping. You're going to be easy."

Colleen became nervous. Kory had no idea about the cupcakes, the morning bakery habit, or the mornings where Colleen could hardly get out of bed. Fixing her was not going to be easy.

"My goal is to help you apply that same appreciation you have for this teapot to yourself. You're beautiful and you need to get off that shelf of yours, brush the dust off, and embrace how special you are."

Colleen's eyes burned. She gazed down at the stacked tables and slightly nodded.

"What do you think you have in common with this teapot?" Kory said.

Colleen's mind was blank. She had no idea how she was like that teapot. Her mind was consumed with holding her tears back. She knew as soon as she opened her mouth, her efforts would be lost. "I don't know." Tears gushed down her face.

"You know. What did you just say a few minutes ago about this teapot?" Kory reached over and gave Colleen's arm a supportive squeeze.

"That I liked it." Colleen hated the way her voice sounded when she cried.

"You more than liked it," Kory said. "When I asked you what you found beautiful, you said and I quote, 'It is so different and unique. It looks like it has a long history with lots of good stories to tell.'"

Colleen accepted a tissue from a box Kory held out to her.

"Colleen, you are lovely, you are different and unique, you

have a great history with lots of great stories to share and because of that you are extraordinarily beautiful."

Colleen cried harder. Kory shocked her by wiping her own tears. She was crying, with Colleen?

"I'm sorry, I don't know why I'm getting so emotional." Colleen shifted her eyes down to Kory's Birkenstocks sitting on the rug in front of her chair. Even the toe indentations on her sandals were pretty.

"I don't want you to ever apologize for how you are feeling. One of the most important things for you to do is to feel your emotions." She guided Colleen's face back up. "I suspect you've been holding a lot in. You're safe here. You're free to release everything that's been held up inside."

Colleen nodded. Everything was a lot. She didn't know if she could handle that.

Kory handed Colleen the Kleenex box. "Let's take a few cleansing breaths before we move on. Just like we did on Saturday, I want you to take a deep inhale and release." Kory took a deep breath in.

Colleen struggled to get air in through her clogged nostrils.

"As you exhale, imagine those feelings, the ones that brought tears to your eyes, leaving your body. Those feelings, whatever they are, are not serving you. Let them go, Colleen, let everything go with each exhale."

Colleen followed Kory in the breathing exercise. She couldn't believe how fast Kory was able to tap into her. She didn't have words to describe what she was feeling. She just tried to focus on calming herself and letting go of whatever it was making her feel so sad. On her final exhale, she felt better and opened her eyes.

"How did that feel for you?"

"I feel better."

"You look more peaceful. Are you ready to get started?" Kory said.

"We haven't started yet?" Colleen said. She felt like she'd opened up more with Kory than she had with anyone.

"Well, so far we've established how extraordinary you are. Now let's make you believe it. "

Colleen drew in a breath.

"I'd like to ask you a few questions," Kory said.

Colleen nodded. Kory lifted a clipboard from beside her chair. She had a purple pen. Colleen found herself wishing she had one.

"Tell me about your life right now."

Colleen didn't know where to start or how much she should say. She wasn't ready to get into how difficult next month was for her.

"I've been trying to get ready for summer. I can't fit into any of my summer clothes," Colleen said.

"Tell me about your health," Kory said.

"I just learned that I have a thyroid problem. I also found out that I'm anemic, and my B12 and vitamin D levels are low. I started taking medication and supplements a couple of weeks ago," Colleen said. She hoped that explained part of her weight problem and Kory would understand some of the weight wasn't her fault.

"That's a lot. You must be tired," Kory said.

Colleen was relieved that someone finally validated her exhaustion. "I'm always tired and I have a hard time sleeping at night. If I had more energy, I would exercise more," Colleen said.

"You'll get there. Sounds like you just started medication, am I correct?" Kory said.

"Two weeks ago." Colleen quickly shifted her eyes away from Kory after realizing she had a pleading look on her face. She hated when she caught herself looking at people that way. It made her look desperate.

"This is something that takes time. You have to be patient and let your body adjust to the drugs," Kory said. "Did your doctor recommend follow-up testing?"

"I'm supposed to go back the second week of May."

"Hopefully, you'll notice an increase in your energy soon." Kory flipped through the form that Colleen filled out. "You're a stay-at-home parent. Do you like that?" Kory said.

"Yes." What kind of person would say no? Colleen didn't have to work. She lived in a big house and never had to worry about her financial stability. She thought about the checkout clerk who worked at CVS and also worked at the Jewel grocery store. Chloe had been the one to notice she worked at both places. While bagging two Hello Kitty Color and Play Activity books, a Play-Doh Party Pack and a box of Fannie May Turtles, the woman told them she had to work both jobs to support her four children. She handed Colleen her change and said, "Their dad left when I was pregnant with the fourth."

Colleen thought about how hard her parents and aunts and uncles had to work just to put food on the table. Colleen damn well better like it. Still, she wondered how her life would have been different if she had continued on with her master's degree. She would have her own career, her own friends and be doing something meaningful. She would have waited longer to have kids. She would have been able to go to Johnny's funeral. Maybe she would be closer with her family.

"What things do you most enjoy about being a full-time, stay-at-home mom?" Kory said.

Colleen was silent. "Just being there for my girls," she finally said. "I guess I'm lucky that we don't need the additional income." Colleen was feeling relieved that the questions were easy to answer and she wasn't feeling emotional anymore. "My husband travels a lot during the week, so it would be hard for me to have a job."

"How old are your girls?"

"Mabel is seven and Chloe is five."

"What sweet ages. Have you ever thought of doing something else?" Kory said.

"No," Colleen said.

"What does your husband do for work?"

"He's a lawyer. He works out of New York and sometimes LA."

"How's your relationship with— What's your husband's name?"

"Jay."

"How's your relationship with Jay?"

Colleen's heart came up to her throat. She didn't intend to give such a long pause.

"He's gone all week, but our weekends are great," Colleen said as convincingly as she could. She wanted to avoid discussing her suspicion about Jay's fidelity at all costs.

"Is it hard to have him gone all week?"

Colleen nodded her head and pressed her lips together as she twirled her hair around her fingers.

"Before my husband Eric passed away, he was gone a lot also. I had to take care of our son, Andrew, all by myself and that made me feel resentful toward him," Kory said. "I have to admit, I felt resentful toward him even more after he died."

Colleen was caught off guard. Kory was too young and beautiful to be a widow. She couldn't help but wonder what happened. "I'm so sorry," Colleen said. She wondered what happened to her husband but resisted the urge to ask. Colleen looked down at her clasped hands. "Jay's been traveling for so long that I don't think much about it." Her voice was soft as she lied.

"It's okay to feel resentful," Kory said.

Colleen nodded. Frizzy-haired women who weighed 185 pounds weren't allowed to be resentful. She was lucky to have anyone stay married to her.

"I'm getting the feeling that there's something you're holding back," Kory said.

Unwelcome tears dropped across the top of Colleen's clenched hands. She took a deep breath as she reached for another Kleenex. "I don't know."

Kory waited for Colleen to collect herself. "Let's come back to Jay in a little bit," she said. "What was your childhood like?"

Colleen's shoulders softened. "It was good. I grew up on a farm in a small town. I had a lot of family around. It was nice," Colleen said. She didn't see the point in bringing up the humiliation of wearing Janet's hand-me-down clothing, or not knowing anything about the videos on MTV, or not understanding the jokes the kids made about *Gilligan's Island* or *The Beverly Hillbillies*, especially *The Beverly Hillbillies*, since some of the kids called her Elly May. That was the past. She was grateful for her life now.

"Are your parents both living?"

"Yes."

"Do you see them often?"

"Not very often, they live about three hours away."

"You must miss having your family around."

Colleen nodded.

"Do you have any siblings?"

Oh no, thought Colleen. She took a deep breath and looked back down at Kory's sandals. Avoiding eye contact was always her first line of defense in trying to gain control of her emotions. It was a step that rarely worked. She wished she could talk about Johnny but every time she tried, she got emotional. "I had a brother, he passed away seven years ago. Eight years ago on May eighteenth." Colleen hadn't wanted to say it. But Kory was just listening. The candle, the teapot, the talk of Kory's husband's death. Her defenses were down.

"I'm so sorry," Kory said. "That must've been about the same time Mabel was born."

Colleen nodded and pulled out another tissue.

"That must have been a very difficult time for you," Kory said. "How old was he when he passed?"

Colleen took a deep breath. "Seventeen."

"My God. How tragic! What happened?" Kory asked.

There it was. She asked. Usually, Colleen became annoyed when people asked about the details. She couldn't understand why people couldn't accept that he died and let it be. Didn't people understand how hard it was to talk about? Now, however, Colleen saw it as an opportunity to ask how Kory's husband had died. "He fell." Her chin began quivering as the tears were once again flowing down her cheeks. She reached for another Kleenex. "He was up high, on our town's water tower with his friends and he slipped."

Kory closed her eyes briefly as she shook her head. She reached across to touch Colleen's arm. "What was his name?"

Colleen blew her nose. "Johnny."

"I can see how painful losing Johnny has been for you and it's obviously hard for you to talk about. Let's take a few seconds to regroup before we move on. I am going to get you a glass of water."

Colleen had not cried so much in one place since Johnny died. She wondered what Kory must think of her.

Kory handed the glass of water to Colleen. "Let's have a drink of water before this next exercise I want to lead you through."

Colleen was grateful for the cold drink. The crying created a rise in body temperature that produced enough sweat to soak through her cardigan. "How did your husband die?"

"Suicide," Kory said. She sat for a few seconds before continuing. "Eric made a lot of money down at the board of trade. He got in over his head and lost everything. Technically, he died of a drug overdose, but he knew what he was doing."

"I'm sorry," Colleen said. She was impressed by the way Kory answered. Colleen wondered how she could be so strong. "That must've been hard."

"It was. But the strength I gained brought me here today. Eric took his life because he was ashamed of his mistakes,"

Kory said. "After he died, my 'big' corporate job no longer made sense to me." Her face softened as she took in a breath. "My goal is to help others develop enough self-love to overcome the struggles in their life."

Colleen didn't know what to say. She wished she could find meaning in Johnny's death. She wished she could find the type of strength Kory had. She wanted to talk about him and share memories of him with Mabel and Chloe. They barely knew anything about Johnny.

Kory handed Colleen a pad of paper and a pen. "I want you to write 'I should' on the top of the paper. Write down everything you think you 'should' do."

Colleen didn't have to think about it. That was why she was here, to get help doing the things she "should" do but for some reason couldn't.

"Okay, what's the first thing on your list?"

"Lose weight."

"Tell me why you should lose weight."

Tears, once again. Colleen gave up trying to control them. She reached across to Kory's table and grabbed the box of Kleenex. "Because I'm fat. I want to fit into my clothes. I want to look better."

"What's next?"

"Exercise more."

"Tell me why you should exercise?"

"Same reasons. I want to lose weight."

"What's next?"

"Be more social."

"Why do you want to be more social?"

"I don't know. I just wish that I wanted to be around people more. I'm always trying to avoid seeing anyone."

"I want you to change the word 'should' to 'could.' Begin each sentence with 'If I really wanted to, I could....'"

Colleen took another drink of water. "If I really wanted to, I could lose weight. If I really wanted to, I could exercise more. If I really wanted to, I could be more social."

"Did that feel any different?"

Colleen dabbed her nose with the wet Kleenex she had been clenching in her fist. Staring back down at Kory's toe prints on her sandals, she remained silent for a few seconds. She wanted to believe that she could, but she wasn't sure. "I don't know." Looking up at Kory, she revealed the fresh tears that filled her eyes. "I've wanted to do these things for so long but for some reason I can't."

"Colleen, I believe in you and I know you can do each one of those things and more. Will you accept my help?"

Colleen nodded. She wanted to believe that Kory could help her. She knew it was ultimately up to her to make change happen, but she didn't know if she could do it.

Kory held up a copy of the Louise Hay book she had given out on Saturday. "Did you get a chance to read any of this?"

"I looked through it," Colleen said.

"Take some time over the next few days and read the first two chapters. While you read it, think about your list. Also, think about other things you want to add. As you get into the second chapter"—she handed the opened section to Colleen—"you'll read about the 'mirror work' exercise. It's very simple and it may sound strange but trust me, it works."

Colleen looked down at the open page.

"Basically, every time you go into the bathroom, look at yourself in the mirror and I mean really look at yourself and look deep into your eyes and say your full name. What's your middle name?"

"Ann."

"Maiden name?"

"O'Brien."

"I want you to love who you were before you were married. I want you to love the true you."

The intense way Kory was looking into Colleen's eyes made her feel self-conscious. She couldn't remember ever having someone besides Jay look into her eyes that way.

"Colleen Ann O'Brien, you are beautiful and I love you, I really, really love you." Kory unlocked her eyes from Colleen's. "I want you to look in your eyes the same way I just did. I know it sounds crazy and I'm not going to lie, it will feel strange at first. Most people haven't stared into their own eyes before." Kory smiled.

Colleen did think it sounded crazy, but it sounded easy enough to at least try.

"I want you to do the mirror exercise as many times as you can until our next meeting. It is important that you do this multiple times every day."

Colleen nodded. She handed the book back to Kory.

"Every time we meet we're going to cover three areas: body, mind, and spirit. So far we've touched on mind and spirit. Now let's talk about physical body," Kory said.

Colleen's eyes felt sticky from her earlier tears. After seeing the clumps of mascara collected on the white tissue, she imagined the black shadow hanging below her eyes and lining her cheeks. She wanted to get in the car and go straight home, but she did her best to stay engaged with Kory. Weight loss was the reason she was in there. The Fourth of July was getting closer and she had to do something. At her current pace, she would never fit into her dress.

"Have you ever done a detox diet before?" Kory said.

"I've tried so many different diets," Colleen said. "Some worked better than others. I've never done well on the ones where you drink your meals."

"This doesn't involve powdered shakes, if that's what you're referring to. It does involve drinking smoothies but you will also be eating whole foods." Kory handed the thick booklet to Colleen. "I don't want to pressure you into doing something you're not ready for. I want you to take your time reading through the program. When you think you're ready, let me know and I'll help you get started."

Colleen didn't have the mental capacity to look through the booklet but she needed the weight loss to happen immediately. "Can you tell me a little bit about the diet?" Colleen said.

"I like to think of it as less of a diet and more of a reset. Your focus needs to be on eating clean foods as an effort to give your body a break and let it naturally detox itself." Kory said. "You'll replace things like gluten, sugar, processed foods, dairy, red meat, pork, alcohol and coffee with vegetables, fruits, lean organic protein, and some gluten-free whole grains."

Colleen wondered if she heard her right. No coffee or wine? "Oh."

"You sound a little unsure," Kory said. She leaned back in her chair as she evaluated Colleen.

"No, I want to do it," Colleen said.

"What part sounds the hardest?" Kory said.

"The coffee."

"If it makes you feel better, everyone has a hard time with the coffee part and more people than you know have a hard time giving up wine," she said. "I am not going to pretend it's easy. The first few days are hard and if you're going to be successful, you need to be ready. By ready, I mean emotionally ready and physically ready."

Colleen sat in silence as she tried to imagine giving up pizza, wine, coffee and vanilla lattes.

"All the information you need is here in this booklet. I want you to set some time aside and read through everything carefully. Right now, you are only reading about the diet, not starting," Kory said. "When you understand everything, have all of your ingredients and the few first meals prepared and most importantly, you are emotionally ready, you can start."

Colleen looked at page one. Even the preparation sounded exhausting. The thought of shopping and cooking food sounded like a huge chore. Colleen wasn't sure if she would ever be ready to tackle that. But, she was tired of planning to change.

"When we decide together that you're ready, you'll do the plan for twenty-one days. Your body will have a chance to naturally clean itself and you'll start to notice more energy, better sleep and hopefully a little weight-loss."

"I'll start now," Colleen said. Of course she wasn't ready. She thought of all the mornings drinking Diet Coke on the way to drop the girls to school, stopping off at Burt's for coffee and a scone, breakfasts at Molly's, afternoon vanilla lattes and her evening wine.

"It's too soon. Work on the mirror exercises for now. Take some time to find a twenty-one-day period that you think works best," Kory said. "When you can really take care of yourself."

Colleen knew if she was going to do it and if she had any chance of doing it right, she needed to do it before the girls were out of school for the summer.

"For now, I want you to take one day at a time and every day tell yourself that you're going to do the best you can every day. If you do that, you'll be on the right path," Kory said.

"Okay," Colleen said, not really listening but calculating how much weight she could actually lose in three weeks. She had once lost seven pounds in a week.

Walking out of Kory's office, Colleen ducked into the bathroom. She dabbed off the mascara streaked under her eyes. She wished she had some concealer in her purse to cover her dark circles and to cover up the red splotches dotting the skin around her eyes and the sides of her nose. She didn't have the energy for her adjustment with Dr. Metzger, didn't have the energy to tell her about the meeting with Kory.

Colleen rounded the reception desk. "I'm going to skip my appointment with Dr. Metzger today." Gertrude was on the phone. She winked at Colleen and waved her off.

Colleen fumbled through her purse for her keys. Her mind felt foggy and for some reason, her body ached, as if she'd been moving it for an hour. The time in Kory's office moved differently than it did in the regular world. Colleen thought about the mirror exercise and the detox and the booklet with its lists of foods and supplements, and she wanted to go home and take a nap.

TWO GALLON-SIZE ZIPLOC BAGGIES FULL of leftover pizza sat next to a tub of butter on the middle shelf of her refrigerator. Three juice boxes were scattered on the shelf below, next to a six-pack of Diet Coke. The oversized refrigerator that Colleen had once looked forward to filling sat mostly empty. She grabbed a Diet Coke before closing the door. She opened the freezer and quickly closed it. She didn't want chicken fingers, tater tots or ice cream. Tugging once again on the refrigerator door, she pulled out one of the bags of cold pizza. She took one piece out and put the bag back on the shelf. She would only eat one, she told herself.

Her throat burned from a large of a gulp of Diet Coke. She had eaten her slice of pizza too fast. She wanted another. One more, she told herself. She pulled the diet booklet from her purse as she sat down at the kitchen table. She loved the soft snap of cold cheese as she bit down into the sweet tomato sauce. Cold pizza tasted entirely different than hot pizza.

The meal plans didn't look bad. Every breakfast was a smoothie, lunch was salad, and dinner was fish or chicken and vegetables. Kory even had grocery lists to accompany the meal plans and recipes.

Colleen stuffed the booklet back into her purse. She could do this, she told herself. She could at least buy the ingredients.

The Whole Foods parking lot was jammed with cars. People were double-parked, waiting for shoppers to load their groceries and return their carts. She read through the booklet again while she waited behind the line of cars waiting for a woman up ahead who unloaded one bag at a time into her car and then slowly walked her cart back to the designated area. The incessant honking behind her nearly drove Colleen out of the lot and back home, but the prospect of weight loss, maybe twenty-one pounds, the slimming silk navy star-spangled dress, Dinah's face and winning Jay back dangled in the air before her. The coffee shop inside the store also had a firm hold of her attention.

Once in the store, a coffee barista whistling along with the song "Love Shack" had a vanilla latte in her hand in no time. Before placing the plastic lid on top, Colleen brought the warm drink up to her lips for a long slug. She breathed vanilla aroma in through her nose while filling her mouth with the frothy goodness. She'd had the barista add two shots of espresso in this one. She was going to suck down every molecule of caffeine before she had to say good-bye for twenty-one days.

She got a cart and pulled the booklet back out of her purse. She flipped to the meal plans section. Kory had the program broken down into three weekly meal plans with accompanying grocery lists, which she carefully organized according to the layout of the grocery store. Colleen began in the produce section. Kale was at the top of the list. There were so many different leafy green vegetables and none of them seemed to be labeled. She skipped the kale and picked up a head of romaine lettuce. She didn't know what bok choy was either. She moved on to the more familiar items — lemons, limes, broccoli, carrots, bell peppers, mushrooms, onions, apples and avocado. Butternut squash? How would she ever cut that? she wondered. The "Love Shack" song grated. She still needed to figure out which bundle of green leaves was kale. She approached a man with a long ponytail unloading a box of bundled leafy vegetables. "Kale?" Colleen said.

"Which kind?"

Colleen stared blankly. There was more than one kind? She pulled out her booklet.

"We only have Curly, Tuscan and Redbor," he said. "What do you plan to do with it?"

Colleen flipped through the booklet; she couldn't find any kale recipes. She had no idea what it was for. "I'll take the most popular one."

He shrugged and handed her a thick bundle of wet leaves. Colleen stared at the stretch of skin he'd exposed as he reached for the kale. There, inked into his skin, was a beautiful mermaid swimming up his arm. Her hair was soft and flowing, and her curves were in all the right places. She would have no problem fitting into Colleen's navy dress. Dinah would proudly lock her arm into hers and weave her through the flocks of women, making introductions to those who were worthy. She'd be the envy of the club.

He shook the bundle of leaves and released a spray of water. She didn't know which kind he had selected, but she wouldn't forget the dark green sturdy leaves with purple veins running through it. Colleen wiped her wet hands across her pants as she admired the beautiful rainbow of produce piled in her cart. The moment was lost quickly as "Love Shack" recycled itself through her mind and her mind churned with apprehension about her ability to do anything with her new bounty. She lifted the paper cup and took a sip. Her latte had become cold.

Colleen sighed and looked at the next section on the meal plan. Meats: smoked salmon, black cod filets, boneless turkey breasts, boneless chicken breasts. She hated touching raw meat, especially chicken, and she had no idea how to cook fish. She imagined her kitchen smeared with fish scales and the pulpy chicken heaped on her cutting board. The sour smell of rotten chicken and pungent fish would permeate the air in her house. As much as she wished she could do this, she knew there was no way she would cook and prepare all the meals listed. The only chance she had of getting through the twenty-one days would be if she hired someone to help her. She left her half-filled cart in between the produce and meat section, slung her purse over her shoulder and left the store.

Back at her kitchen table, the room still unmarred with what would certainly have been her failed attempts at butchery. Colleen picked up her phone and texted Kory.

Colleen: I'm not much of a cook. Do you know anyone that I can hire to help prepare food for me?

Colleen pressed send before her fear of Kory's judgment stopped her.

> *Kory: Don't worry. When we decide you are ready to start, I'll connect you with Nothin' but Nutrition. Billy cooks for a few of my clients. Sorry I didn't mention that as an option earlier. I will give you his card when we start the detox.*
>
> *Colleen: I'm ready!*

Colleen put the phone away and pulled another slice of pizza from the refrigerator. Obviously, Kory was right. She wasn't ready. She would never be ready. She loved pizza and Diet Coke. If given the choice, she would never give those things up. Something had to change, something more than she could manage on her own.

Colleen pulled the under-counter-mounted trash can out and threw the remaining leftover pizza in the garbage. She imagined Mabel and Chloe telling Jay, "Mommy threw perfectly good pizza away!" She also imagined an hour from now, seeing herself taking a slice out of one of the Ziploc bags in the trash can and eating it. She shuddered at the image. But she knew she was capable of eating it, the girls' leftover food, burnt food from the trash. When had it gotten so bad? She pulled the plastic bag from the garbage container and took it out to the dumpster in the alley.

Her phone rang. It slipped out of her hand as she pulled it from her cardigan pocket. Sweat ran down her back as she bent over to pick it up from the gravel. Somehow the screen wasn't shattered.

Kory's number.

"Colleen, please listen to me. It's not a good idea to rush into this. I'll send you Billy's information but he usually needs a week's notice for new customers. Spend the week focusing on the mirror exercises and reading the book I gave you."

Colleen grunted a sound that could have been yes, could have been no.

Colleen looked down at her swollen belly and the pizza crumbs caught in the nubby Lycra stretched across her breasts, and she knew she couldn't wait any longer.

"Something you could do — so you feel like you are taking action — pick up the herbal supplements at Whole Foods. The list is in your booklet," Kory said. "Do you have a good blender?"

"There's a Get Juiced near my house," Colleen said.

"That's a perfect place. I'll pull up their menu and text you a few smoothies to choose from," Kory said.

Colleen's phone dinged. Kory had sent Billy's contact information. She dialed the number.

"Nothin' but Nutrition, Billy speaking." His voice was soft and feminine.

Colleen paced around the kitchen, twirling her hair around her fingers with her free hand. "Kory Stone suggested I call you about preparing meals for me?" Colleen said.

"Would tomorrow be too soon? I had a cancellation this morning from one of her other clients," Billy said.

Colleen paused a few seconds. "That works." She inhaled and moved her hand up to rub her scalp that had become sore from her excessive twisting.

"I don't do the smoothies, just lunch and dinner. I'll have your food ready for pickup tomorrow morning."

Colleen wasn't mentally prepared for this. She hoped the diet went as smoothly as it had come together.

She feared upsetting Kory and considered not telling her. But she needed the smoothie suggestions.

> Colleen: Billy had a cancellation and will have
> food ready for me tomorrow.

She held her breath as she pressed send. Her phone began to ring.

"I know you said I should wait, but I really want to start." Colleen bit her lip as she waited for Kory to speak.

After a long pause Kory said, "You know I think you are rushing in to this, but I respect your desire to begin. Do you have a pen and paper handy?"

Colleen dug around in the drawer in the island where she kept note pads, pens and a collection of other random things she didn't know where to put.

"Write, 'I will do the best I can do today.'"

Colleen hated her handwriting. She would rewrite it neater later and with a nicer pen, not a red one.

"Keep this note with you at all times. I want you to look at it the first thing every morning. Look at it all day if you need to," Kory said. "Take one day at a time. If your best isn't what you hoped for, don't judge it. Let it go. Get up and do your best the next day."

Colleen found Kory's words of encouragement reassuring. She put the note on the counter so she would remember to rewrite it later.

"Promise you'll call or text with any questions or concerns that come up along the way," Kory said. "The first few days are hard, but you can do it."

Colleen hung up the phone. She wondered if she should she wait until next week like Kory had suggested. She wasn't sure what she had just gotten herself into. She wanted to fast-forward past what was ahead.

Her phone pinged.

Kory: Smoothies: Green Monster (my fav!), Protein Power, Liquid Sunshine, Berry Power. I hope you enjoy them!

Her phone pinged again.

Kory: I'm hosting a workshop next Monday evening called, Kick Start Your Day. If you're free, I think it would be really good for you. I'll be doing a green smoothie demonstration in addition to other tips about starting your day with success. I'll have Gertrude forward you the flyer.

Colleen didn't like doing things in the evening. She might not even make it that far into the diet. Even if she was still on the diet, why should she learn to make smoothies when she could just pick one up from Get Juiced? But she typed a message to Kory anyway.

Colleen: I'll try to get a sitter.

EIGHT

The eight ounces of lemon water grew as it sat in her bladder. In a desperate search for a restroom, Colleen pulled away from the drop-off line. This is why she hated drinking water. Making a right-hand turn at the light would take her straight to Burt's Pastry Shop. The bathroom there was always clean, but she didn't trust herself. Her mouth tasted of coffee just thinking of the place. She thought of a buttery scone combined with the creaminess of the chocolate chips melting in her mouth. Her stomach gurgled over the car radio.

Her phone pinged.

> *Dinah: The girls' dresses are waiting to be picked up.*

Dinah's building was close and the bathroom in the lobby was nice, but the risk of running into Dinah wasn't worth it. She would get the dresses another time. The dirty little gas station at the corner of Hollywood and Lakeshore Drive was her only option. She wished she could make it home. The southbound traffic on Lakeshore Drive at eight-thirty on a weekday morning was always congested. The mounting pressure and pain she was feeling couldn't be contained much longer. She hoped the dirt and grime in the gas station would turn her stomach enough to resist buying a Diet Coke.

She weaved through the line of customers waiting to pay for their gas, lottery tickets, packaged breakfast and stale coffee. She would have given just about anything for a package of chocolate-covered donuts or the powdered-sugar ones. She kept her head down as she made her way through. Straight to the restroom and straight back to the car, she told herself.

The hour and a half that she had lived through this detox diet led her to question how she could possibly get through the next twelve or so ahead. She didn't dare think about tomorrow or the next day or the nineteen after that. Her head was beginning to ache and her stomach begged for food. She pulled the booklet from her purse. The corner of the first page had become curled over and there were oil marks from yesterday's pizza crumbs. "During the twenty-one days you will be making changes in your lifestyle that may be uncomfortable but will help you move toward a healthier lifestyle. This program isn't meant to turn your life upside down." Healthier lifestyle better mean extreme weight-loss. The one-day-at-a-time thing was encouraging yesterday. Today, it sounded impossible. She wished the booklet gave techniques for an hour at a time. Even a few minutes at this point was excruciating without caffeine.

Cars stretched out from both ends of the fifteen-minute-loading zone in front of Get Juiced. She didn't have the patience to look for a parking space. The energy required for her to park at home and walk three blocks didn't exist. The no parking zone in front of the fifteen-minute loading would have to work. She pulled in across the striped lines and put on her hazards. A parking ticket was worth not having to walk.

The line of juice-drinking women flaunting their flat stomachs and tight bottoms were a stark contrast to the line of people at the gas station. Colleen almost went back to her car. She preferred the company of the various-sized donut-eating people. She wondered what planet these thirty- and forty-something-aged women came from where they were able to have the body of a teenage athlete. Perfectly sweaty and perfectly dressed, they looked like a Lululemon catalog. They had obviously come straight from a workout. She wondered if it was the juice or the fitness class that sculpted these women.

The grassy smell of the juice bar irritated Colleen's aching head. She scrolled through Kory's text messages until she found the list of smoothies. The Green Monster was her favorite. A drink made out of kale, coconut milk, almond butter, dates and banana sounded horrible. She couldn't drink that. The Power Protein was the only one without spinach or kale. Even though she wasn't sure what chia seeds or hemp seeds were, she knew they weren't leaves. She didn't want to know what the maca root was. The almond milk, almond butter, cacao (she hoped was chocolate), banana and dates sounded the most drinkable.

Colleen took her Power Protein Smoothie back to her ticketless car. She was lucky. Next time, if there were a next time, she would walk. She spied the parking police crossing the street. She kicked the car in gear before the uniformed woman could make out her license plate and drove toward home.

Maria's car blocked the garage. Colleen turned off the

engine and sat in her car. She couldn't deal with Maria's inquisitive eyes watching her, assuming Colleen was drinking a milkshake. She wished that were what she had. Her favorite was an Oreo milkshake from Potbelly's Sandwich Shop. She sniffed the beige-colored smoothie. Her stomach growled. The coolness of the smoothie coming up through the straw brought momentary relief to her pounding temples. She pressed the plastic cup against her forehead. She ran her tongue over her teeth. The smoothie left a nutty banana aftertaste. She took another sip and waited for the flavor of nuts. She didn't hate it.

She noticed a missed call on her phone. "I'm calling from Nothin' but Nutrition. Your meals are ready to be picked up," the woman's voice said on the voicemail. Colleen had forgotten. Hopefully, this detox would do something for her ability to focus.

She managed to push through her exhaustion and her splitting headache to pick up her future meals. Billy was a small man. His head was shaved and he wore a small hoop earring in his left ear. He reminded Colleen of a petite version of Mr. Clean. He seemed too fit to be a chef. He had six boxed meals waiting for her when she arrived. From what she understood, the meals could be eaten in any order. They were labeled with ingredients and cooking instructions. The throbbing of her head made her eyes hurt as she strained to read the ingredients. Some were to be eaten cold while others needed to be heated. Seaweed, quinoa, yams, Swiss chard, and more kale were a common theme on most of the labels. The chilled salmon salad with spring vegetables and lemon quinoa sounded the best of the six meals. She dipped into her bag and pulled out two Tylenol. She swallowed them dry while Billy ran her credit card. The pills stuck in her throat but they'd relieve her head in the next hour. Colleen wondered if Billy reported back to Kory on her clients. She needed relief from her headache — even if Tylenol was against the rules.

On the days that Maria cleaned, Colleen never ate at home. She grew tired of Maria's need to be in the kitchen the minute she sat down. Maria liked to see what she was eating. Her incomprehensible commentary was always decorated with disapproval. The Gonzalez family believed every meal should be made up of meat, vegetables and a starch. Drinking soda instead of milk with a meal was sinful. Colleen's habit of diet soda and pizza received a lot of muttered words Colleen couldn't understand in Spanish.

Colleen cleared the middle shelf in the refrigerator. She placed the boxes into three piles, stacked in twos except the one she left out for lunch. Maria gave an approving smile as she eyed Colleen's plate of food and the half dozen white plastic bottles of supplements. She wiped her hands on a towel. "Señora?" She hovered over Colleen. "¿Estés enfermo?"

"Not sick. Just a headache." Colleen closed her eyes as Maria's cold hand pressed into her forehead. She thought of the way her mother used to use her hand the same way to check for a fever. She wished Maria could follow her around, kneading her cool hands into her temples. The minute Maria removed her hands, the pounding resumed. Colleen began to worry that she was sick. What she was feeling couldn't be normal.

Maria returned to dusting the pictures hanging in the hall and shook her head while mumbling something in Spanish.

Colleen chose the salmon on top a bed of lettuce for lunch. The pink, flaky fish tasted better than she expected. Billy had added lemon and dill to the side of salad dressing. Her belly was content, but her head continued to ache. Leaving the empty salad container behind on the table, she headed to the back living room. She closed the blinds and stretched her legs up on the couch. The pain that crossed the front half of her skull forced her eyes closed. She let her head sink into the overstuffed down-feather pillow. Maria began vacuuming.

Colleen retreated to her bedroom. If the Tylenol didn't help in the next ten minutes, she promised herself that she would go to Southport Grocery & Cafe for a double vanilla latte. She would leave out the vanilla to make it healthier, she told herself. She had less than an hour until her two o'clock hair appointment. She wrote these events in capital red letters in her calendar. SS Beauty Bar had a waitlist every day of the week. If she didn't go, her hair would expand and frizz until it floated above the headrest in the car.

Her phone pinged. She moaned as she raised her arm to bring the phone into the view of her blurry eyes.

Kory: How's it going?

Colleen: really tired and have a terrible headache

Kory: That's normal. I'll send you an article on caffeine withdrawal. Take a nap if you can. Make sure you drink plenty of water.

Colleen would have killed to take a nap. And she had

forgotten about the water requirement. The only water she drank so far was the lemon water when she woke up and the little bit she had with her supplements at lunch. Nowhere close to the amount that Kory had listed in the detox booklet.

Colleen clicked on the link to the article Kory sent. She had never thought caffeine withdrawal was a real thing. She skimmed through the article. *Headaches could last one to three days,* it said. Colleen was quite certain she wouldn't make it three days. *Maybe more water would help*, she thought. She felt as though she had the flu. She reached down into the cabinet of her nightstand where she kept large bottles of Evian water. She had stocked those in there six months ago when she was trying to drink more water. All she wanted to do was lie in total darkness. The light made her eyes constrict, creating a stabbing pain through her eye socket.

Colleen picked up her phone.

"Hi, this is Colleen Adler, I need to cancel my appointment with Sandy today."

"You'll be charged the full amount of your service," the receptionist said, seeming to enjoy the power of her position.

Colleen should have reminded the snippy woman of her loyalty. She had been seeing Sandy twice a week for almost ten years and had never canceled before. Too exhausted to argue or be mad, she said, "Okay," and hung up the phone before the woman could respond.

The coolness of her pillow comforted her aching head. Her brain felt as though it was bruised and the slightest motion caused it to bang against her skull. She brought her arm up to rest the crook of her elbow up against her burning eyes. A cold washcloth would have been better, but her exhausted body couldn't move. As her body sank further into the mattress, she remembered she forgot to do the "mirror work." That would have to wait until later, she told herself. It sounded like nonsense, anyway.

A beeping sound entered Colleen's dream. She was in Brockville riding the bike she had as a little girl. Her grown body struggled to pedal without hitting her knees on the handlebars. She had to grip tight with both hands to keep from losing balance. The wind whipped her curly hair into her face. She couldn't see where she was going. The back-up beeping noise sounded like it was coming toward her. She needed to move her hair out of her eyes, but if she took her hands off the handlebars she would fall. The beeping became louder and louder until it eventually woke her up. Her hand shook as she reached across Jay's side of the bed to turn the alarm off. Her clothes were damp with sweat. She fought against the dead weight of her sleepy body to lift up out of bed.

Dazed, she left her bed unmade and walked into her bathroom. Her headache was gone. Her eyes felt grainy and were bloodshot. Digging around her medicine cabinet, she found some eye drops. She dotted the corner of each eye, accepting the burn as she closed them. Maybe in the wake of relief as the pain eased from her scalp she was imagining things, but looking at herself once again, she thought her eyes looked bright and clear.

The comb felt good on her itchy scalp. Getting through the next three days was going to be interesting. The comb marks revealed her greasy roots. A hat was her only option. As she adjusted a blue Cubs baseball cap over her hair, she thought of the looming "mirror work." What could it hurt? She removed her hat.

Remembering what Kory said, she looked deep into her eyes. There was a sadness that she had never seen before. "Colleen Adler." She stopped herself. "Colleen Ann O'Brien." She paused. "You are beautiful and I love you. I really, really love you." She thought she would find the exercise stupid. It was stupid. But a lump swelled in her throat and her eyes filled with tears.

SHE USED SUNGLASSES TO FURTHER camouflage the sight of her makeup-free eyes. She didn't care if it was cloudy. She watched the gaggle of moms using the rainy weather as an opportunity to show off their Burberry raincoats and matching rain boots. The ones wearing fedora hats appeared to be particularly pleased with flaunting their ensemble.

Of course, Chloe was the first one to come skipping out of school. Mabel came out more timely than normal. She didn't skip to the car, but she had a smile on her face.

"Mommy, why do you have sunglasses on when the sun isn't out?" Mabel said.

"Yeah, and where did you get that hat?" Chloe said.

The girls weren't used to seeing Colleen looking so disheveled. For once, her looks reflected the way she felt. "I had a headache earlier and the sunglasses helped," Colleen said. "How was your day?"

"We learned to knit. Rebecca and I were the only ones who could do it." Mabel beamed.

Colleen wished she saw Mabel this way more often. "That's great."

Not to be outdone, Chloe said, "I am three books ahead of my whole class in silent reading time."

Colleen wondered what had gotten into the girls when they went straight to the kitchen table to start their homework. They never did that without being told. She wondered if she would wake up tomorrow and discover everything since being at Get Juiced was a dream. If it was a dream, she was going to enjoy the good parts.

The landline rang, and Mabel jumped to answer it. "Okay, let me ask my mom," she said. "Mom, can we go over to Stella and Sarah's?"

Mystery solved. Colleen remembered being shocked when her own mother knew her motives. She smiled thinking of Noel Bellman's pool party.

Colleen hesitated for a moment. Having the girls out of the house until dinnertime was usually a cause for celebration, but not tonight. Tonight she needed to be distracted with helping with homework, sorting through the DVRs for their favorite episode of *Hannah Montana* and helping Chloe get her American Girl Doll's clothing changed.

"As soon as you get your homework done," Colleen said.

Chloe slammed her math book closed. "Done!" she said.

"We'll be over soon," Mabel said into the phone.

Mabel sat back at the table and flew through the rest of her work. "Done!" she said.

The girls were running toward the door when Colleen stopped them. "Put your homework back in your backpack so it's ready for tomorrow."

The obedient little girls did as their mother asked. Chloe stuffed her math booklet into her Hello Kitty bag and quickly zipped it shut. Mabel was more careful as she closed and zipped her binder before placing it in her plain backpack.

"Be home by six," Colleen yelled behind the girls as they ran through the front door. She stood in her empty house and watched them as they crossed the front yard. After rearranging the velvet throw pillows on her Chesterfield sofa, she looked at the girls' baby pictures that decorated the bookshelves along the wall. She loved the one with Jay and the girls at the Cubs game. That may be the last game they went to as a family. Colleen wished she had asked someone to take the picture. It would be nice to see her slimmer self in a picture with her family. The picture had been taken two years ago. Colleen recognized how much the girls had changed. And how, unfortunately, she had too.

The five o'clock news validated her fear of the evening before her. The beginning sounds of the evening broadcast created a gaping need for a forbidden glass of wine. She turned the TV off. She wasn't sure how she was going to get through the night. Would one glass of wine really sabotage her efforts? The problem was one glass would turn into two and possibly three.

She had to have something. Anything. Her body ached for relief. She walked into the pantry. Everything was off-limits. She walked out. Got a glass of water. Chugged it. You can do this, she told herself.

She sat down at the kitchen table and stared out the window into the Wilsons' yard. Stephanie had been busy planting over the past few days. She now had window boxes lining her back deck. They were full of pansies and English ivy. In a few weeks, she would replace the pansies with some sort of summer annual, probably begonias. In the fall she would replace the summer annuals with mums. The English ivy was the only plant that remained in place from the first planting of the spring to the final cleanup after Thanksgiving.

Colleen's ears began to ring from the quiet in the house. Closing her eyes, she began Kory's breathing exercise. After inhaling and exhaling slowly ten times, she opened her eyes. The first thing that came to her mind was to put on a different channel on the TV. She needed some noise, a distraction, something other than the news.

Scanning the channels, she came across the TV show *Seinfeld*. It made her miss Jay. They'd watched *Seinfeld* with Ryan and Harper every Thursday night at seven, up until their two best friends broke up. Then, it was just Colleen and Jay watching. They knew which episode contained Man Hands and The Competition and Assman. Tonight's episode was The Chicken Roaster. She was grateful to Kramer for making her laugh and to forget, at least temporarily, about having a glass of wine.

The continuous ringing of the doorbell let Colleen know the girls were home. They thought it was hilarious to push the button over and over while waiting for their mom to let them in.

"Ew, what's that smell?" Chloe squeezed her nose closed.

"Curried chicken." The pungent smell concerned Colleen as well.

"Do we have to eat it?" Mabel said and cupped her hands over her mouth.

Chloe scrunched up her nose and brought her eyebrows together. "Why are you eating that?"

"I'm trying to eat healthier," Colleen said.

The curried chicken was spicier than Colleen had expected. At least, it helped her drink three glasses of water. After adjusting to the strong spicy flavors, she began to like it. She had never liked sweet potatoes before but the spicy curry sauce made them edible. She was satisfied and full but not stuffed like she usually was after dinner. She needed to learn to stop eating before she became uncomfortable. So far, she liked two of the six meals Billy had prepared.

The girls each only finished half of their plates. Colleen always made too much food. Clearing their plates from the table, she mindlessly tossed a leftover chicken finger into her mouth. Halfway into chewing it, she realized what she had done. She spit the chewed pieces into the sink. It didn't have flavor like her curried chicken but the saltiness of it made her want another bite. Did she always eat from the girls' plates while she cleaned up?

She wished her craving for a glass of wine could be as fleeting as being full and satisfied had been. The herbal tea Kory suggested was of no use. Her headache was back. Wine was the only thing she wanted.

She heard her phone ping from across the kitchen.

Chloe ran through the house screaming as Mabel chased after her. "Mom, tell Chloe to give my diary back!"

"Chloe!" Colleen yelled. She looked at her phone to see another message from Dinah about the dresses.

Chloe threw Mabel's diary at her and ran off. The diary hit the floor. Mabel picked it up and charged after her little sister.

Colleen heard her bedroom door slam.

"Tell Chloe to stay out of my things!" Mabel screamed as

she ran up the stairs. The screaming continued, along with her pounding on the locked bedroom door.

The high-pitched screaming sounds from upstairs were more than Colleen could handle. Instead of going up the stairs to help the girls settle their argument, she went down the stairs to the wine cellar.

Reaching the top of the stairs with her bottle of cabernet, Colleen heard silence. The ruckus had stopped. She hoped the quiet lasted for the rest of the evening. In the likelihood that it wouldn't, she was now better equipped to handle it.

In preparation for the next battle between the sisters, she twisted the wine opener into the cork. The small popping sound indicated the release. She brought a wine goblet down from the leaded glass cabinet and slowly poured the deep, dark purple liquid into the glass. She stopped halfway up. Only half, she told herself. She corked the bottle and put it away in the pantry. An open bottle in plain view would be too much of a temptation.

She swirled the glass until a perfect tunnel formed in the center. Letting the deep color settle back into stillness, Colleen watched the legs of the wine drip down the sides of the glass. She hadn't spent so much time observing wine since she was in Napa with Jay. This was a standard procedure for Jay before taking the first sip from a new bottle. He relished every step leading up to the first drop of wine that hit his palate.

Colleen usually just drank it. Not tonight. Tonight she was going to cherish it. Burying her nose in the glass, she paused to inhale the rich herbal scent that was about to come across her lips. She vowed to hold the wine in her mouth for a couple of seconds before swallowing the few sips that awaited her.

The glands under her tongue salivated as she brought the flavor inside. She created a well with her tongue as she savored the small moment of pleasure.

She looked across the counter and saw the piece of paper she had written on yesterday. The red ink with her sloppy handwriting said, "I will do the best I can do today." She held the wine on her tongue. Was this her best? Up to now, she felt she had done her best. Was swallowing this tongueful of wine doing her best? Was wanting wine this badly normal? The thought of being an alcoholic forced her to spit the wine in the sink. She retrieved the bottle from the pantry, uncorked it and listened as one of her favorite liquids gulped down the drain.

She flipped through the calendar hanging on the refrigerator. Seventy-six days until the Fourth of July. There were at least twenty-five pounds standing between her and her stunning silk dress. She locked the powder room behind her before cradling her face into the palms of her hands. Inhaling and exhaling deeply, she stood to look at herself. "You can do better," she said to her tearful reflection. She looked deep into her eyes. "Colleen Ann O'Brien, I love you, I really, really love you." Her heart warmed a little as the tears ran down her cheeks. How did she end up so broken?

She went to her desk, took out one of her personalized stationery note cards and with her best pen, the one with black ink that always made her handwriting look better, she wrote, "I will do the best I can do today."

NINE

Colleen changed the alarm setting from six to seven. She had given up on the early wake-up call. Waking without the guilt and shame about not getting out of bed to run was a nice change. The sudden urge to go to the bathroom caught her by surprise, since she forgot to drink her laxative drink. She wondered if her body eliminating on its own was a fluke. *If nothing else came out of this detox, this was something worth doing it for*, she thought.

She parked her car at home and walked to Get Juiced. The sun had broken through the clouds and the fresh spring air felt nice. The throbbing behind her eyes had returned before she opened her eyes that morning. The hat she was now forced to wear didn't help her aching head. She had made it through yesterday, but the withdrawal article said day two could be worse. She walked gingerly, trying not to move her head too much as she glided to a bench across the street from Get Juiced. The Power Protein Smoothie sweated in her lap. Her phone pinged.

Kory: How was day 1?

Colleen didn't have the energy to respond. The little energy she felt upon waking was seeping into the bench. Colleen's phone rang. Kory's number appeared on the phone.

"Hi, how much water did you drink yesterday?" Kory said.

"Not sure. Probably not enough."

"Your body weight, one hundred and eighty-five, divided in half is ninety-two and a half. That's how many ounces of water you need to be drinking."

Colleen cringed when she heard that number. Kory seemed to enjoy playing around with the numbers. This may be fun for Kory, but it was hell for Colleen. She definitely hadn't drank that much water. Colleen looked down at her smoothie and thought of her lemon water. "Does my smoothie and lemon water count?"

"You can count one-third of your smoothie toward your goal and all of your lemon water," Kory said.

Colleen sat silent with the phone pressed up against her ear. She pressed her index finger into her throbbing temple.

"Colleen, these first few days are the hardest. I promise by day four or five, things will be easier."

Colleen wasn't sure she could make it to day four or five. "Okay."

"The two-inch pile of supplements will help you get some water in your system," Kory joked.

Colleen didn't appreciate Kory's humor. She obviously had no idea how much she was struggling.

"It's normal to feel tired the first few days. Your body is going through withdrawal from sugar," Kory said.

Sugar and caffeine withdrawal. It was like she was a drug addict. Her body ached for a coffee and a scone. It wasn't fair that something so delicious and small could be so bad. Shame filled her. She was now more determined than ever to see this thing through.

"I find it helpful to measure out the water for each day. Leave it out on your counter so you are reminded to drink it," Kory said.

"Okay." Colleen thought of the look on Maria's face seeing all that water on the counter. She would definitely think Colleen had lost her mind.

"If you're tired, take a nap," Kory said. "We'll talk about adding exercise next week."

Exercise? Colleen wasn't sure her legs had enough strength to carry her home, let alone exercise.

"Don't worry about that now. Sweating will help, so try sitting in a hot bath, a steam shower or sauna, if you have access to one. I'm going to text you a detox bath recipe."

"Okay, thanks." A hot bath sounded nice but Colleen wasn't up for any kind of recipe. Colleen sat in the sun and relaxed a while longer. She took a big slug of her smoothie before she closed her eyes up toward the sun. Her phone pinged again. It was Kory with the detox bath recipe.

Kory was a machine. Colleen wasn't sure she was cut out to work with her. She wasn't sure she could ever keep up. Colleen looked up from her phone and watched the bouquet of tiny women flood the juice store across the street. Colleen pried her body off the bench. She wasn't going to look like those women if she stayed sitting there. She looked at the text again. She didn't have any of those ingredients Kory had listed. The last thing she wanted to do was to get back in the car. She wanted to go home and stay there until it was time to get the girls later. Maria wasn't there cleaning, so she had the house to herself. The only thing she had to do besides eat and take a nap was to gather the dirty laundry into a bag and leave it by the door for Suds Laundry Service.

"I can do this," she said, using the same strategy she used yesterday. She forced herself through the necessary motions in order to get it over with as quickly as possible. She grabbed her keys and set off to Whole Foods, where she hoped they had all those unheard of ingredients.

Colleen held her breath as she walked past the coffee counter. She weaved through the shoppers and their carts, avoiding the sample of Brie cheese topped with fig jam and marcona almonds and headed straight to the vitamin section. She handed the pink-haired girl who appeared to be an employee her phone to see the things Kory had listed. The girl walked Colleen over to the bath salts. Colleen was faced with an assortment of detox bath mixtures, Seaweed Mineral Detox — cleanse, rejuvenate, relax; Purr Bliss Red Poppy Detox; Moisturizing Epsom Salt Detox and Cleanse. There were more variations than Colleen cared to sort through. Wishing she had gotten a cart instead of a basket, Colleen lugged the bags to the checkout counter.

Upstairs in her seven-foot Jacuzzi bathtub, Colleen's tired body sank into the warm bath mixture. She looked around at the nearly forty thousand dollars' worth of Italian Calacatta marble covering the bathroom walls and floor. She wondered if Arthur still thought it was the best. The lavender aroma encompassed her body as she leaned her itchy head back against the towel she had rolled into a pillow up against the acrylic tub. The Tylenol kept the headache at a dull throb, but her scalp was sore from having her greasy hair pulled back in a ponytail.

Her phone pinged.

She wiped her wet fingers across the towel behind her head.

Dinah: Harrold said you still haven't picked the dresses up!

Those dresses were going to have to wait until she had her hair done on Friday. There was no way she could go into Dinah's building with the current condition of her hair.

Colleen: I'll get them Friday.

It had been six days since she last had her head washed. Unable to take it any longer, she pulled out the ponytail holder and submerged her head into the water. The warm water brought instant relief to her irritated scalp. The only shampoo within reach was the tear-free baby shampoo she used on the girls. She filled her palm with as much shampoo as she could hold and massaged the liquid against her scalp until a thick layer of suds formed across her head. The force of the warm water coming out of the handheld nozzle against her head felt heavenly. Positioning the towel once again, she released the weight of her head against the towel while using her toe to press the button to turn on the jets. Her body felt weightless as it floated in the swirling water.

The lavender-scented Seaweed Mineral Detox bag recommended soaking for twenty minutes. Flinching awake after dropping off for the third time, Colleen got out before the elapsed time. She wrapped her head in a towel and her body in a matching soft terry cloth robe. The crispness of her sheets under her heavy duvet comforter lured her body into a deep sleep. She awoke to the beeping of her alarm. The last thing she remembered was climbing into bed.

SHE CONTINUED TO BE IMPRESSED with Billy's food. It had taken her a while to work up enough courage to try the seaweed salad that came with the grilled chicken she had for lunch. After twirling the awful-looking green seaweed around on her fork, smelling it and inspecting the sesame seeds, scallions and either parsley or cilantro leaves dotting the seaweed, she finally took a bite. It was delicious. For the first time in a long time she looked forward to dinnertime. For once, she felt prepared.

Tonight, she was going to cook something for the girls that didn't come out of the freezer. She wondered what Stephanie was making Stella and Sara for dinner. Most likely it would be something that Colleen didn't have the ingredients for. Digging through her pantry, she found a box of farfalle noodles. The girls loved the bowtie shape. She didn't have any sauce but did have butter and Parmesan cheese.

"Mabel, let's go!" Colleen heard Chloe yelling through the fumbling of pots and pans. She found Chloe slumped against the powder room door. "She won't come out," Chloe said.

Colleen tapped on the door. No answer. "Why don't you put your homework away while I talk to Mabel," Colleen said.

Colleen tapped the door again. This time there was a click on the door handle. Colleen gently opened the door. Mabel sat in a little ball, hugging her knees up around her middle on top of the toilet lid. She had her face buried into the top of knees. Colleen knelt down beside her. If she was smaller, she would have scooped her up in her arms and held her on her lap. Colleen stroked the top of her hair, pushing back the stray hairs that had escaped her ponytail holder. "Rebecca?" she said.

Mabel shook her head and brought her red eyes up toward her mother. "She said I'm ugly." Her chin quivered.

Colleen fought back her tears and tried to soothe the hatred she felt toward Ashley and Rebecca Barr. "You are beautiful. You are smart and you are strong. Don't listen to that mean little girl."

Colleen held Mabel until she was ready to pull away. It was only four in the afternoon and the aching for a glass of wine had already begun. She closed the bathroom door after Mabel walked out. It was her turn to sit on the closed toilet seat. She brought the lavender candle sitting on the edge of the pedestal sink up to her nose. The lavender bath had put her in such a good place earlier that she hoped taking in the scent of the candle before doing her breathing exercise would help also. At the end of her tenth exhale, she opened her eyes and whispered, "I will do the best I can do today."

"Bye, Mom," Mabel yelled.

Colleen's exit from the bathroom was too slow. The girls closed the front door before she could catch up to them. She watched out the front window as they ran across the yard to the Wilsons' house. She went back to the mirror in the bathroom and did her mirror work. She still wasn't sure if it helped, but she was glad she no longer cried when she did it.

Colleen had allowed the girls to monopolize the past few evening phone conversations with Jay. The less she spoke to him the easier it was to ignore her thoughts of him being with the blond woman from LA. Her exhaustion over the past couple of days had allowed her to temporarily forget about her suspicions. She also wasn't ready to tell him about her new diet. She wanted to make sure she could get through the week first. She would tell him about the diet on Friday night when he got home, but the conversation about the woman in the picture would have to wait until this diet was over.

COLLEEN SAT UP IN BED. She looked at the clock for a second time. *Amazing*, she thought as she sat up and leaned against her headboard. She had woken on her own, felt rested and it was only five after six. Other times when she had woken at this hour, her body felt heavy and tired. Instead of going downstairs for a Diet Coke, she drank her eight ounces of lemon water that she had left on her nightstand before going to sleep last night. Another new habit she hoped to keep.

There was a text message and missed call from Jay at two a.m.

Jay: Sorry for the call – pocket dial.

Quickly shaking the thought of what Jay was doing up at two a.m., Colleen focused on how far she had come in four days. She couldn't believe how different her body was behaving. Her new regularity, without a laxative, combined with her healthy eating had left her feeling much lighter. Her clothes were actually beginning to feel looser. As much as she wanted to see how much weight she had lost, she was scared to check. She didn't want the number on the scales to ruin her positive thoughts. She decided to wait a full week before she allowed herself to get on the scales.

While a headache had lingered through much of the day yesterday, it was better than it had been the first two days. The detox baths after lunch followed by a nap in the afternoon seemed to have made a big difference. She feared the naps would make it hard for her to sleep at night but the opposite happened. She had been sleeping better than ever.

The girls had remarked on her ability to stay awake during all of the bedtime stories. Chloe said, "Mommy, you are reading just like daddy."

At first Colleen didn't know what she was referring to. Then she realized that Chloe was picking up on her alertness. She was able to read all the requested stories and tuck the girls in without falling asleep. Last night, she even had enough energy to read a few chapters of *You Can Heal Your Life* after she got the girls to bed.

Colleen was proud of her progress, but she worried about the day ahead. There wasn't going to be time for a bath or a nap. She was embarrassed to go into the salon with her hair looking the way it was, but that was a better option than Jay seeing it in its current condition. The appearance of her hair after washing it in the bath the past few days followed by taking a nap with wet hair reconfirmed the importance of the salon's professional services. Going to bed with a wet head was never a good idea but Colleen realized it was a really bad idea when she was overdue for another Keratin Treatment. She woke with part-straight, part-wavy, and mostly frizzy hair.

Just as she had been doing after her naps the past few days, she pulled her mass of hair back into a ponytail before twisting and twirling it into a bun on the back of her head. Accepting that it was as good as it could be, she put the final bobby pin in her hair and walked out of her bathroom.

The chirping of the house alarm announced Maria's earlier-than-normal arrival. Colleen thought of how this was the first time she could remember not being annoyed with Maria getting there earlier than she was supposed to. For once, nothing sat unfinished in the washer or dryer; all the clothes had managed to make it in the bag for Wednesday's laundry pickup.

The girls' bedroom was empty. She wasn't the only one to wake up early on her own today. Pride radiated through Colleen as she walked downstairs. Being awake, in a good mood and ready for the day was a rare occurrence; one she hoped would become regular.

Maria was in the pantry with Chloe helping her find items for her lunch. Mabel sat on the couch watching TV with her backpack ready and by her side.

"Señora!" Maria reached up to Colleen's bun. Then she stretched her arm up to feel Colleen's forehead again. "*Bueno, bueno,*" she said in an approving tone.

Colleen wondered if Maria really liked her hair or if she was just happy that she was ready ahead of schedule.

"Mommy." Chloe ran over to Colleen and gave her a long hug.

"How would you like to try a smoothie for breakfast today?" Colleen wondered if the girls would like Get Juiced.

"Yes!" Chloe said.

"What about you, Mabel? Would you like to stop by Get Juiced on the way to school and try one of their smoothies?"

Mabel shrugged as she sat in a trance watching *SpongeBob SquarePants*.

"Let's go. We're all ready." Colleen sat down by Mabel, wrapping her arm around her shoulder. Colleen leaned down and kissed her cheek. "Let's do something different."

Without a word, Mabel turned the TV off. She leaned into her mom and nodded her head into Colleen's chest.

Maria helped the girls get their backpacks on. She gave Colleen a nod of approval as she embraced both of the girls.

"We're going out for smoothies!" Chloe announced to Maria.

"Bueno, bueno," Maria said.

Chloe hopped out of the car before Colleen had the keys out of the ignition. Mabel followed behind her and Colleen had to hurry to catch up to them. Chloe charged into Get Juiced like she had been going there every day of her life. Colleen hoped the girls could find something they liked, but just in case, she threw a package of Pop-Tarts in her purse.

Get Juiced was quieter than the other times Colleen had visited. The store had just opened and besides the girl behind the counter, they were the only ones there.

"Why's your hair purple?" Chloe's inquisitive eyes took in the juice woman's interesting locks.

Colleen cut in before Chloe said something else that may offend the poor woman. "I'm sorry," she mouthed. The woman's purple hair did complement her pale blue eyes.

The woman laughed. "Don't be sorry. I love your honesty!" she said looking at Chloe. "I just really like purple."

Chloe smiled. "Mommy, can I make my hair purple?"

"Let's stick with getting smoothies for now," Colleen said.

"I'll have the Protein Power. Do you have any kid-friendly smoothies?"

"How about the Breakfast Blast?" the woman said. "It has oats, yogurt, OJ, berries and bananas."

"Yummy!" said Chloe.

"And it's purple!" the woman said.

Colleen glanced in the rearview mirror to see whether Mabel's and Chloe's silence was a good or bad thing. Seeing both girls with their lips wrapped tightly around the straws made her smile. Incredibly, they were enjoying their breakfast. Her girls deserved better than she had been giving them. The smoothies were a good start, but she needed to figure out how to replace all the other junk she fed them. She was going to throw out the Pop-Tarts when she got home.

The craving for a cup of coffee and a scone still hung heavy in Colleen's body all morning. Her mind was relentless as it teased her taste buds with the imagined flavors of cedar and cloves in Burt's breakfast blend. The relief she felt each morning, knowing that she had made it through the day before, gave her an added layer of strength. Her experience this week made her aware of how she had been mindlessly fueling her body with caffeine and sugar until the clock deemed it appropriate to have a glass of wine. As much as she missed having those things, she was beginning to realize how much she relied on caffeine, sugar and alcohol to get from one day to the next. The past few days had been difficult, but she had managed. She'd cried more than she had in a long time, slept a lot more than she could ever remember sleeping and wanted to pull her hair more times than she could count. She may have come close a time or two but she still hadn't cheated. In all the months of berating herself for not working out and for not eating healthier, she'd finally accomplished something. She'd made it four days and hadn't cheated or yelled at the children.

TEN

"Everything looks amazing!" Colleen handed Pedro a check. She was sorry she'd waited so long. The decaying evergreens in her window boxes attached to the railing of her front porch had been replaced with bright yellow daffodils, blue muscari and orange tulips. Pedro had filled the urns on each side of her front door with white tulips, orange pansies, pink hydrangeas and pussy willow branches. Her dark decaying front porch was now cheerful and full of life. Her yard had been cleaned of the scattered debris and manicured into perfection. The freshly laid mulch and spring blooms filled the air with scents of cedar and sweetness. The smells of dust and mildew were long gone. She wished she could pay someone to accomplish the weight loss and sculpt her body into the perfect size for her Fourth of July dress, as she did with her hair, nails and yard. The week had been full of changes. The easy ones were visible; the hard ones were not.

Kory had been right when she said things would get easier. Not only had Colleen remembered to pick up the girls' dresses from Dinah's doorman, she also managed to get through the day without a nap, and, surprisingly, it felt good.

"Pedro, you're a miracle worker!" Jay said, pushing his hair back as he walked up the front steps. The knot of his tie was slid a quarter of the way down his partially unbuttoned shirt.

His crumpled suit coat and pants were just as tired-looking as he was. He shook Pedro's hand before stepping inside and dropping his keys in the steel bowl on the entry table.

Colleen held her breath as she followed Jay back to the kitchen. Wet circles had formed under the arms of her grey cardigan sweater. She wished she had worn black so it wouldn't be as noticeable. Tilting her chin down toward her left shoulder, she did a subtle smell evaluation and was relieved there wasn't an odor. The blond woman from LA with the beautifully sculpted arms probably never had wet circles under her arms. She couldn't compete with the beautiful women that surrounded Jay all week. Still, she felt better than she had in a long time.

She wondered how he was going to take the news that she wouldn't be drinking with him for the next few weeks. Sharing a bottle of wine was one of the few things they enjoyed doing together. With the looming temptation in front of her, she prayed to hold on to her current state of mind. She reached into the refrigerator and chose chicken salsa verde with zucchini and broccoli for tonight's dinner. She'd had Billy make extra for Jay. He'd also packaged up homemade chicken and noodle soup and mini roast beef sandwiches for the girl's dinner. Colleen was grateful to him for offering a quick solution that included transforming the girls' diet. He made a note to prepare some kid-friendly dishes for her next pickup.

"What's all this?" Jay said. Seeing the table set, candles burning and the girls nowhere in sight was not something he was accustomed to. "Where're the girls?"

"They're up in our bed watching a movie. They already

ate," Colleen said. "I promised them you would come up when you got home. I've got dinner for us when you're ready." Colleen smiled at her husband. Feeding them early worked out nicely for her impromptu dinner date with Jay.

"I'm impressed," Jay said. "You look different, did you get a haircut?"

"Just my usual blowout at the salon earlier today." Colleen was touched that he noticed a difference in her. She still hadn't weighed herself, but she knew she had lost a few pounds. She wondered if she really looked different. She felt different, that was for sure. "Are you letting your hair grow?" Colleen asked.

"Yeah, why not? I thought I'd try something different. You look great, by the way." Jay kissed Colleen. His lips were salty. The taste combined with his compliment made Colleen's cheeks flush.

Jay pecked her cheek and headed upstairs to see Mabel and Chloe.

Colleen tuned in Van Morrison Radio on Pandora and synced her iPad to the portable speaker in the kitchen while she waited for the food to heat. She had never listened to Van Morrison until she and Jay began dating. "Moondance" had always been one of their favorite songs. She placed the large bottle of sparkling water that Kory had suggested she use in place of wine on the table next to her empty wine glass.

Jay smelled of rosemary when he came back into the kitchen. He had showered and changed into a clean T-shirt and sweatpants. "I'll get us a bottle. What's on the menu?"

"Chicken salsa verde with zucchini and broccoli. I'm not drinking tonight, so get whatever you want."

"No wine? Wait...please tell me you don't think you are pregnant." Jay leaned his head back.

"I'm definitely not pregnant," Colleen said. She tried to count back but couldn't remember the last time they had sex. She avoided him seeing or touching her fleshy body at all costs. She wore baggie pajama pants and oversized T-shirts to bed, locked the bathroom door every time she took a shower and always kept the lights off in the bedroom just in case. She wondered if that was what drove him outside the marriage as much as her size? "I'm not allowed to drink while I'm detoxing."

"Oh." Jay tilted his head and took another look at Colleen. "You know... I'm not going to drink tonight either. I had a late night last night and a night off from drinking would probably be good for me."

Colleen couldn't believe what she had just heard. She couldn't remember a night ever, except maybe if Jay was really sick, that he didn't have a glass of wine with dinner. "Are you sure? I'm okay if you have wine. I have sparkling water."

"Positive. I want to hear all about this detox you are doing," Jay said as he approached Colleen from behind. She flinched as he brought his arms across her hips. She went from feeling great about her changing body to feeling insecure about the width of it. His hands remained clasped across the front of her pelvis while his fingers hung dangling, brushing against her. He nuzzled his nose through her hair, breathing in her ear and kissing the tender skin below. She fought against the flicker of arousal he was creating inside of her. She would like nothing more than to join him in their bed, door locked for a few minutes of ecstasy but she couldn't shake the thought of him being with that woman from Los Angeles. Maybe sex would be good for them? It might help him stop thinking about the woman in LA. But she couldn't bear him seeing her naked, touching her rolls of skin.

"The herbal supplements I have been taking have made me so bloated," she said as she pulled away.

ELEVEN

"Don't you look rested and relaxed this morning!" Gertrude said.

"Really?" Colleen smiled. She had noticed a difference in her reflection this morning also. Her eyes looked bigger and her face looked smaller. The whites of her eyes didn't need eye drops to erase the redness. Gertrude was right; she felt more rested than she had in a long time.

Gertrude cocked her head and continued to stare. "Were you on a vacation last week or something?"

"No," Colleen laughed. She definitely wouldn't call last week a vacation. "I've been doing Kory's detox program." Colleen thought about how much had changed since she sat in the same spot one week ago. The anxiety and desperation were gone. She was well on her way down a path that was changing her life. Six days may not be that long, but they had been transformative.

"Oh, I've been hearing about that. How do you like it?" Gertrude said.

"I'm getting used to it," Colleen said. "I didn't think I was going to survive the first two days, but every day since has gotten a little easier." Gertrude was now the third person to know.

"I can tell you're doing something different. You look more rested than I think I've ever seen," Gertrude said.

Jay's support over the weekend left her feeling energized. She couldn't believe it when he insisted on following along with her diet for the entire weekend. Going without coffee and wine seemed to be easier for him than it had for Colleen. He was his normal cheerful self all day and night. Looking back, she realized how hard sticking to the plan would have been if she had to watch Jay enjoy the things she was not allowed to have. His support meant the world to her. She knew she would have cheated without it.

Kory came around the corner to greet Colleen. "You look amazing," she said as she opened her arms to give Colleen a hug.

Colleen accepted the hug from the woman who hadn't judged her, never reflected back that she wasn't good enough to work with her. "I feel good." Colleen felt lighter than a week ago, and even though her clothes were loser, she was still afraid to weigh herself. Colleen gladly accepted herbal tea as she settled into the same chair as the week before.

"I can't wait to hear how everything is going." Kory sat back in her chair, bringing her legs up in a crisscross position like the week before.

"Things have gotten easier. I can't believe I made it to the seventh day."

"You look so different from a week ago. Your eyes are brighter and your face's less puffy. The biggest difference is you're smiling." A wide smile spread across Kory's face. "What's been the hardest?"

Colleen had to think about that for a minute. So many

things had been hard. "The headaches, the exhaustion…not having coffee in the morning…or wine in the evening."

"All the normal things." Kory's laugh made it seem so simple and basic. "The morning coffee and the evening wine will return, but in a more balanced way. The headaches and exhaustion should be a thing of the past," Kory said. "What's been the best part?"

"I'm sleeping better than I've slept in a long time."

"Taking out caffeine and wine makes a huge difference."

"Billy's been a lifesaver. I'm going to keep using him even after the detox is over."

"Billy's amazing. At some point, though, we do need to get you to embrace some cooking but we'll get to that later."

Colleen wasn't interested in cooking; she didn't care what Kory said, she wasn't giving up Billy. If she never cooked again, that would be okay.

"For now, let's celebrate your completion of the first week," Kory said. "You've made such great progress. I'm so proud of you."

Colleen's cheeks flushed. She was proud of herself and knew she couldn't have done it without Kory.

"I hope you are still planning on coming to my workshop tonight," Kory said.

Colleen had forgotten to ask Mia or Gabby. "I hope to come."

"You have spent the last week showing up for yourself by taking steps to take care of yourself and improve your life. You have spent time respecting who you are and the needs you have. Have you noticed a change in your relationship with Jay?"

Colleen thought about how she wanted to be closer to Jay over the weekend but had resisted. "He was so enthusiastic to join me in the detox."

"What about the girls? Have you noticed anything different in your time with them?"

"I was able to get through their bedtime stories without falling asleep." Shame filled Colleen's system. She was embarrassed about always passing out before she even finished one book with her girls.

"You showed up for yourself and Jay showed up for you in return. By showing up for yourself this week, you were able to show up for your girls."

Colleen sighed and looked up at Kory; her eyes were moist.

"I hope you can come to the class. It's another step in showing up for yourself, and it's a great opportunity for you to learn to make a few smoothies on your own," Kory said.

"I'm not sure I'll ever make a smoothie, since Get Juiced is so close."

"I think it's wonderful that you have a place to get your smoothies, but it's good for you to learn how to make them yourself," Kory said. "I'm a big believer in self-sufficiency."

Colleen liked how things had been going. She wasn't ready to change anything.

Kory took a sip of her tea. "The hardest part is over. Now it's time to slowly add in some things so you can continue to progress on all levels — physical, mental and spiritual. How are you doing with the mirror work?"

"It felt strange when I first did it, but now I think it might be helping," Colleen said.

"I know it's helping. You're a different person than I saw

last week. Isn't it amazing what a week of loving yourself can do?" Kory reached over and squeezed Colleen's hand. "You not only professed your love to yourself multiple times a day, but you let yourself rest when you were tired, didn't put things into your body that weren't good for it and resisted all the urges to do so," Kory said. "For once, you loved yourself like you love those beautiful little girls of yours. Do you tell them you love them?"

"Yes," Colleen said.

"Do you let them eat candy and ice cream for every meal?"

"No." Colleen couldn't help but to laugh at that.

"Do you make them sleep when they're tired?"

Colleen got the point.

"If you can keep up with the level of work you did last week, you're not going to recognize yourself when we're done."

Colleen didn't know if she could keep up with what she did last week. It had been awful, but the way she felt now was incredible. She would try.

"You've given yourself a week of rest and nutrition. Now, it's time to get your body moving. Tell me what kind of exercise you like to do," Kory said.

Colleen hated all of the exercise classes she had done. She never liked working with a trainer. "I like walking," Colleen said.

"Walking's great. Let's start there," Kory said.

Colleen let out a breath of relief. She had feared Kory would recommend one of those sweat-laden workout classes that all those women from Get Juiced came from. She'd seen a couple of the women with Mo's Army Fit written across their T-shirt. She was not interested in anything associated with a boot camp.

"We want to proceed gently. You're teaching your body a new way to live. If you find yourself tired, take a break and take a nap," Kory said.

She could probably handle gentle. Although if Kory thought the food changes were gentle, she would probably be a puddle on the floor.

"Do you think you can commit to a time every day to walk for at least thirty minutes?"

"I think so."

"Keep things simple at first. Go for a walk and do some light stretching, nothing more," Kory said.

Last week, thirty minutes of exercise would have been out of the question. This week, she felt different. This week, she believed she could do it. If she needed a nap afterwards, she would take a nap.

"Exercise doesn't need to be hard, but it needs to be consistent. The people who have the most success do it the same time every day," Kory said. "You need to make it as routine as brushing your teeth. What time do you think you could commit every day, a time without any conflicts?"

Colleen had to think. Getting up before she took the girls to school had never worked. "I'm not sure," she said. "I've tried to get up early to run, but it never worked. I was always too tired," Colleen said.

"Do you think you were too tired because of your old lifestyle or do you think it was just too early?" Kory said.

"I'm not sure. I stopped trying to get up early last week when I started the detox," Colleen said.

"What do you do right after you drop the girls off to school?" Kory said.

"Most of last week, I stopped for my smoothie, but Friday and today the girls and I got smoothies on our way to school," Colleen said.

"What a great way for your girls to start their day!" Kory said.

Colleen wasn't used to having moments to be proud of, especially around her parenting. "I'm not sure what I'll do when the girls are out of school for the summer," Colleen worried all of her hard work would be lost.

"One step at a time. We are only focusing on next week. We'll work through changes one week at a time," Kory said.

Colleen took a deep breath.

"Your journey's just begun." Kory looked up at Colleen as she lit a candle on the small table sitting between them. "We've been focusing on your body, but now we're going to focus on your mind and spirit. I'm going to lead you through a chakra meditation. Each chakra acts as a passageway for a certain type of energy. Starting here at the base of your spine"—Kory stood in front of Colleen and pointed toward her pelvis—"and traveling up to the top of your head." She slowly moved her hand up her body to the top of her head.

Colleen had no idea what she was talking about. She had never heard of "chakra" before.

"Your first chakra, your Root chakra, is located at the base of your spine. It's your source of survival and keeps you grounded." Kory placed her hand on the lower part of her stomach as she sat down. "Here below your belly button is your sacral chakra, the second chakra. The energy of this chakra allows you to feel emotion, pleasure and is your source of creative energy." She moved her hand up just under her rib cage. "Your Solar Plexus, your third chakra, sits just below your rib cage. It's your place of power and ego and where you hold stress." She moved her hand up higher, over her heart. "Right here at your heart is your fourth chakra and is also called your Heart chakra. It's your place of love." Kory placed her hand at the base of her throat. "This area is your fifth chakra, your Throat chakra and it's your place of expression." Placing her fingers above her nose, between her eyebrows, "Your sixth chakra is here, also referred to as your Third-Eye and it's your source of intuition." She placed her hand at the top of her head. "Your Crown, your seventh chakra, is your connection to spirit."

Colleen was lost. There was no way she could remember all those areas. What did she mean connection to spirit? Colleen was afraid to ask.

"Got all that?" Kory laughed.

"Some of it." Colleen's voice wavered.

"No need to remember all of the details. I'm going to guide you through. Just relax and follow along. Your feelings are what we're after here, not memorizing."

Colleen tried to relax.

"Certain areas may be harder than others to breathe into. Don't worry, just keep your breath steady," Kory said. "Ready?"

Colleen didn't know why she felt so nervous, but she did. She was afraid she was going to mess the meditation up.

Kory began speaking softly and slowly. "Close your eyes. Bring your focus to your breath. Feel it coming in and out.

Relax your jaw. Let go of any lingering thoughts. Soften your belly on your next inhale."

Colleen hadn't realized how much she had been clenching her jaw. Letting it drop was a relief.

"Feel where your body meets the chair. Feel the ground at your feet. You are supported and you are safe. Let your body relax."

Being tense was Colleen's natural state. Her body fought against her efforts to relax it.

"Focus on your breath. Let it come in. Let it go out. Place your concentration on the base of your spine. Imagine your breath coming into your spine — your root chakra — chakra of belonging. Breathe into it and allow it to soften with each breath."

Colleen struggled to follow Kory. What did she mean breathe into it?

"Follow it as it connects to the earth below. Imagine the color red and allow it to empower you. Allow it to give you strength."

Colleen didn't get the connections. She wasn't interested in this spiritual stuff. Her family stayed far away from church. Her great-grandfather cut ties during the depression when he was told not to come back until he upheld the financial commitment he had made before the depression started.

"As you breathe into your crown, think of a giant ball of white light entering from the top of your head. Allow the light to travel through your body, going down your spine into your root chakra. Then, send it down your legs and allow it to go down to the bottom of your feet and out into the ground."

Kory's soothing tone helped Colleen continue to relax.

Before Colleen knew it, she was following along without much effort.

"When you are ready, open your eyes," Kory said.

Colleen slowly opened her eyes. She felt as though she had taken a nap, sleepy but refreshed.

"How'd that feel?" Kory asked.

"Good." Colleen's voice was groggy.

"This a good meditation for you to repeat at home. Creating a meditation practice will help you gain better perspective on the things outside your control," Kory said. "I will email you a written version of the meditation you just did so you can try it on your own."

Colleen hoped that would replace her need for a nap.

"I would like to jump ahead a bit, if you don't mind," Kory said.

"Okay," she said with reluctance.

"Let's jump to a time in the near future when your weight is where you want it to be. What then? What will you be missing in your life then?"

Colleen remained silent. She didn't know. She thought solving her weight issues would solve everything. She looked down at the burning candle. All she could think of was her mom, dad and rest of her family in Brockville. She missed them all so much, especially her mom. "My family," she said quietly. She brought her eyes up to Kory. "My mom and dad, my aunt Susie and the rest of my family in Brockville."

"What keeps you from having them in your life?"

"We have a complicated relationship."

"What makes it complicated?"

Colleen exhaled loudly and bit her lower lip. She didn't

know where to begin. So much had become complicated over the years. She could feel her nose begin to clog and her chin began to quiver uncontrollably. "My family doesn't like to spend time discussing how they feel. They don't like to waste time dwelling on their feelings. They believe in staying busy. I'm not sure we have enough time to get through it all," she said as she reached for the box of tissues.

"Please, take your time and share whatever you feel comfortable."

"Ever since Johnny died…" Colleen closed her eyes and drew in a deep breath. "…things have been hard between us. We talk about once a month, usually on Sunday afternoons. My mom reports on the hours my dad has put into the field or the price of corn and soybeans. I tell some anecdote about Mabel or Chloe. We get off the phone and I feel guilty for not taking the girls to visit more than once a year." She brought a Kleenex up to her dripping nose. "Going home is too hard. When I visited last year, I was so exhausted trying to keep the conversation going, doing anything and everything to avoid talking about Johnny. His ghost appeared in his empty seat at the table, on the couch playing video games, out on the tractor goofing off — every turn, it seemed, I felt his absence."

"Have you tried talking to your parents about it?"

Colleen shook her head convulsively. "It's too upsetting. They've been through so much. I don't want to upset them anymore." Colleen looked back down at the burning candle. All the peace she had created inside was gone. Her chest felt as though it were closing in.

"I want you stop for a moment and take a couple of deep breaths," Kory said. "Breathe deeply into your chest, opening it up as much as you can. Don't allow your sadness to close off your chest. Breathe through it and keep the energy flowing."

Colleen fought her body's instinct to close up. She wanted to curl up into a ball and go to sleep until the pain went away.

"You're stuck in your grief. What types of things have you done to work through the loss of your brother?"

A painful lump sat at the base of Colleen's throat. She redirected her breath from her chest to her throat. "I don't know. Nothing really. Just waiting for time to pass."

"How many years did you say it's been?"

"Seven years, almost eight. He died on May eighteenth."

"In the almost eight years that you've been waiting, how much better has it gotten?"

"A little, I guess."

"I want you to think about something. You've gained fifty-five pounds, alienated yourself from your parents and extended family, and developed a thyroid disorder in the process. Have things really gotten better?"

Colleen had never thought about her grief in relation to her current problems. "I guess not." She paused, feeling confused. "How would that affect my thyroid?"

Kory placed her first three fingers at the base of her throat. "Your throat chakra is located in the same place as your thyroid. This is your place of self-expression. It's where change takes place. You've spent the last eight years resisting the change your family has undergone."

Colleen understood what Kory was saying but wasn't convinced her words were true.

"What were you taught as a little girl about expressing yourself? Were you ever told things like, if you can't say something nice, don't say anything at all?" Kory said, hooking her fingers in the air to form quotations around those words.

Colleen's gaze met Kory's as she contemplated what she just heard. That message replayed in Colleen's head for as long as she could remember. "Yeah," Colleen said faintly.

"As much as we need to be thoughtful and kind, we also need to express how we feel. Where else in your life are you holding back your feelings and emotions?"

Colleen had become an expert at holding in her feelings and emotions. Her most recent withholding burned on the edge of her tongue. She wanted to tell Kory about the woman in the picture with Jay, but she was afraid to say it out loud. "I guess I do it a lot."

"Have you ever done any journaling?"

Colleen shook her head. She had tried to write in a journal a time or two but had filled out a page and shoved the book in her nightstand. She never had anything interesting to say.

Kory handed Colleen a hard-covered black spiral notebook that had a gold sun up in the far corner shining its golden rays across the cover with small golden words that read, "Embrace the glorious mess that you are. —Elizabeth Gilbert."

"Inside the cover of the notebook, you will see several writing prompts that I pasted on for you to journal about."

Colleen ran her finger across the pasted writing prompts. She read along as Kory read the first one out loud, "Make a list of all the important people in your life and next to each person's name, write about situations where you held back your feelings. What do you wish you would have done or said? Then write what you would say or do now, if you had the courage."

Colleen stared down at the blank page below the prompt. She imagined Jay's name written in her handwriting with her nice pen. Next to it she saw, "Who was the woman you were with at Alexis's party?" and then, if she really had courage, "Do you love her?"

"In addition to continuing your detox and mirror work this week, you are going to add in the meditation we just did, spend some time journaling and begin walking every day." Kory paused and looked at Colleen carefully. "Does that sound like too much?"

It did but Colleen didn't want to say so. "No, I think I can do it."

"Our time is almost up but if you have a few extra minutes, I would like to share a story with you." She paused and looked at Colleen.

Colleen looked at Kory with curiosity. "I don't have to be anywhere."

"It's about my husband's death." Kory sighed and sat upright. "Learning that Eric was dead was hard, learning the details of his death were unbearable. I was shattered. He was the love of my life."

Colleen could see the pain in Kory's eyes as she spoke of her late husband. Her eyes became moist with tears just as Kory's were.

Kory sniffed and looked down at the floor before bringing her eyes back to Colleen. "A prostitute named Shelly found him in a hotel room surrounded by vodka and cocaine. The shame, betrayal and heartbreak were just too much." She paused for a few seconds.

Colleen sensed the pain that lingered within Kory. She

knew the pain. She didn't know the betrayal, but she had been imagining it enough lately to be able to empathize. The strong and confident woman who sat across from her suddenly seemed wounded and vulnerable.

"Andrew was so little and he needed me. I had no choice but to find strength to take care of him. I got through those early days with the help of a therapist. My life no longer made sense. My job, which I'd once loved, seemed meaningless. I followed my therapist's suggestion of going away to a yoga retreat. My parents took Andrew and off I went to California. The trip saved my life."

Kory ran her fingers through her hair and shifted in her chair. She paused and smiled at Colleen. "This is where the story gets a little crazy. After one of the yoga sessions, a woman named Rachel asked me if the name Eric meant anything to me. You can imagine my shock." Kory paused. "She explained to me that she was a psychic medium, someone who was able to communicate with the dead. She said a spirit by the name of Eric has been coming to her since she arrived. I couldn't believe what she was telling me. It all sounded so far-fetched, but I also couldn't make sense of how she would know about Eric. She brought up the bar, Charlie's, where Eric and I met, she brought up running with Eric at North Avenue Beach for our first date, and she knew we went to Benedicts for breakfast afterwards. She knew about Andrew's love of the Curious George books and the picture of Eric on his nightstand that he made me kiss every night before I tucked him into bed and a lot of other personal stuff that she had no way of knowing. I was left with no choice but to believe her."

Colleen sat still in silence, hanging on every word Kory

spoke. What she would do for such an opportunity to talk with someone like Rachel.

"Rachel communicated the guilt and sorrow Eric felt for doing what he did. She helped me see the importance of forgiving him and she said once I do, I would be set free. Eric communicated through Rachel that my purpose in life is to help others overcome what is holding them back."

Colleen believed her. She didn't think it was crazy. She wished more than anything she could get a message from Johnny.

TWELVE

"M-o-m-m-y," Chloe yelled, "Gabby's here!"

Just as Colleen started down the hall toward the front door, she heard Mabel barreling down the stairs. The sour mood she brought home from school with her vanished once she heard Chloe announce Gabby's arrival.

"Hi, Mrs. Adler," Gabby said.

"Hi, honey, thanks so much for coming over tonight. Hope you don't have too much homework."

Gabby's eyes were bright with relief. "No homework tonight," she said with a broad smile.

"That's good." Colleen felt sorry for Gabby. Being dyslexic made school incredibly difficult for her. Colleen wished there was more she could do to help.

"Come on, Gabby," Chloe said as she pulled on Gabby's arm. "Let's go down to the art room."

"There's cash on the counter for the pizza. I ordered it a few minutes ago, it should be here in about forty minutes," Colleen said to Gabby. "Please make sure it's gone before I get home. I don't need the temptation," Colleen laughed.

Gabby gave her a confused look. "Okay," she said.

"My mom's on a diet," Chloe said.

"Oh, yeah, my grandma said you were eating better," Gabby said.

"I'm trying to," Colleen said. She wondered what else Maria said to Mia and Gabby.

KORY HAD TRANSFORMED THE WAITING room of Dr. Metzger's office into a classroom. She had a large table set up in front of Gertrude's reception desk. The center of the table held a large industrial-looking blender that was surrounded by an assortment of vases containing large green and purple leaves and a large bowl full of lemons, limes and oranges. There were already several women sitting in the front two rows of folding chairs that lined the rest of the room. Colleen was relieved to see empty chairs in the back corner.

As soon as she sat down, Fran walked in. She looked younger than Colleen remembered her looking at the meeting a few weeks ago.

"I was hoping to see you here," Fran announced as she navigated her way through the folding chairs to reach Colleen.

Standing halfway, Colleen awkwardly returned Fran's unexpected hug.

Fran dropped her purse on the floor and draped her sweater around the back of the chair next to Colleen. "Can you believe what Kory has done to this room? She is just amazing, isn't she?"

"Yes, she is," Colleen said. Colleen thought about the betrayal and heartache Kory experienced. She couldn't imagine losing Jay in such a horrible way. Even if Jay was cheating, she was on a new path now. The face of that sun-kissed woman with blond, beachy hair flashed through her mind. They still had a chance. She hoped they did.

"My friend Alice, the one who introduced me to Kory, said

that Kory loves to make green smoothies. They sound terrible to me, but Alice said once she got used to them, she can't live without them. She said you just have to get over the idea of blending lettuce in with your fruit. Her skin just glows from all those drinks," Fran said.

"I've been drinking smoothies every morning for a week, but I haven't tried any with lettuce yet," Colleen said. "I was hoping to avoid them."

"I think we're going to try them tonight!" Fran laughed.

Kory walked up behind the table and asked everyone to take their seats. Every seat in the room was full. "Welcome, ladies, please come up and help yourself to some warm lemon water. For those of you who haven't started the detox yet, lemon water should be the first thing you drink every morning."

"What does the lemon water do?" a woman in the front asked.

"Lemons are high in vitamin C and potassium and they help balance the pH in your body. Research shows that people with a more alkaline diet have less illness and more success with weight loss," Kory said.

Colleen was surprised with how much she enjoyed the lemon water in the morning, especially once she began adding a drop of honey. She would probably continue drinking it even after the twenty-one-day period was over, but it would be followed by a double latte.

"A lot of you here expressed concern about drinking the green smoothies. The first thing I'm going to ask is for you to stop thinking about what's in it and just focus on the taste.

I promise you'll like it. How many of you've had a green smoothie before?"

No hands went up.

"We're in good company," Fran whispered to Colleen.

Colleen was glad she wasn't the only one scared to try the green things.

"How many of you have reservations about trying a green smoothie?" Kory asked.

Nervous laughter filled the room as the rows of women raised their hands.

"How lucky for me that I get to be the one to surprise you!" Kory said as she passed trays of small cups of already-prepared smoothies down each row.

"If it's a green smoothie, why is it purple?" a lady in the middle row asked.

"Before I tell you what's in it, everyone has to take a drink."

Somehow, the purple color made it seem more appealing. Colleen watched Fran as she took her first sip.

"It's really good," Fran said.

Colleen was skeptical but focused on the beautiful purple color. She hoped Fran was being truthful and not just being polite. Reluctantly, she took a drink. Fran was right. There wasn't a sign of any weird lettuce flavor.

"The smoothie you just tried had Swiss chard, mixed berries, banana and lemon water." Kory began assembling the next smoothie. "You always want to start your smoothie with a liquid base. There's a smoothie chart being passed around the room but it's also in the detox materials most of you have. You can mix and match the various ingredients to create different smoothies. The liquid base can be anything from coconut water, lemon water, regular water, almond/ rice/coconut milk, or fresh-squeezed juice. I personally like using water with a squeeze of lemon or lime. Tonight, you're trying two of my favorite smoothies." Kory had to stop talking because the blender was so loud that no one could hear her. "I find that the first thing you put into your body sets the tone for the rest of your day. If you start with a cinnamon roll, most likely you'll crave carbs and sugary foods for the rest of the day." She poured the smoothie into several small cups before passing the trays around again.

The high-powered blender that Kory used sounded like a chain saw. Colleen cringed over the noise but was amazed at how fast it pureed everything. There wasn't a lump to be found in the drink. If she were to ever attempt making her own smoothies, she would have to buy a blender like Kory's.

This time, Colleen didn't wait for Fran to take the first sip. She took a drink right away and once again, she couldn't believe there wasn't a bitter lettuce taste. Based on the energetic chatter happening in the room, everyone seemed to be enjoying the smoothies. Relieved and surprised that she actually liked these drinks, Colleen decided she would try one from Get Juiced the next day.

THIRTEEN

Colleen heard her phone ping while she was turning the key to unlock the front door. Struggling to get the door open while wrangling her phone out of her coat pocket, she saw it was Kory. She had been checking in every morning since Colleen began the twenty-one-day program.

Kory: How did you like the class last night?

Colleen had just finished walking for forty-five minutes. Her face was flushed and she was slightly out of breath. She couldn't remember the last time she had walked for that long. Colleen took a seat on her front porch to rest her tired legs while she texted Kory.

> *Colleen: It was great. Got the Green Monster at Get Juiced this morning. Loved it! Can't stop thinking about your friend Rachel. I wish I had someone like her to talk to.*

> *Kory: She's coming in town on Thursday. She is usually booked but would you like me to find out if she can meet with you?*

Colleen sat up straight. Her hands shook as she held her phone.

Colleen: YES

Kory: I will let you know.

Colleen stared at her phone. Kory needed to understand how important this was. She wondered if offering a large sum of money would make a difference. She took a deep breath and decided to wait until tomorrow to say anything more to Kory. She set her phone on the table next to her chair. She closed her eyes and pointed her face toward the sun that was shining down through the trees. She inhaled deeply and allowed the light to come in through the top of her head, travel down her neck, her arms, surround her heart and pass its energy through the rest of her body all the way down to her feet. As her body absorbed all the beautiful energy and light that the sky was offering her at that moment, she reflected on how far she had come in such a short time. The doubt that had consumed her not that long ago was gone. She had newfound confidence in knowing that she could get through the emotional mountain sitting before her just as she had gotten through the last two weeks.

She tried to manage her expectations about the meeting with Kory's psychic friend. Even if there was an opening for Colleen, there was a possibility that she may not connect with Johnny. There wasn't a dollar amount too high, even for a chance.

Sometimes she would have dreams about him that were so real. She would wake up feeling as though she were just with him. Every once in a while, he would pop into her mind out of nowhere, and she would sense he was near her. One time when that happened, she could smell the earthy stench of dirty, wet dog. Her mind flashed to the memory of him as a little boy climbing all over her after he'd been outside playing all day. The more she told him he smelled and pushed him away, the more he would laugh and hug and hang. Colleen's dad would say, "Johnny quit wallowing Colleen to death." Everyone, including Colleen, would laugh. Her mom would drag Johnny to the bath, fighting every step of the way. Colleen had forgotten all about that smell.

Her phone pinged.

Kory: Does Thursday at 10 work?

Colleen: Yes! Thank you!

"Don't look too far ahead. Baby steps. Baby steps," she said to herself. With that, her heart filled with gratitude. "Thank you," she said silently. Unsure where the "thank you" was directed, she sent it out into the unknown place that her strength had come from over the past few weeks.

Her pants slid down as she stood up. She had to roll the waist down during her walk to keep them up. Re-rolling the waist tighter, she hoped they would stay in place for a little longer. She would spend time in her closet later to find a pair of smaller pants to change into. She wondered how much looser her pants needed to get before the zipper on her new dress would close.

ON THURSDAY MORNING COLLEEN WALKED into Dr. Metzger's office at quarter to ten. She was early. The office was quiet. The reception desk was empty. Colleen wondered where Gertrude was. She was always there to greet her when she came in. Now, more than ever, she could have used her company. Taking a few deep breaths to calm her nerves.

Kory escorted Colleen to her office, where Rachel was waiting. Sitting in the chair that Colleen normally sat in, Rachel looked younger than Colleen imagined. Like Kory, she had on workout clothes and looked very fit and athletic. She wore a baseball cap over her long dark hair and didn't appear to be wearing any makeup. She looked like any other woman walking down the street. No one would have ever guessed she was a psychic medium.

"Hi, Colleen." Rachel's warm and friendly demeanor was similar to Kory's.

Colleen looked at Rachel nervously. Her eyes darted between Kory and the empty chair. She wasn't sure how this was going to go, but she hoped Kory would stay in the room with them.

"I'm going to step out while Rachel does your reading. I can't wait to hear all about it," Kory said as she closed the door behind her.

"It's okay with me if Kory stays in the room." Colleen wished she would stay.

"It's better for her to leave. I only want your energy," Rachel said. "I'm not sure what Kory has told you about me, but I want to tell you a little bit about what I do so you understand the process. I'm a medium, which means I'm able to communicate with the dead. I get messages from your deceased loved ones and spirit guides."

Colleen's jaw was clenched and her heart pounded. She had no idea what spirit guides were.

"I can't guarantee a connection with a specific spirit. I can only work with those who are interested in coming through," Rachel said.

Please come through, Johnny, please, Colleen thought.

"Spirits come to me and express themselves through images I see in my head, words I hear and feelings that I get." She paused. "Ready to get started?"

"Yes," Colleen said weakly. She sat in disbelief as she tried to prepare herself for the unknown before her.

Rachel lit the candle on the table between them. "I want you to close your eyes and take some deep slow breaths. Do your best to relax and open yourself up."

Colleen closed her eyes. Relaxing was impossible. Her heart raced. She felt Rachel moving around as she sat with her eyes closed.

"I'm smudging our space with sage to help rid any negative energy that may be lingering in the room," Rachel said.

Colleen opened one eye enough to see that Rachel had sat down. She continued taking deep breaths, but her anxiety persisted.

"I only work with positive and loving spirits, so there is no need to be afraid," Rachel said. "In your mind, I want you to send a prayer of gratitude to your spirits for the love and protection they provide to you. Thank them for the messages they are about to offer." She paused for a few seconds. "Now, think of the people you want to hear from. Take a moment to fill your mind with their faces as you remember them and, when you are ready, open your eyes."

Colleen concentrated on Johnny's image. She first thought of him as a little boy running around outside all day, covered in dirt and sweat. She thought of him on the farm with her dad. Then she thought of him the very last time she saw him, on Christmas Day opening presents, eating almost an entire sausage and egg casserole by himself. She envisioned him standing next to her mom and dad on the porch of the farmhouse waving good-bye as she and Jay drove away. Tears ran down Colleen's cheeks as she opened her eyes.

"Spirits typically start by offering validation. They want to make sure you know it's really them. I need you to just listen to what I'm saying and answer as simply as possible when I ask you a question," Rachel said.

"Okay."

"I don't want to confuse what you're saying and what that makes me think with what they are trying to tell me," Rachel said. "I'll offer clues that I'm getting. They won't make sense to me but should make sense to you. If things don't make sense right away, please be patient. I'll keep trying to say it in different ways as the spirit offers me more options to convey the correct message."

"Okay." Colleen struggled to make her voice loud enough to hear. She seemed to have lost control of her ability to speak.

Rachel closed her eyes and smiled. "I'm seeing a dog, a golden retriever. I know it seems crazy that a dog is coming through, but our pets cross over too. It seems to be on a farm or near water or something. Did you lose a dog?"

Colleen thought of the dog they got for Johnny right before she left for college. Could it be Leo? She didn't come to hear from a dog, she wanted to hear from Johnny.

"This may sound even crazier, but I hope it makes some sort of sense to you. He's showing me a turtle," Rachel said.

"Oh my God. Teenage Mutant Ninja Turtles." Colleen

cleared her throat. "My brother named his dog after his favorite ninja turtle, Leonardo. We called him Leo."

"Leo's with a teenager. Why am I seeing the character J.R. from the TV show *Dallas*?" Rachel smiled. "Do you know who this is?"

Colleen struggled to speak. She was overcome with emotion. Swallowing deeply, she said, "My brother." She paused.

"Your brother is really playful and happy. He's showing himself outside. He looks sweaty and he is with his dog." Rachel paused. "He looks as though he has been playing outside all day."

Colleen had an overwhelming sense of peace come over her. She felt as though she was in a dream.

"He's with an older woman, a grandmother, maybe. She's really beautiful. She's showing me the mass of curls on her head and showing me a mirror image. She's showing me a reflection of you?"

"My grandmother," Colleen said. "I never knew her, but I look just like her," Colleen said.

"She's smiling," Rachel said. "She's one of your guides. She's there to help you. You need to reach out to her more."

Rachel closed her eyes and brought her hands up, squeezing the space at the bridge of her nose. "Your brother wants me to tell you he's fine," she said. "I'm seeing a picture of a farm in the summertime."

Colleen shook her head. "We lived on a farm."

"Your brother must have loved the farm. He's on a farm now. Spirits show themselves at an age or time in their life when they were the happiest. Even though they're in another realm, they're in an environment much like the one they lived in or traveled to that they loved," Rachel said. "Do you dream about him?"

Colleen brought her lips together to stop them from twitching and nodded her head. More tears spilled from her eyes. "Sometimes I wake up and the dream feels so real, I feel as though I was just with him."

Rachel nodded. "He visits you in your dreams. It's hard for spirits to get through to us. When we sleep our minds are in the most relaxed state, so it's easier for them to come through. When you dream of him, know it's really him. I'm getting my sign for smell. Did you think you smelled him recently?" Rachel said. "I'm seeing a wet dog. Does that make any sense?"

Colleen smiled and said, "Just a few weeks ago, a smell surrounded me that reminded me of him as a little boy."

"He's smiling. That was him. He wants you to know that he's with you all the time," Rachel said. "I'm seeing two little girls. Does one of them have a big opinion about her clothes and what she wears?"

"My youngest. She is very stubborn about her clothes," Colleen said.

"Your brother thinks it's cute. Spirits like to watch us in our lives — they get a kick out of certain things we do," Rachel said.

"He wants me to tell you that he thinks you are a great mom and to keep doing the work you are doing," Rachel said. "Have you started a new job?"

Colleen shook her head.

"Your purpose in this life isn't to be a caregiver. The work you're doing now is helping you get closer to where you are supposed to be. You have a higher purpose in this life and you need to get on with it." Rachel closed her eyes again.

Colleen had no idea what she was talking about. Panic began to set in. Higher purpose? She was afraid to disrupt Rachel's concentration by asking for more details.

"Now he's showing me a man — your husband? Is he gone a lot?"

"He travels for work," Colleen said.

"Your brother wants you to know that your husband loves you and wants you to be happy," Rachel said.

Colleen resisted her desire to ask about Jay's fidelity.

"He wants you to know that his life was complete here and it was his time to pass over when he died." She closed her eyes and pressed two fingers to her temples. "Your brother's showing me an urgency with your parents. He wants you to go visit them. How long has it been since you saw them?"

Colleen shook her head. "It's been a while."

"He doesn't want to alarm you, but he wants you to go see them as soon as you can," Rachel said.

Colleen was filled with worry. She had a pang in her stomach for not visiting with them more.

"He doesn't want you to feel bad about not visiting. He knows it's been hard for you to visit because you miss him, but he wants you to know that he's there with you even though you can't see him," Rachel said.

Colleen's heart pounded during the brief silence. She couldn't figure out what the urgency would be. They were both healthy as far as she knew. It was probably about them missing her. Guilt poured over her.

"Part of his death was meant as a lesson for you and your parents to learn to overcome grief and to learn to share your vulnerability with each other. You need to open up and share your feelings with them. Don't feel guilty about letting them know how hard things have been for you. It will be healing for them to help you through your challenges." Rachel's eyes stared straight ahead, and she spoke as though she were in a trance. "Your brother wants you to forgive yourself for not going home more. He wishes you all wouldn't be so sad. He's showing me something with the radio?" She blinked and looked at Colleen. "Do you ever have a song come out of nowhere that reminds you of him or the station suddenly plays a song that speaks to what you are thinking about?"

"Not that I can think of," Colleen said.

"Maybe it hasn't happened yet, but it's going to happen. Spirits love to play with songs on the radio," Rachel said.

Colleen made note to play the radio in the car.

Rachel smiled and said, "Your grandmother has been patiently waiting for her turn. Does one of your daughters remind you of her?"

"I named my oldest after her. She resembles me and my grandmother."

"That makes sense. She keeps showing me a mirror image but with two like her. She's honored." Rachel closed her eyes again before continuing. "Your strength will come from the love and acceptance you give yourself. She is showing me people who hold you back. Is there an older woman in your life that is difficult for you?"

Dinah! Colleen thought. "My mother-in-law?" she said.

"Your grandmother is showing me her curls again and

telling me that you need to be yourself. Ignore your mother-in-law," Rachel said.

Colleen sat up straight in her chair, trying to stop her legs from shaking.

"Your brother is with your spirit guides and wants you to know that he is always there for you. He's showing me darkness. Have you been fighting depression or extreme sadness?" Rachel asked.

"I've had a hard time since he passed." Colleen's chin quivered as she spoke.

"He's showing me that's behind you. Moving forward, things are going to be a lot easier. You've overcome a lot and he is proud of you. He's showing me several people surrounding you on the other side who love you very much," Rachel said. "He's showing me a manila envelope. Does that make any sense to you?"

Colleen stared ahead, trying to think about what that could mean. "My mom gave me a manila envelope right after he died. She said it was a keepsake for me to remember him. I couldn't bring myself to open it. I left it in Brockville."

"If you come across it, open it," Rachel said. "Do you have anything you want to ask?"

Colleen wanted more details about Jay but tried to focus on what was most important. "Should I be worried about my parents?"

"He's showing a sense of urgency for you to go see them. I can't see any more than that," Rachel said.

Rachel took a sip of water. Colleen imagined her dad having a farm accident or her mom developing cancer.

"Johnny has something else he wants to say. We all enter

this world with lessons to learn so our soul can evolve. Everyone has a team up above helping to guide and protect them as they go through life. Your brother shows me that he only had one exit point and his soul's contract was to die at that exact time that he did."

Colleen's eyes remained fixed on Rachel. She wanted to take in every word she was saying.

"He came here as a teacher for you and your family, as well as many of his friends. He taught you all many things about love and loss and how to overcome the unimaginable," Rachel said. "The biggest thing to take away from all of this is that he is still here — in a different form, but he's still here."

Colleen finally had the validation she had longed for.

"When in doubt, say a prayer to your brother. Ask him to show himself to you. If you are open and pay attention, you will see signs of him."

Colleen felt her brother's presence. She had a sense of peace and comfort about his death that she never dreamed was possible. She missed her parents more at that moment than she ever had, and she was mad at herself for not sharing her grief with them. They were a family and were supposed to help each other. She had been a coward. She let her strength slip away. But maybe she could stop. She was at least going to try. Now was the time to do whatever she could to make things right in her life.

FOURTEEN

Mabel and Chloe had been starving on Friday afternoon when Colleen picked them up from school. Instead of taking them to Southport Grocery and Cafe for cupcakes like she did on most Fridays, she brought them home and fed them an early dinner. While Colleen heated up the macaroni and cheese with broccoli and chicken sausage that Billy had prepared for them, the phone rang at the usual time.

"We're on a diet, so have to eat before we can come over," Chloe said into the phone.

"You are not on a diet, you're eating healthy. There's a big difference," Colleen said.

The girls gobbled every bite of the food Colleen put on their plates. They were thoroughly enjoying the meals Billy prepared for them.

Colleen promised Mabel and Chloe that she would send Jay over to the Wilsons' as soon as he got home. Normally, the girls wanted to stay home and wait for Jay's arrival, but painting the new playhouse in the Wilsons' backyard trumped Jay's welcome home greeting.

Colleen was out on the back deck when she heard Jay calling for her from the kitchen. She popped her head inside through the French doors. "Mabel and Chloe are waiting for you over at the Wilsons'. We can eat when you get back," she said. She continued to set up the patio table with two wine glasses decorated with lemon wedges, silverware on top of cloth napkins, a stainless steel wine cooler containing a bottle of chilled sparkling water, and a candle burning in the center. Firewood was stacked in the fireplace ready to be lit and the new set of Edison lights that Pedro had strung across the top of the pergola were plugged in.

She was glad to have Jay to herself. She needed his undivided attention. It was going to be hard enough to erase his skepticism of her meeting with a psychic medium even without the girls' distraction. If nothing else came from their conversation, she needed his cooperation about going to Brockville. He needed to understand that it wasn't negotiable and that it needed to happen soon. She had to see her parents.

She stood at the kitchen island transferring the brown rice, roasted broccoli, carrots, mushrooms and spinach onto plates to be heated in the microwave. Per Billy's suggestion, she had heated the salmon that accompanied the vegetables and rice in the oven. She covered it in foil to keep it warm while she heated the rest of the food.

Jay's phone pinged. Colleen's eyes shifted to his phone a few inches away.

Holly Brinkley: Did you tell her yet? Call me!

Colleen stared at the phone. Who was Holly Brinkley?

Colleen took her phone and went into the powder room, locking the door behind her in case Jay came home. She clicked on Facebook. She typed in Holly Brinkley. Three came up. The blond one listed a mutual friend. Colleen clicked on the blond Holly Brinkley. Her heart raced when she saw that the mutual friend was Alexis. There she was. Holly Brinkley was a perfect name for a skinny blonde from Los Angeles. Her hair blew in the wind as she stood up against the backdrop of the California coastline. Her willowy body radiated with light as the giant orange sun behind her prepared to plunge itself into the ocean.

Her Facebook albums were full of images of teenage girls. They all appeared to be Latin American. Her profile indicated that she worked at Wyatt Galleries, graduated University of Southern California in 2004, lived in West Hollywood and was from Santa Monica.

Her husband was having an affair. For all Colleen knew, he was going to be telling her about it soon. At least, that's what Holly Brinkley wanted him to do. Now what? What should she do? Colleen's heart was in her throat; she was dizzy and felt as though she may vomit. Her eyes were dry but stinging. She needed to go further with her detox. The navy blue dress hanging on the hook in her closet still didn't fit. She wasn't ready to confront him. She felt betrayed by her husband but also by Alexis.

She heard the front door shut. Jay was back.

"I'll get the fire going," he yelled down the hall toward the powder room.

Colleen couldn't speak. She closed the toilet seat and sat down. Beginning with her root chakra, she worked her way up to her crown. Breathing deeply and drawing in the light she imagined above her head. "Johnny, help me find the strength to get through this," she said silently.

Shaking as she stood, she looked at her reflection. Her eyes were red, her mascara streaked and her face was blotchy.

She darted into the kitchen to grab her purse containing her makeup. Jay had left his phone on the island. She wondered if he saw the text.

"COME SIT NEXT TO ME," Jay said as Colleen walked out to the deck.

Colleen bit her lip and took a deep breath. "You can do this," she said silently to herself.

"There's a woman named Holly who works for Alexis," Jay said. Colleen's ears started ringing. She wasn't ready to hear what Jay was about to tell her. "They started a program that helps aspiring Latin American teenage artists."

Colleen's thumbs ached as she pressed them harder and harder into her fists. Did Jay think telling her about all the good this woman does was going to help her understand his affair?

"Holly does most of the work with the program. I sent her pictures of Gabby's paintings."

Colleen gave Jay a confused look. "Our Gabby?"

"She's really talented, honey," Jay said.

Colleen wasn't questioning Gabby's talent. She was confused that Gabby was part of this conversation.

"Holly started a summer program to help underprivileged teenage Latin American female artists. She formed a partnership with USC's Art School. They're offering month-long camps this summer. All expenses paid. They have a spot for Gabby in July if she wants it."

Colleen's eyes widened. "For Gabby?"

Jay smiled, "There's a very strong chance Gabby will get a scholarship to USC's Art School. I told Holly about her learning differences and her family history. She said that if Gabby liked California and USC, she would see to it that she got one of the scholarships — Eli and Alexis are the primary donors."

"This is going to be life changing for her, for Mia, and for Maria," Colleen said. Her body softened as she sank her body into the chair next to Jay.

Jay shook his head in wonder. "There's more. Alexis wants to buy the two paintings that I sent her. She is offering five hundred dollars for each piece." Jay reached over and wrapped his hand around Colleen's fingers. "I waited to tell you because I didn't want you to get your hopes up and be disappointed if it fell through."

Colleen felt her emotions rise. Jay spoke Holly's name with such ease. He had smiled each time he had said it. She was someone he had a real relationship with, more than he implied. Colleen retreated back to the powder room, grabbing her purse on the way. She couldn't let Jay see her cry. She was genuinely happy for Gabby. She wanted to support Jay's venture, even if they were not okay yet. Her support would help her win him back. She was closer to fitting in the dress every week. This might give her a little more time.

Jay tapped on the bathroom door. "Let's have the Gonzalezes over to celebrate tomorrow night." Jay said. "I'm going to go get the girls from the Wilsons'."

COLLEEN WAS HAPPY FOR GABBY. She wondered how many other kids who struggled as students had gifts that went unrecognized. She wished schools would do a better job looking at the whole child and not measure a child only in core subject matter. Gabby was a smart girl with an unbelievable talent. She hoped Gabby was able to embrace the amazing opportunity before her and pursue her life as an artist.

Colleen had texted Mia to ask her and Maria to come with Gabby on Saturday night. "We have exciting news that we want to share with the three of you. It will only take a few minutes and then you guys can leave Gabby here with the girls," Colleen had texted.

After a family trip to Get Juiced on Saturday morning, Jay, Mabel and Chloe sat around Jay's laptop and created a slide show to present to the Gonzalezes. The girls were so giddy with excitement for Gabby that they could barely stay seated on their chairs as they selected pictures.

Jay connected his laptop to the TV in the back room. The slide show was ready to go. Mabel and Chloe fought over who was going to hand Gabby the check for her two paintings. "I'm going to present the check to Gabby," Colleen intervened.

The Gonzalez women arrived at five. All three appeared to be nervous as Chloe led them to the back living room and instructed them to sit together on the couch facing the giant plasma television. "Three, two, one." Jay directed Chloe's little index finger to press the start button.

As Miley Cyrus's song "The Climb" began, Chloe's smile was so wide her eyes became slits. Hannah Montana was one of her favorite shows. Colleen and Jay agreed the song was the perfect choice for the slide show. The first slide was of a group of Latina teenage girls each with a paintbrush in their hand standing in front of a propped canvas at a beach along the California coast, then a picture of Wyatt Galleries. Next were pictures of Gabby's two paintings that Jay had sent and finally slides of USC's campus and art school.

Gabby sat with her mouth open and her eyes fixed on the TV. Maria and Mia exchanged looks of confusion.

Jay and Colleen stood before the three women. "Gabby, I hope you will forgive me, but I sent pictures of your paintings to my sister-in-law. She would like to purchase the two paintings you saw on the slide show for five hundred apiece," Jay said. Colleen handed Gabby the check made out for one thousand dollars.

Large teardrops fell from Gabby's eyes as she stared at the check with her name written on it. Maria began speaking in rapid, incomprehensible Spanish as she stood to hug both Jay and Colleen.

"There's more," Jay said. His eyes glistened as he looked at Gabby. "They're offering you an all-expenses-paid, month-long art camp at University of Southern California."

Colleen couldn't tell which of them was more excited, but she suspected Maria held the most pride. She was the one who had packed up her pregnant daughter and moved to the United States. She wanted more for her daughter and soon-to-be-born granddaughter. She had suffered greatly as a single parent raising Mia in Guatemala. She didn't want her daughter to face the same harsh judgment. The family cycle of cleaning other people's homes and taking care of other people's children was going to be broken. Colleen wasn't sure why, but her excitement for the Gonzalez family was coupled with envy.

"I'LL CALL YOU LATER," JAY said softly into Colleen's ear.

Half asleep with her eyes closed, she wrapped the duvet across her. The cold light of morning had crept in.

Jay sat on the edge of the bed next to Colleen. "Thanks for the great weekend. I'm so proud of your detox work. You've literally blown me away."

Jay's comments fueled her hope. Hope that she could win him back and hope she could forgive him. Colleen finished the last of the lemon water she had sitting on her bedside table.

Colleen had spilled every detail about her conversation with Rachel. She had watched for signs of fear or guilt. Jay was so collected. But he listened to every detail, fully supporting her need to visit her parents. He'd committed to come home early that week so she could drive to Brockville. Why hadn't she asked Rachel about Jay? She wanted another reading.

Colleen leaned across her bed to straighten the duvet cover. Standing up straight as she placed the last quilted pillow on her bed, her pajama pants slid down to her ankles. She kicked them off. Now on her fourteenth day of the detox program, she decided it was time to get on the scales.

After emptying her bladder and stripping off all of her clothes, she stepped on the scales. She stood with her eyes closed for a few seconds before she had the courage to look down at the number. Looking down, Colleen saw she was fifteen pounds lighter than when she started. Her dress had to be getting close to fitting. Still, she wasn't ready to try it on. Instead, she brought her hands together in front of her heart and focused her breath into her heart chakra. Love and gratitude poured into her chest. She couldn't have gotten this far without Kory's help. Things in her life might not be perfect but they were definitely changing.

Colleen ran her fingers over the shiny silver stars embroidered into the navy blue silk fabric. She envisioned herself walking into Harborview Country Club. Her aqua blue eyes would pop next to the navy blue dress. Everyone would ask where she got the dress. Women would talk to her. The look on Dinah's face would be one she would always remember. She needed to talk to Kory about arm exercises. Toned arms hadn't occurred to her before but now fifteen pounds lighter, she wanted more. Five more pounds and she would try the dress on.

"COLLEEN, MY GOODNESS, YOU ARE melting away!" Gertrude said. "You look fantastic."

Colleen beamed at Gertrude.

"Colleen Adler." Colleen looked up and saw Dr. Metzger standing in front of her. "I heard about your progress, but my word, you look amazing," Dr. Metzger said as she led Colleen back to her office. "Let's get your adjustment done so you can get to Kory."

"I'm so glad I finally listened to you. You really helped change my life." Colleen gave Dr. Metzger a hug.

Colleen lay faceup on the adjustment table. She relaxed her head as Dr. Metzger began to rotate it from side to side. A quick rotation to the right and Colleen heard the biggest crack she'd ever heard.

"That was a good one!" Dr. Metzger said.

The left side did the same thing. Colleen felt everything relax.

"Your body was ready to release," Dr. Metzger said, shaking her head in disbelief.

Before Colleen made it back to the waiting area to wait for her appointment, Kory walked into the hallway. "Gertrude's right, you are melting away." She laughed and gave Colleen a hug. "You have changed. Not just the weight. There's more. You're a different person."

The beautiful old clay teapot steamed on the table next to two glasses of water and a new box of Kleenexes.

"Dare I ask what's new?" Kory said with a smile full of pride and admiration.

Colleen shook her head as she smiled at Kory. "Rachel was more than I'd imagined. I don't even know how to thank you for introducing us." Colleen's eyes were moist with gratitude. "I gained a sense of peace about Johnny's death that I never thought was possible. He told me I needed to go see my parents right away."

"Are you going?"

"I'm leaving on Thursday right after my doctor's appointment." Colleen was skeptical at how easily Jay had decided to come home a day-and-a-half early from New York. The girls were thrilled to hear their daddy was going to be the one to pick them up from school on Thursday.

"That's wonderful news," Kory said. "I said it earlier and I'm going to repeat, you're so different. You're waking up inside."

"I never realized how much I shut myself down. Johnny's death affected every part of my life. Part of me died with him and so did my relationship with my parents." Colleen channeled her breath into her chest and throat as her emotions rose.

"You are taking control of your life. Rebuilding your relationship with your parents and taking the necessary steps to find things that feed your soul are the two things you need to focus on now." Kory paused for a few seconds. "You've come so far in such a short time and for that I'm grateful. So with that, I want to lead you through a gratitude meditation."

Colleen closed her eyes. She focused on her breath coming in and out of her body. Her jaw relaxed along with the rest of her body.

Kory spoke softly, "As you exhale, think of your body releasing all of the stress and negativity — all of the toxins you cleaned out during the detox — anything left that is not serving your highest good. Let it go."

Colleen imagined her fat melting away as she allowed her body to release the stress and negativity that she had been carrying around for too long. She tried to let go of the image of Holly Brinkley drinking champagne and brushing her bare shoulder against Jay's arm, her willowy silhouette outlined by the setting sun.

"Taking another deep cleansing breath, focus on the peace you have created for yourself — feel all the good energy that you have created in your body. Take in the radiant sunshine that fills the sky outside — become one with the new life and beauty being created. Take the energy being offered to you now. Let it penetrate into the areas that need healing. Stay connected to this divine energy as you spend time with your parents this weekend."

Kory sat quietly for a few minutes while Colleen began

to open her eyes and come back to the present place. "The next time I see you, you'll be on the last day of your detox and you'll have begun rebuilding your relationship with your parents."

Colleen's smile faded as she thought about her trip to Brockville. "I'm concerned about staying on the plan while I'm in Brockville. I'll be taking food from Billy with me, but I won't have the smoothies," she said.

"Do your best while you're visiting your parents. If you have to eat something outside the guidelines, don't worry about it. You've come so far. We'll get you back on track when you return," Kory said.

"What will I do after the detox is over? I'm afraid of slipping back into my old habits," Colleen said.

"Next week, we'll go through the steps about how to re-introduce things back into your life. I will help you come up with an everyday plan that isn't as restrictive as the plan you're doing now but will keep you healthy and feeling good." Kory looked Colleen in the eye, pleading for her trust. "Colleen, you're going to be fine. You're not going to go back to where you were. Keep your eyes focused ahead."

FIFTEEN

Colleen resisted the urge to skip as she left Dr. Bradley's office. A week would pass before she knew the results of her blood tests. She agreed with Dr. Bradley; she didn't need to see test results to know she was doing better. She couldn't remember ever feeling so good. Normal test results or not, she was thrilled to learn that she had lost another eight pounds.

"Whatever you are doing, I don't want you to stop," Dr. Bradley had said.

Colleen opened the back of her Range Rover to get the chopped salmon salad out of her cooler. Billy had prepared enough boxed meals to get her through Sunday. She hoped her mom wasn't going to be offended. Mary Ann would have a hard time understanding why Colleen was choosing to eat food out of a cooler instead of a meal Mary Ann had cooked herself. Carefully placing a paper napkin across her lap to protect her pants from salad drippings, she reminded herself to stay focused on her weight loss. Her mom would have to understand that this packaged food was helping her.

Pulling out of Dr. Bradley's parking lot, her knuckles where white as she gripped her fingers around the steering wheel. The reality of seeing her mom and dad in just a few short hours had begun to set in, but not as much as her regret over not telling them. She didn't want them making a big fuss over her coming. Earlier in the week she thought a surprise would be nice especially since Sunday was Mother's Day.

The line of traffic waiting to get on the expressway presented a good time to call. The salmon salad came up to the base of her throat as the first ring came through. With a hard swallow, she listened to the phone continue to ring. Her dad must already be finished with lunch and back in the field. The house phone was the only place to get ahold of him. He still wouldn't carry a cell phone. Her mom, on the other hand, did carry a cell phone but would have it turned off and stashed away in her purse. She always told Colleen to call the bank's main number if she needed her during the day. Colleen couldn't bring herself to call the bank.

Wishing to not have let so much time go by since last visiting, she hoped they could forgive her for being an absentee daughter. She looked forward to having an easy and casual weekend with them. She hoped to slide right into their life and do whatever it was that they were doing. If her dad were still working in the field in the evening, she would help her mom get his supper ready and drive it to him. They could eat off of the tailgate of his pickup truck like they used to.

Her phone pinged.

> *Jay: Just landed. Jumping on conference call as soon as I get off plane. Will call you later. Drive safe.*

Exiting I-57 just south of Kankakee, Colleen got off the interstate. The cars all seemed to be in a hurry as they rushed around her. The seventy-five-mile-per-hour speed limit felt too fast. Her mounting anxiety couldn't take more pressure.

The few times her parents had come to visit her in Chicago, her dad had insisted the back roads were a much better route. Colleen argued it was fifteen minutes slower. John said he didn't care if it were an hour longer; he hated the interstate. She now understood where he was coming from. She searched for a country radio station. Country music always made her feel close to her dad.

Fields of corn, soybeans and wheat divided small towns. Two-story farmhouses sat in the distance surrounded by a line of trees. Tarnished silver silos stood tall next to the modern-sided sheds that surrounded them. Only a few old barns remained, most so dilapidated that they couldn't be salvaged. Colleen thought of the long conversations between her dad and uncles about the restoration of the old barn at Farm Five-Thirty-Five.

The small towns were all the same; water towers and gas stations greeted travelers from the north followed by the local bank, grocery store, family restaurant and the VFW. Many towns had small signs perched under their town name and population sign. Little towns loved to announce the achievements of their young people. Seeing a sign announcing Millbrook High School Football 2009 State Champions made Colleen think of the sign at the edge of Brockville — Home of the late Johnny O'Brien — 2003 Track State Champion.

The sight of Brockville's water tower had been hard enough to see as she approached town that first time after he died, but she had mentally prepared herself for it. Seeing the words "the late Johnny O'Brien" had been a dagger to the heart that she wasn't ready for. That was just one of the many things she hadn't been prepared for during that first visit with Mabel.

Her parents hadn't mentioned Johnny once during that first visit. She told herself she didn't want to burden her parents with her pain. She gladly let her mom and dad put Mabel in their bedroom for the two nights she stayed. When she barricaded herself in her old bedroom, her grief was allowed to spill out in private. She let her parents believe that she was catching up on her sleep.

The predictability of the small-town life brought a sense of safety and acceptance to Colleen, something she hadn't felt in a long time. The isolated old farmhouses she saw in the distance reminded her of home. Nothing was going to force her to hide out in her bedroom on this trip.

Just as Colleen approached her hometown, Garth Brooks's song "Friends in Low Places" came on the radio. Maybe Rachel was right about spirits playing with the radio.

Welcome to Brockville, population 1,500. Johnny's sign was gone. It had been replaced by the next generation of State Champions. She reminded herself that she was connected with him now. She didn't need to see his name on a sign to feel his presence. The sight of the water tower still made her heart heavy. She said a silent prayer, "Johnny, show me a sign of your presence." She rolled her windows down as she slowed down to the 25 mph town speed limit. After a quick sneezing fit, her nose adjusted to the fertile air.

Right at the edge of town sat the Brockville Grain and Feed Store. Colleen wondered if her aunt Linda was inside. As a little girl, she loved going to the grain store with her mom and dad, especially when her aunt Linda was working. Aunt Linda always took Colleen to the back room, where they had a hearty supply of donuts for the employees to snack on. As a teenager, though, she loathed the grain store, and did everything possible to avoid being seen surrounded by livestock supplies, tractor parts, agriculture seed and the unfashionable bib overalls hanging on the racks nearby. When she left Brockville, she hoped to never have to set foot in that store again.

Driving through the town square, she slowed nearly to a stop as she approached the Brockville State Bank. Kids on bikes rushed alongside her. She realized school must have just let out. She didn't see her mom's red Oldsmobile in the parking lot. Even if her mom was inside, she didn't want all the attention she would get if she went in and surprised her. She drove on south through town, passing by old people sitting on their porches in rocking chairs, little girls jumping rope on the sidewalk and people bent down tending to their newly planted gardens. She paused at the stop sign at the edge of town to watch a group of horses munching on the new spring grass with their newborn colts standing by their side. She was the only car on the country road that led her to Farm Five-Thirty-Five. The fields surrounding her were full of farmers finishing up the spring planting. Colleen had forgotten how strong the smell of manure was this time of year. For the first time, she actually enjoyed the scent.

Colleen turned left onto the gravel road that led to the lane up to the farmhouse. She rolled her windows up to protect herself and the interior of her car from the cloud of dust that surrounded her. She had forgotten how dusty things were out in the country.

There were three tractors in her dad's field. She wondered who was helping him. He rarely accepted help. He prided himself in doing his own work. Rolling almost to a stop, Colleen made the sharp turn down the lane toward the house. Two light-colored dogs began chasing her car as she slowly made her way down the lane. Colleen wondered when they had gotten the two dogs. Coming to a stop in front of the old farmhouse, Colleen parked her Range Rover next to her dad's old Chevy pickup truck. She was pleased to see her mom's Oldsmobile sitting on the other side. Colleen turned off the ignition and sat in silence for a few seconds before opening up her car door.

Both dogs were dancing around her legs sniffing and begging to be pet. She was surprised no one came out of the house to see whom the dogs were barking at. Was her mom in one of the tractors, she wondered.

Colleen smiled as both dogs sat obediently by the front door, not daring to go in. She remembered how hard her dad and Johnny had worked to train Leo to do the same thing. She wondered how long it took her dad to train these two. Not being able to resist them any longer, she reached down and stroked behind their ears. They loved it as much as Leo had. She wondered what their names were.

Wiping the fresh-cut grass off her shoes, she hooked her fingers around the cool metal handle of the screen door and pulled it open. If the barking of the dogs hadn't announced her arrival, the creaking of the old screen door would. She was met by the familiar scent of Dawn dish soap as she entered the empty kitchen. The day's newspaper sat unopened on the kitchen table. *They must be really behind*, Colleen thought. Her dad always read the newspaper at lunch while he waited for the twelve o'clock news to give the farm report. Two plates and two coffee cups sat in the strainer next to the sink. She couldn't believe they still washed their dishes by hand. She marveled at the old rotary phone that still hung on the kitchen wall. Once, it had been her lifeline to the outside world. Besides a new white refrigerator, everything down to the bunny ears on top of the old TV was exactly the same.

The air was warm against her back as she walked to her car to get a water bottle. Retreating to her favorite spot on the porch to wait, she took in all the updates that had been made since her last visit. The entire porch, it seemed, had been redone. The house no longer had paint chipping off. No more missing floorboards or patches of various shades of unpainted wood filling in the gaps of the floor. The house looked better than Colleen had ever seen it look. It finally matched the new steps that had been added years before.

Although repainted, the original old porch swing hung as it had for so many years. Colleen sat down on the slick new paint and gave a strong push with her legs. Enjoying the soft breeze created by the swing, she looked up and smiled as the new chains moaned just as the old ones had.

Colleen stood at the sound of the grumbling tractor motor approaching the back side of the house. She held her breath as she waited for the engine to turn off. She couldn't wait to see the look on her dad's face when he saw her standing on the porch.

"Colleen?" a man's voice said.

Colleen walked around to the other side of the porch. "Nate! I didn't expect to see you here." After an awkward embrace with her younger cousin, she asked, "Where's my dad?" The sounds of two other tractors approached the house.

Nate raised his eyebrows and gave Colleen a look of concern. "You don't know?" He took his hat off and ran his fingers through his hair.

"Know what?" Colleen said.

Liam and Michael walked up on the porch, each giving Colleen an awkward hug just as their older brother Nate had. They both looked so much older than the last time she saw them. Nate had blond hair and a long, narrow face like her aunt Linda, but Liam and Michael looked more like her dad and Uncle Patrick, thick wavy dark brown hair with sky blue eyes. Johnny, Liam and Michael all resembled each other enough that they could have been brothers instead of cousins. Colleen always found it hard to be around Liam and Michael for that very reason, but something had changed. Seeing them made her happy.

"I assumed your mom called and that's why you're here," Nate said as he looked over at his brothers. "Your dad had to go to the hospital. He was having chest pains this morning and couldn't catch his breath."

Colleen swallowed as though she had something stuck in her throat that wouldn't go down.

"Dad came over to borrow the manure spreader and found him sitting in his truck." Nate wiped his brow before putting his hat back on. "Uncle John thought he just needed to rest a bit, but Dad insisted he go to the hospital to get checked out. Dad called about an hour ago and said they took him in for surgery. It's got something to do with his heart."

Colleen continued trying to swallow with her jaw clenched. She couldn't believe what she was hearing. She couldn't believe no one had called her. "I have to go to the hospital," she said.

"We were just getting ready to head that way. We've just about finished the last of the fertilizing," Nate said.

"Why don't you guys drive her to the hospital? I'll stay and finish up," Michael said.

Colleen followed Nate and Liam to Nate's dusty pickup truck. Liam held the door while she climbed in. Colleen felt claustrophobic sandwiched between her two cousins. Her chest tightened as she tried to process what was happening. She could only think of the sense of urgency Rachel had picked up from Johnny. She hoped she hadn't gotten there too late.

"Why didn't anyone call me?" Colleen said.

She caught the glance Nate gave Liam.

"Probably just wanted to get some answers before they called and worried you," Nate said.

"I've been such a terrible daughter." Colleen said. She stared ahead into the cloud of dust as Nate drove over the gravel toward the blacktop road leading to the hospital.

Her cousins remained quiet.

"Thanks for helping my dad out," Colleen said.

"Anything for Uncle John," Nate said.

"He needs to slow down," Colleen said.

"Been trying to rent his land but he won't hear of it," Nate said.

"Impossible for the three of us to make a living off Dad's piece," Liam said.

The three cousins sat in silence the rest of the drive to the hospital. Colleen was too worried about her dad to process the conversation with her cousins about the farm.

Aunt Susie stood outside the double doors in front of the

hospital. Michael had called ahead to announce Colleen's arrival.

Colleen let her body relax into Aunt Susie's familiar and comfortable arms.

"How did you know?" Susie said as she released Colleen.

Colleen's face was soaked with tears as she stood face-to-face with her aunt. "I didn't. I wanted to surprise them," Colleen said. She wasn't about to say a psychic told her to come. At some point, she planned to tell Aunt Susie but that would have to wait until later.

"They just finished doing a cardiac catheterization to see what kind of damage was done to his heart." Susie handed Colleen a tissue. "Your mom is meeting with the surgeon now."

Colleen wiped her tears and her nose. She didn't want her mom to see her upset. "How did she get her car home?" Colleen said.

"I drove it out to the house for her," Nate said. "Liam drove me over to the grain store to meet Mom. I rode with her to the bank to pick up your mom. I didn't want her to worry about her car later."

Colleen missed being part of the O'Brien family operation.

Aunt Susie led them to the waiting room. Colleen felt as though the three of them were holding her up as she walked.

"Look who I found," Susie said.

Mary Ann was unable to contain her emotions as she embraced her daughter. "You just made my day." She quickly regained her composure. "I didn't believe Susie when she told me that you were here. How in the world did you know to come?"

"I don't know. I hadn't been home in a while and wanted to see you guys."

"Your dad's coronary artery was blocked about 80 percent. They put a stent in to open it up." Mary Ann's face looked tired but relieved. "They're keeping him for the night but he can go home tomorrow," she said. "Honey, you couldn't have picked a better time. Your presence will be the best medicine for your dad."

Uncle Patrick, Aunt Linda and Uncle Jimmy all stood waiting their turn in giving Colleen a hug. Colleen was proud to be part of this group. The love and protection from her family was missed. She knew that her coming home at this particular time was more than a coincidence. She couldn't stop thinking about if she had waited.

Colleen heard a familiar laugh outside of the waiting room. She couldn't place who it was, but she knew she recognized it. She saw someone who looked just like Tara Meyers's mom standing near the doorway talking to another woman. Could that be Tara? It was so weird to see her in a nursing uniform and looking so old. The last time they had seen each other was at Tara's wedding a couple of years after high school. After Tara had gotten married, they lost touch. Like Colleen, she had gained a considerable amount of weight. Her once beautiful, long blond hair was now cut into a short bob.

Mary Ann walked over to her as she entered the waiting room. "Is he ready for us?" she asked.

"They are getting his room set up now. I'll take you back," Tara said.

"Colleen O'Brien? Is that really you?" Tara came over and gave Colleen a big hug. "God, I miss you!" she said.

Colleen didn't realize it until that moment, but she missed her too. "It's so good to see you," Colleen said. Holding her tight, Colleen took in the smell of fresh-cut flowers. Tara smelled the same as she had when they were younger. Colleen remembered the Christmas that Tara received a bottle of Beautiful perfume by Estee Lauder. "You smell the same."

"You know I could never part with my bottle of Beautiful! I barely recognize you without your curls," she said.

"I barely recognize you with your short hair," Colleen said. "When did you become a nurse?"

"After I divorced Wes. I'll tell you all about it another time." Her eyes flittered as she shook her head. "I've been working here about three years now," she said. "Don't worry about your dad. He's in good hands here. We may not be fancy like the people in Chicago, but our doctors know what they're doing."

"It's so good to see you girls together again," Aunt Susie said.

"Don't be a stranger. We need to catch up," Tara said. She gave Colleen another hug before leading the group to John's room. "I'm here if you guys need anything," she said as she watched them enter the room.

The smell of Pine-Sol layered underneath rubbing alcohol went straight to Colleen's stomach, leaving her queasy and uneasy on her feet. She was glad when Aunt Susie motioned her over to sit next to her on one of the three seats in the room. Her mom took the other one while the men stood, arms crossed, doing their best to remain patient. Being indoors under fluorescent light must have felt like poison to them. Especially when there was work waiting to be done.

Susie spoke softly as if not to disturb the awkward silence in the room. "How are the girls?"

"Excited for summer," Colleen said.

"I sure do miss them," Mary Ann said. She straightened up in her chair and crossed her legs.

Colleen felt the words. "They get out of school in a few weeks. I plan to bring them then," she said.

The family remained silent as they waited. Silence was their way when something was wrong. No one spoke. They preferred to keep busy when difficult situations happened. Sitting around wasn't their thing.

Colleen felt all eyes follow her hand as she reached into her purse in search of her phone.

> *Jay: Tell your mom and dad hello. The girls want me to tell you they want to go with you next time.*

She hadn't had a chance to let Jay know what was going on. She would call him later, when she wasn't under everyone's watchful eye.

After what seemed like forever, a small commotion came from the hallway. The hospital bed squeaked as a nurse pushed John into the room. Colleen stood next to her mom as they positioned his bed in the center of the small room.

"He's pretty tired but will be as good as new tomorrow," the nurse said.

John lifted his hand as though it had weights on it. He lay flat on the bed with his eyes half closed. Colleen had never seen her dad look so grey and frail. She barely recognized him without his false teeth. His chin was pushed up under his nose in an unnatural way that made his nose look bigger than it was.

Mary Ann took hold of his hand. "Colleen's here," she said.

Colleen walked to the other side of his bed. She wiped her tears before bending down to kiss his forehead. "Hi, Dad," she said.

"My sweet girl," he croaked.

"We're going to let you get some rest. We'll be back in the morning," Mary Ann said.

He nodded. His eyes were closed and his breathing was heavy as they picked up their purses and followed the rest of the family out of the room.

COLLEEN HADN'T EATEN ANYTHING SINCE the salmon salad in Dr. Bradley's parking lot earlier. Mary Ann pulled a large Country Crock butter container out of the refrigerator. She transferred the leftover chicken noodle soup into a pan on the stovetop. Colleen had forgotten about her mom's collection of Country Crock butter containers. She thought Tupperware and other types of storage containers that people spent money on was a waste of money. In her opinion, it was wasteful to spend money on storage containers when empty Cool Whip and Country Crock butter containers provided perfectly fine storage and she refused to use anything else.

Colleen didn't have the heart to tell her mom that she couldn't eat her homemade soup. Mary Ann already had a hard enough day. How bad could one meal off the detox plan be? She was grateful that her mom didn't drink alcohol. After seeing Johnny's name wiped off the Brockville welcome sign, the sanitation smells of the hospital and a day full of fear, a glass of wine would have been impossible to refuse.

Colleen swallowed several spoonfuls of the soup. She did her best to navigate her spoon around the oil that pooled in shiny circles. The starchy noodles and rich broth began to upset her stomach. She put her spoon down. Her teeth felt fuzzy.

"You didn't eat much," Mary Ann said.

"I've been on a diet for the past few weeks. I think my stomach shrunk," Colleen said.

Mary Ann nodded. Her hunger was apparent.

"I've lost twenty-five pounds." Colleen looked at her mom. She wanted Mary Ann to notice that her face was no longer puffy, her eyes were bigger and brighter or that her skin looked better than it had in a long time. But Mary Ann wasn't the type to comment on appearance, and because Mary Ann hadn't seen Colleen in over a year, she had never seen Colleen balloon up with the last thirty pounds.

"I think you just eat out too much. Why don't you try cooking your own food? We've never had any weight problems in our family. We all work hard and cook our own food," Mary Ann said.

Colleen didn't have the energy to debate with her mom. She wished it were as easy as Mary Ann thought. Colleen wanted to tell her mom about the rest of her life, about how kind Jay had been to help Gabby. About how he might be, was probably, having an affair. About her fears that the woman he would leave her for was pretty, thin, blond Holly Brinkley. Instead, she unloaded the meals from her cooler into the refrigerator. She now had one extra. She couldn't burden her mom with more worry.

Mary Ann stood over Colleen's shoulder watching the various rectangular meals get stacked in her refrigerator. "So you paid someone to make all those for you?" The fancy black containers created more skepticism than the foreign-sounding meals.

COLLEEN PICKED UP HER PHONE to call Jay. Her cell phone didn't have a signal. She had no choice but to call from the old rotary phone. No answer. She left Jay a message highlighting the details of her dad's surgery.

Mary Ann wiped her hands on a dishtowel after she finished washing the bowls, spoons and glasses. "I'll see you in the morning," she said as she bent down to kiss the top of Colleen's head.

Colleen climbed up the dark stairway to her old bedroom. The room smelled musty and the air felt stagnant. Colleen hung her cardigan across the chair and cracked open the window. She stared out into the darkness and noticed the millions of stars up in the night sky. Johnny used to take his constellation map and a flashlight outside on clear nights. Most nights, frustration arose from his inability to find every single constellation on his map. Colleen wished she'd bought him a telescope. Besides the Big Dipper and Little Dipper, she didn't know any of the shapes. The light pollution from the city of Chicago prevented her from seeing the stars. Now, she realized, she missed them.

She hung her clothes in the closet and placed her two cardigans on the shelf above the clothes rod. Her sweaters wouldn't go back all the way and hung from the shelf. She pushed harder but there was something on the shelf. She reached her hand back as far as she could. There was a package of some sort, but she couldn't get a grip on it. With the help of an empty wire hanger, she pulled the package down. The large manila envelope, the one her mom had given her during that first visit with Mabel. The one Rachel had mentioned. Johnny's name was written with a black marker across the front side. She couldn't bring herself to open it back then. She wasn't sure she could now, either.

She sat down on top of the floral quilt covering the bed, the same one she'd slept under every night growing up. The once vibrant colors were now faded into soft muted reds, purples and greens, giving it a fashionable vintage look. Her mother didn't replace quilts, sheets or bath towels until there were holes in them. Colleen closed her eyes and took a deep breath into her chest, counting to eight, the way Kory taught her. She pictured Johnny's face the last time she saw him. His teenage face was no longer round like it had been when he was a child. It was chiseled like Liam's and Michael's. Except for the innocence in his smile, he looked grown-up. A breeze through the window sent a chill across her skin. She stared at the dusty manila envelope on her lap, took another deep breath and carefully pinched the gold clasps.

Inside were the contents Colleen hadn't ever had the courage to look at — Johnny's obituary, tributes written in the *Brockville Press* from his many friends, teachers and coaches, articles about his life and love of farming and his valedictorian speech. Colleen's hands shook as she held the page Johnny typed in this house eight years earlier.

Courage. Perseverance. Loyalty. These three words describe the people I most admire. My great-grandfather, the original John Robert O'Brien, the man my grandfather, dad and I are named after — he put these words into action. His courage brought him to Brockville all the way from Ireland. He was only fourteen when he climbed aboard the boat that sailed him across the Atlantic. I'm not sure how much money he had in his pocket, but I know it wasn't much. His perseverance saved his farm from being lost during the Great Depression. The loyalty to the land he inherited out of his Irish luck was passed down to the future generations. My family honors his courage by continuing to persevere through the difficult years spent farming. We honor him by maintaining our loyalty to the land he worked so hard to keep. My sister, Colleen, had the courage to leave and set off on her own adventure. She persevered and found a life in a new city, a happy marriage, now motherhood. Her loyalty to her unborn child is why she isn't here today. Our teachers had the courage to take on the task of teaching difficult teenagers. They persevered through the challenges we presented them on a daily basis. Their loyalty is why we are gathered here today in our caps and gowns preparing for the next chapter in our life. To the class of 2003, have courage to try something new, persevere when

*things get hard, stay loyal to who you are and
never forget where you came from.*

Colleen let the letter drop to the floor. Until what felt like
late into the night, into the next morning, she lay on her bed
and wept.

SIXTEEN

Colleen looked at the clock. Mabel and Chloe would be awake and getting ready for school by now. She hoped Maria had gotten there early today, as she had the past few Fridays. French-braided pigtails had been the latest third-grade fad. Colleen had instructed Mabel to have Maria help her with her hair. Jay wouldn't know where to begin with a French braid. Getting three people out the door by eight a.m. instead of just himself was going to be hard enough.

Colleen flipped the light switch in her old bathroom. There was barely more light with it on than with it off. She heard the clanking of dishes downstairs and knew her mom would be ready to leave for the hospital soon. She remembered that the shower took a while to heat up and reached to the old silver knob to turn it on. She struggled to find a place to set her face products, makeup and toothbrush on the small pedestal sink. She had forgotten how frustrated she used to get in high school when trying to get ready in this house. The lighting was so terrible that it made the mirror almost pointless. As she focused on her reflection in the mirror, she thought of how she used to see a girl with unruly curly hair looking back at her. Her hair was smooth and straight. The way she used to dream it would be. She slipped out of her pajamas and stood in front of the mirror naked. Although she couldn't quite see into her eyes, she spoke quietly, "Colleen Ann O'Brien, you are beautiful and I love you. I really, really love you." She no longer felt silly talking to her reflection. She took a deep breath and said a silent thank you before getting in the shower, then dressing and walking down the creaky old stairs toward the kitchen. She found her mom standing at the kitchen sink rinsing off the blue and brown eggs she had just collected.

"Didn't you bring any other clothes?" Mary Ann said.

Of all people to ask about wearing the same clothes, Colleen thought. "I did. I just brought all the same ones," Colleen said. She wasn't about to explain her reasons for it.

"Guess that's one way to keep things simple," Mary Ann said. "You need to eat before we leave," Mary Ann said. "Sit down while I make you some eggs."

Colleen thought of Kory's words: *If you eat badly while you're away, we can get you back on track when you return.*

Mary Ann put a cup of coffee in front of Colleen. "I'm not supposed to have coffee," Colleen said.

"Well, have some anyway." Mary Ann seemed pleased to veer her daughter off the strict diet she had just learned about.

"When did you guys get the dogs?" Colleen asked.

"Oh, it's been about a year I reckon," Mary Ann said. "Don't you remember when we found that litter down by the creek? Your dad had me getting up every two hours to bottle-feed those dang pups." Mary Ann smiled. "We gave three away and your dad couldn't part with the two outside."

"What are their names?" Colleen said.

"Nelson and Cash," Mary Ann said with a chuckle.

"Like Willie and Johnny?" Colleen laughed as she

remembered how much her dad loved Willie Nelson and Johnny Cash.

"You got it," Mary Ann said.

Colleen didn't dare say anything as she watched her mom drop a chunk of butter into her old cast iron pan that she was about to scramble her eggs in. Her back ached as she reached for her forbidden cup of coffee. If she was going to be here more than a few days, she was going to have to replace her old mattress. That would mean another battle with her mom on spending money needlessly.

They drank the coffee in silence. The stale, watered-down version of coffee Mary Ann brewed didn't compare to Burt's, Southport Grocery & Cafe or even Whole Foods. Colleen drank it quickly to get it down. The weak coffee managed to give Colleen the happy buzz she'd been missing. She needed to remain strong for her mom. If that meant breaking the detox with some coffee, then so be it.

Mary Ann finished her last sip.

"I'll drive," Colleen said. "Do you think he will remember seeing me last night?" Colleen said.

"We'll see in a few minutes. I just hope you don't give him another heart attack," Mary Ann said.

Colleen laughed. Mary Ann making jokes was a good sign. Colleen liked her mother best when she relaxed; maybe they could all start to not be quite so serious.

John was sitting up reading the paper with a cup of coffee on the bedside tray. He looked up when he heard the door open.

"Well, I'll be darned, you really are here," he said. "I should've had a heart attack a long time ago."

Working around the IV in his arm, Colleen was finally able to give him the type of hug she had thought about since she left Chicago the day before. She was glad to see his face was pink, his eyes were bright and his frail body seemed to have inflated overnight.

"Where are my beautiful granddaughters?" John said.

"They're at home with Jay. I promise to bring them as soon as they are out of school for the summer," Colleen said.

"You meet Nelson and Cash?" John asked with a proud smile.

Colleen was happy he had his false teeth back in place. "The girls will love them," Colleen said.

They waited for the nurse to bring in the discharge paperwork. Despite the nurse's orders to let someone help him get dressed, John grabbed his clothes and locked himself in the small bathroom attached to his room. He was fine, he insisted — still as stubborn as he'd ever been.

The nurse came in and cleared her throat until they all stopped speaking.

"You need to take it easy for a few days. Avoid lifting more than ten pounds or pulling heavy objects for the first five days. You may climb stairs but go slowly. Your cardiologist will contact you for a follow-up appointment," the nurse said.

John and Mary Ann didn't seem interested in writing down what the nurse was saying. Colleen dug through her purse to find a pen. Had the nurse said ten days and not more than five pounds? Or was it the opposite? She used the backside of one of the discharge papers to write rapidly, trying to capture all the instructions.

"Make sure to drink eight to ten glasses of clear fluids

today and tomorrow. Moving forward, you need to decrease saturated fats and trans fats, eat more fiber-rich foods, and try to eat more plant protein than animal protein." John and Mary Ann sat politely listening to the lady. Colleen was certain they had no intention of following a single one of these instructions.

Colleen pulled her car around to the entrance of the hospital. Her dad stood next to the wheelchair they forced him to ride in. He told them it was nonsense and he was perfectly fine to walk. After more discussion than was necessary, Mary Ann convinced him to follow along with the nurses if he wanted to go home.

"Whew wee, what kind of car is this?" John said.

"What did you say it was called, Colleen?" Mary Ann said.

"Range Rover," Colleen said. She changed the subject before he asked how much it cost. "Let's stop by the grocery store and get some of the food the nurse suggested."

"We've got plenty. You know how the folks are around here. We're going to have more food than we will know what to do with," Mary Ann said.

"How much did this Range Rover set you guys back?" John said.

ALL COLLEEN WANTED WAS TO be alone with her parents out at the farm. She wanted to sit around the kitchen table or out on the porch talking with her dad while her mom fussed over them. Hearing from Johnny through Rachel had shaken her awake, made her see how every second was precious. She wanted to open up and share her struggles with them, as Johnny had communicated to her. But one car after the next drove down their lane. The men visited with her dad while the women delivered covered dishes, each of them cooking the same dish they brought to every celebration or crisis. Mary Ann's contribution was always banana walnut muffins, Aunt Susie's was crunchy chicken casserole, and Aunt Linda always brought a meatloaf. Colleen wondered what her dish would have been if she had stayed in Brockville. Once the freezer in the kitchen was full of casseroles, zucchini bread, blueberry muffins, two lasagnas and a shepherd's pie, Colleen began carrying the remaining dishes out to the deep freeze in the machine shed.

Colleen pondered the ritual of bringing the dishes. No one wanted to be the one who didn't bring something, but more than that, everyone wanted a firsthand account of her dad's health. They cared and wanted to help. The O'Brien roots ran deep through the heart of Brockville.

COLLEEN WOKE BEFORE THE SUN made it to her bedroom window. She looked forward to the full day ahead at home with her parents. An entire day spent at the farmhouse used to feel like a nightmare, but today, it seemed like a dream. She didn't bother getting dressed before she made her way down to the kitchen. She was eager to finally have a minute alone with her parents. Coffee and mealtimes were the only times during the day they sat down. The rest of the day was filled with chores — cleaning out the chicken coop, pulling weeds from the garden, turning the compost, working on tractors, mowing. Not today, though. Her dad wasn't allowed to do anything.

"There's our girl," John said as Colleen walked into the kitchen.

Colleen declined her mom's offer for a cup of coffee. "Colleen's on a diet," Mary Ann said to John.

"It's a detox. I'm giving my body a break from hard-to-digest food," Colleen said.

"D-what? Sounds like someone's pulling your leg, honey," John said.

"I found out I have hypothyroidism. The detox is helping me lose the weight I've gained," Colleen said.

"Colleen's lost over twenty pounds," Mary Ann said. She didn't hide her shock about her daughter recently weighing a lot more than she currently did.

"Did you ever know Betty Elmer?" Mary Ann asked Colleen. "She had a similar type of thyroid problem you do — same type of weight gain. She still isn't thin but once she got her medication straightened out, she trimmed down."

Colleen was surprised by her mother's knowledge of hypothyroidism and was grateful to whoever Betty Elmer was for laying the foundation for her medical condition. Her parents were skeptical of most "conditions."

"Whatever you're doing is working. Keep it up," Mary Ann said while giving Colleen's forearm a squeeze.

Colleen watched her dad smear margarine across the top of a piece of toasted white bread. She wished the nurse had gone into more detail or at least helped them understand what things in their everyday diet weren't heart-healthy. Saturated fat and fiber-rich foods didn't mean anything to her parents. "Kory, the woman that I told you about, knows a lot about nutrition. If you want, I can ask about heart-healthy recipes for you," Colleen said.

"That would be real nice, honey," John said.

Colleen knew how unlikely it was that her parents would change their eating habits, but she had to try.

"I never thought about how food was affecting my body until I started working with Kory," Colleen said. She left out how much alcohol she'd been drinking. "I've really gotten used to eating differently over the past nineteen days."

"You going to keep buying the already-made food from that place you told me about?" Mary Ann asked.

"Those little containers? What's in those things?" John said, pointing toward the refrigerator.

With a combination of vulnerability and pride, Colleen collected the containers to show her dad their contents.

"I never heard of anyone eating seaweed before," John said. "You sure it's safe to eat that stuff?"

"It's better than you think," Colleen said. "You should try it."

"We can't afford to eat that way," Mary Ann said.

"I can help you eat that way," Colleen said. "Now that I'm starting to get my energy back, I'm going to start preparing some of my own food," she said. She didn't mean to lie, but somehow it just came out of her mouth. Jay had suggested they help her parents out more times than she could count. "I could find a company here who would deliver healthy meals. Or help you hire someone for the farm — give you time to grocery shop and cook new things, take it a bit easier."

"You know how we feel about that," Mary Ann said.

Without a word, she began clearing the breakfast dishes and moved on to the rest of her Saturday chores.

Colleen washed and rinsed the last fork from the breakfast dishes and placed it in the dish rack to dry. She couldn't remember the last time she had hand-washed dishes.

"I can stay longer than tomorrow, if you guys need me to," Colleen said, even though she knew it would be almost impossible to leave Jay alone with the girls longer.

John set down his newspaper. "Those little girls need their mama. You need to get back to your family, where you belong. Your mom and I can manage just fine." He stood up. "We have a nice day ahead of us here, even though your mom won't let me do anything." John winked at Colleen as he raised his voice to make sure Mary Ann heard him. Facing Colleen, he put his hands on her shoulders. "Having you to myself one more day should do my heart good."

Colleen didn't argue with her mom when she sent her out to the porch to keep her dad company. He'd already broken the agreement with the nurse. He had a broom in his hand reaching up to knock down a spiderweb from a far corner above the front door.

Colleen took the broom from her dad's hand. "You need to sit down." Colleen finished clearing the spiderweb.

John took a seat on the porch swing and Colleen sat next to him. "I don't ever remember seeing you sit out here on the swing," Colleen said.

"Honey, once I'm gone, I'm afraid this old farmhouse is just going to crumble away. Or even worse, get sold off to someone outside of the family." John ran his finger over the purple spot on his arm where his IV had been.

Colleen listened to the air blowing through the leaves of the old oak tree next to the house. Her dad had reason for concern but she didn't want to say so. "That's never going to happen."

"You do know, it's supposed to go to you? Was supposed to go to my oldest child upon marriage," John said. "Our portion of the farm too, when I'm no longer around."

Colleen watched her dad smooth his pants with his palms. He left steaks of sweat. "Well, you aren't going anywhere, so we don't need to talk about that now," Colleen said. She didn't want to think about him dying. Her chest tightened and a lump formed in her throat, making it painful to breathe.

"I know you don't want to hear this, but the fact of the matter is I'm not going to be around forever. It's probably safe to say that I'll go before your mom."

"Dad—"

"When I go, this house is going to be too much work for your mom," he said.

Colleen looked on at the field in front of them. The cornstalks creeping out of the soil looked taller than yesterday. The manure smell had subsided and the sounds of tractors were gone. Colleen focused her ears on the owl *hoo-hoo*ing in the distance over the moaning of the chain of the porch swing as it swayed Colleen and John back and forth. She wished she could tell her dad about her marriage problems. She hated pretending everything was great between her and Jay.

John put his hand on Colleen's knee. "It's good to have you home, sweetheart. Promise me you won't wait so long to come back again," John said.

"I promise," Colleen said. A tear rolled down her cheek.

She did her best to brush it off without her dad noticing but wasn't successful. John moved his arm around to her shoulders. He brought her in close and let her head fall onto his shoulder.

Colleen relaxed against her dad. She closed her eyes and breathed in his Irish Spring soap smell. "I'm sorry that I've been gone for so long."

"Did your mom show you what she did with Johnny's old room?" John said.

Colleen had been afraid to look in his room since she had arrived. She wasn't sure she could handle seeing it. The last time she had been home, his room was exactly as he left it the afternoon before his accident. The towel he used for his last shower was thrown across his unmade bed. His track medals were lying across his desk on top of a paper that he'd been working on for school. She was definitely more at peace with things, but she didn't have any interest in traveling back to the painful past.

"She made it into a little study and framed up all of Johnny's pictures, all the newspaper articles written about him and his valedictorian speech. She even framed his acceptance letter to the U of I." John got up and motioned for her to follow him.

Colleen thought of what Rachel said about it being Johnny's time to pass. Things were the way they were meant to be. She walked behind her dad into Johnny's room. The room had been transformed. A couch, surrounded by the framed pictures and articles, now sat where his bed once was. A wall of shelving filled with books, photo albums and more pictures replaced the area where his desk once sat.

Colleen smiled. "It feels peaceful." She stood staring at his speech. She was going to frame her copy, also. "I can picture Johnny sitting right here listening to music."

John joined her on the couch. "Nice, isn't it?"

"Mom did a great job," she said. She thought of Rachel saying that Johnny was with her all the time. "This may sound crazy, but I feel like Johnny is here with us now."

"I know he is," John said. "I've been coming in here a lot since the room's been redone. I've found it to be the best medicine for my broken heart." He choked on his words.

Colleen reached over and gave her dad a hug. So, they all still had broken hearts. Shouldn't that be even more of a reason that they do what they could to mend them, even if only a little at a time?

THE ROOM WAS DARK. COLLEEN brought her hands up to her hair. She let out a sigh of relief as her fingers ran down the length of the thick mass. She realized it was just a dream, not real. She brushed the loose strands away from her face and twisted her hair behind her head. Colleen remembered hearing the snip of the scissors, then another and another. At first she couldn't see who was doing the cutting. Chunks of long straight hair fell into her lap and down on her feet. Hair clung to her ankles, tickling the exposed skin. Her great-grandmother Mabel danced before her, then circled around her, laughing. The woman gently brushed the hair off Colleen's lap with a small broom she held in her hand. The broom found its way to Colleen's ankles and relieved the itchy tickle. Her grandmother slid her warm hands into Colleen's and pulled her to her feet. She twirled Colleen around and around. Colleen felt light and free. She twirled around again and felt her grandmother's hand slip away.

Colleen reached over to her nightstand for her cell phone: 3:52 a.m. She flipped her pillow over and laid her cheek on the cool side of the pillow. She closed her eyes and tried to recapture the wonderful feeling she'd had before she'd lost her grandmother. "Come back to me, Grandma," Colleen said in her head. The image of her grandmother was so vivid.

Colleen tried the breathing exercise that Kory taught her. Her mind wouldn't cooperate. Johnny's words kept replaying through her mind. Courage. Perseverance. Loyalty. Had he really thought she possessed those things or was he just being kind? He had been a naive teenager when he wrote those words. She tried to think of all the things in her life that would warrant those labels. There weren't many. She supposed her leaving Brockville could have been seen as courageous, but at the time she'd felt it was more out of desperation. She had felt her family always viewed her move as betrayal. School had always been easy to her, so there was no perseverance there. She had persevered in her efforts of not coming back to Brockville and in trying to fit in with the women of Harborview Country Club and Northside Day School. What kind of life had she really created? She hadn't followed her calling to work with students, to become a mentor or a guide. She hadn't been a good mother to her girls. She hadn't been attractive enough for Jay. The only thing she was proud of since giving birth to the girls was getting through this detox and that she had finally found the courage to come home. That was something.

Colleen stared up at the ceiling. Shadows from the oak tree

branches outside her window formed along her wall and crept up to the ceiling. She needed courage to confront Jay about Holly. She didn't know if she had the strength to persevere without him. Was she strong enough to be a single mom? How would she manage financially? Would she really get half of everything they had if they were to divorce? She'd never learned the basics, never had a reason to talk to a divorce attorney. The words sounded strange. Divorce. Single mother.

She thought of the envy she felt when Jay presented Gabby with the keys to her future. At the time, her feelings had confused her. She wasn't envious of Gabby — she realized now — she was envious of Jay. She wanted to be the one to help Gabby. She wanted to help other teenagers, ones who didn't have the great fortune of working for someone as generous as Jay. She wanted to teach those kids to be courageous, to persevere and to stay loyal to themselves. She knew what Kory would likely say — that Colleen needed to master those things herself.

She made up her mind; she would confront Jay about the affair when she got home. She wasn't going to wait for the security of her beautiful dress. She would call the Gonzalezes on her way back to Chicago to see if one of them could babysit the girls while she and Jay went out for dinner. She would speak to him in the car before they got out. Regardless of the outcome, she would persevere. She would get back on her detox. She would sell the house if she had to. She was no longer going to live a lie.

Before she could go back to Chicago, she had to set the most important thing straight. She had to make things right on Farm Five-Thirty-Five. She tiptoed down the wooden stairs and left a note on the table that she was going to find a cell signal to call Jay. Then she slipped her shoes on and slowly opened and closed the screen door. She drove down the lane as slowly as she could to keep the dogs from barking and hopefully, quiet enough to not wake her parents. She had no intention of calling Jay. Nate was the one she had to talk to. She hoped her cousin didn't kill her for visiting so early.

The crops in the fields surrounding her were still low enough to allow a clear view for what seemed to be miles in any direction she looked. In the west, the sky was the color of a ripened plum. In the east, it was a pale soft pink. The young crops hung with the weight of the dew clinging to their leaves. The sun would lift them up as soon as it crept up above the green crop line in the distance.

She drove slowly down the lane leading to Nate's house. She saw his truck parked along the fence line near the pasture. She drove her Range Rover down into the ditch and across the grass. She saw him walking in the distance. He had a syringe in his hand. He looked worried. "Everything okay?" he said.

"You're the one with the syringe," Colleen said. "Calves?"

He shook his head. He stood waiting, syringe dripping with yellow liquid, waiting for Colleen to explain her presence.

Colleen shivered as she wrapped her sweater tightly across her middle. "My parents are going to need help with the farm at some point. I don't know anything about it. They won't want to know I'm asking around, but I hoped you could help me," Colleen said.

"I've been trying to get your dad to rent his portion of the farm to me for a couple of years now," Nate said. "He won't hear of it."

"He isn't one to sit around," Colleen said.

"Uncle John knows more about farming this land than anyone. I would insist that he was part of the annual production," Nate said.

"At some point, this will be my responsibility," Colleen said.

"When the time comes, Michael, Liam and I will be the first in line to buy the land from you, or if you prefer, we'll rent it from you," Nate said.

Colleen was relieved her cousins would be there to step in when the time came.

"You sell it to us and it'll be in good hands. You won't have to be bothered with it. Better, though, to transition things with your dad's guidance. Will make things easier down the road," Nate said.

Colleen couldn't imagine selling her dad's portion of the farm, but what would she do with it? She wasn't ready to agree to anything and planned on her dad living for several more years. "If he rented to you, would he make enough to live on? He won't accept money from me," she said.

"No need to worry about that. Farm rent's consistent, farming isn't," Nate said. "He'll be better off. We'll force him to take pay for helping out, also."

"I'm going to work on him," Colleen said. Renting was a good next step. She had zero interest in following the price of corn and soybeans or worrying about the lack of rain. She was grateful she'd have someone like Nate to take over when the time came.

Colleen climbed back in her car. If the farm rent was enough and Nate let her dad help, why wouldn't he do it?

Colleen walked through the front door into the kitchen. Her note sat next to her dad's newspaper on the kitchen table.

John stood at the stove. "I'm cooking eggs for my two favorite moms this morning."

Mother's Day. Colleen had forgotten. Her heart panged with guilt. This was the first Mother's Day she hadn't been with the girls. If she were at home in Chicago, she'd be having breakfast in bed. Mabel and Chloe would be swooning over her, fluffing her pillow, offering her a napkin and watching her take each and every bite of whatever they had chosen to make her — except this year, it would have been a smoothie.

"You're not supposed to be doing anything," Mary Ann said. "I'll cook the eggs. And, Colleen, honey, you should have used our phone to call Jay. No need to run all over the county trying to find a signal."

Colleen sat with her parents and tried to decide how to bring up her concerns about the farm. "Dad, yesterday you told me you wanted to make sure this farm stayed in our family and I was the one it was supposed to go to, right?"

"That's right," he said. After taking a long sip of coffee he sat back and looked at Colleen. His eyes were caring and patient, eager to hear what she was about to say.

"I saw Nate while I was out. He said he's talked to you about renting," Colleen said.

"We'll get it all figured out when the time is right," John said.

"What about now? Why don't you transition things to Nate now? Then when it's time for me to be more involved, it's already done," Colleen said. "I won't have to worry about making the wrong decisions — doing something you wouldn't have approved of?"

"We can think on it a while. I'm not going anywhere any time soon," John said.

Colleen finished the last bite of her mom's scrambled eggs. The yolks of the farm-fresh eggs were more orange than yellow. Her mom's technique of heating her cast iron pan over high heat, turning the heat off, melting the butter and then slowly cooking the eggs in the warm pan resulted in the creamiest texture. No one scrambled eggs better. She would get back on her smoothies tomorrow. She put her hands around her waist. Her pants were still loose, but after a few more rich meals they would become tight again.

John looked out the window over the kitchen table when the dogs began barking. "Jimmy and Susie." He walked out to the porch and Colleen followed behind. Mary Ann cleared the dishes before heading outside. Four more trucks were making their way down the long lane toward the house — Colleen's uncle Patrick, aunt Linda and cousin Nate with his wife, April; Michael with his wife, Heidi; and Liam with his girlfriend, whom Colleen had yet to meet.

"Looks like you have a whole crew here to see you off," John said.

Colleen's cheeks flushed. She was obviously touched that they all came out to see her before she left.

Colleen walked over to April and Heidi, giving them each a hug. She hadn't seen either of them in a long time. She didn't make it to either of their weddings.

"Colleen, this is my girlfriend, Kate," Liam said.

Colleen reached out to shake her hand.

"We're getting married this summer," he said.

"Here at the farm, I hope!" Colleen said.

"You'd better be here," Nate shot back.

"I'm done missing things around here." Colleen said.

COLLEEN MADE HER WAY DOWN the stairs and back out to the porch with her bag and cooler in hand. Her dad stood and made his way over to help his daughter with her things. "Stop, John. I've got her bag," Patrick said.

"You guys better keep a close watch over him while I'm gone." Colleen laughed. She hoped he was almost recovered because there was no way he was going to sit still much longer.

John gave Colleen one last hug. "You give those girls a big hug from their grandpa and tell them I love them, okay? Oh, and tell Jay I said hi, too."

Aunt Susie gave Colleen a long hug. "You better get back down here real soon with those sweet girls!" she said.

Mary Ann came out with a large Country Crock butter container in her hand. "Sorry it took me so long inside. I was getting some chocolate chip cookies ready for Mabel and Chloe. Luckily, I had some made up in the freezer. They should be thawed out by the time you get home. Hopefully, the frozen cookies won't tempt you!" Mary Ann said.

Colleen squeezed her mom tight as she gave her one last hug. "Happy Mother's Day, Mom. The girls will love the cookies."

Colleen pulled away and on her way down the lane she paused as she looked in her rearview mirror at the old farmhouse in the background. That was her house. It was as much a part of her as anything was. Next time she drove on these roads, Mabel and Chloe would be with her and they would be staying longer than a couple of days. She knew they were going to love it here. They had been deprived of their grandparents' love and quirkiness for too long.

Tuning in to her dad's favorite radio station, the one that she'd hated as a teenager because it only played country music, Colleen listened as Johnny Cash sang "Man in Black."

The words struck her. She was the woman in black. She had worn black or charcoal grey since Lyla put her in the "until my weight is gone" outfit. Her appearance did have a somber tone but, unlike Johnny Cash, she wasn't wearing the dark colors for all of the darkness in the world. She wasn't bringing attention to other peoples' misfortune. She was highlighting her own misfortune — as her dad would say, "wallowing" in her own darkness. Suddenly Colleen felt suffocated by the clothes on her body. She wanted to peel them off and throw them out the window as she drove. She was done wearing what Lyla, Dinah or anyone else, for that matter, deemed as acceptable.

She sang loud with Johnny Cash until Jay's ringtone on her phone broke through.

"Happy Mother's Day!" Mabel and Chloe sang.

"We miss you and can't wait so see you when you get home," Jay said. "I called my mother and canceled our Mother's Day dinner with her tonight."

Colleen had forgotten all about the Mother's Day dinner with Dinah.

"The last thing you need is to spend the evening with my mother. The girls and I are meeting her for brunch instead," Jay said.

Colleen could only imagine Dinah's anger about having her plans changed. About not having Colleen there to lord over and disapprove of.

"I arranged for Gabby to babysit the girls tonight so we can go to dinner," she said.

"I'll get us a reservation," Jay said.

"Anywhere but Harborview," Colleen said.

She took a deep breath as the reality of confronting Jay loomed in front of her. For all she knew, her life was about to change. She may be moving, getting a job, becoming a single mom. The only part that didn't feel terrible was getting a job.

JAY AND THE GIRLS STOOD waiting for her in front of the garage. "MOMMY!!!!!!" Chloe jumped up and down.

Mabel grabbed ahold of Chloe's arm to guide her out of Colleen's path as she pulled into the garage. Already protective, thinking of others, she was a sweet girl. The gesture made Colleen smile. Regardless of what happened between her and Jay, they would be okay. As she climbed out of the car, both girls grabbed ahold of her waist and squeezed. She was nervous but couldn't wait to tell them about their summer visit to Brockville.

Jay opened the back of the Range Rover and pulled out Colleen's bag and cooler. "To say the girls missed you would be an understatement," Jay said. "Okay, girls, it's my turn now."

As the girls released their mother, her pants began to slide down. Jay hadn't seen her for seven days and she had lost another seven pounds. "My God, honey, your clothes are

falling off. We need to take you shopping for Mother's Day."
He helped her roll the waist to keep them from falling down.

Colleen kept her eyes fixed on the waistband of her pants.
Even with her weight loss, her waist still wasn't as tiny as
Holly Brinkley's. Her waist would never be as tiny as Holly
Brinkley's. She didn't care. She wasn't Holly Brinkley. She was
Colleen Ann O'Brien Adler. Tonight she would find out who
Jay wanted to be with.

THE FOUR OF THEM WEAVED their way in and out of the various
boutiques that lined Southport Street. Mabel and Chloe
helped select clothing for Colleen to try on.

"Make sure it has an L or XL on the tag," Colleen said.

Colleen walked out of the dressing room. The girls began
giggling and Jay looked at her with a smirk.

"What?" she said.

"Mommy, those clothes are too big for you," Chloe said.

The sales associate was summoned by their laughter.

"Would you like me to help you find some clothes for your
mom?" the salesgirl said to Mabel and Chloe.

The girls excitedly trailed the salesgirl. They returned with
several black articles of clothing. "The girls said your favorite
color was black," the salesgirl said.

"Not anymore. My new rule is 'no black.' I need color,
lots and lots of color," Colleen said. The joy that brought the
girls was unexpected. With the help of the salesgirl, Mabel
and Chloe filled Colleen's dressing room with various outfits.
Colleen stood in utter disbelief as she looked at her reflection
in the full-length mirror, comfortably wearing a size 10.
"Colleen Ann O'Brien, you are beautiful and I love you, I

really, really love you," she said into the mirror softly as she looked into her tearful eyes.

FRESH OUT OF THE SHOWER, Colleen sat wrapped in a towel on the settee in the center of her closet. She glanced over at her navy Raina Rose dress. The navy blue embroidered silk fabric was gorgeous. She didn't care if she was overdressed tonight, she would look beautiful. She unzipped the back, and one side at a time she slid the dress off the hanger. She stepped into the dress and it pulled up over her hips. She reached back and zipped the dress. It sagged off her shoulders, gapped in the front and back, and there were inches between her waist and the waistline of the dress. It didn't fit. She looked like she was playing dress-up in someone else's clothes. She slid her arms out from the sleeves and let the dress fall to the floor. All the worrying, the fantasy of blowing everyone away, the hating herself when she bit into pizzas and scones and ate leftovers from the kids' plates... All that, and the dress was too big. She'd gone right past the exit and hadn't even seen the sign. The dress folded on itself, folds of navy embellished silk curling over on itself like a fading flower. She bent forward, lifted the rich material into her hands one last time and flung the dress over to the corner of her closet.

She felt strange and liberated. Looking around her closet, she grabbed her new jeans. Despite being skeptical of the "new technology" in designer jeans that the salesgirl told her about, she went ahead and tried them on. The salesgirl was right; she looked great in the jeans. Paired with oversized blouses or a tunic, the dark denim had an incredible slimming effect.

She selected the flowing eggplant purple rayon blouse for tonight. Of the five new tops she'd purchased, this one was her favorite. Her heart fluttered when she read medium on the tag. The blouse lay perfectly over her jeans. She loved the design of the floral embroidery across the top of the blouse and loved it even more when the salesgirl told her it was inspired by traditional designs of Latin America. Its bold colors popped against the dark color of the top.

In homage to Brockville, she pulled down her old dusty cowboy boots from a high shelf in her closet. She hadn't worn them for at least eight years, since the night she'd naively worn them to a dinner with Dinah. Horrified by the boots, Dinah asked if Colleen had mistaken the dinner for a country hoedown. Well, she no longer cared what Dinah thought. She dusted the boots, revealing the floral cut-out design in the distressed brown leather. She smoothed her hair back into a bun, applied navy blue eyeliner, another layer of mascara and some raspberry pink lip gloss. She was ready.

She admired her new clothes while she thought about what she was going to say to Jay. She didn't care if she ever went to the Harborview Country Club again. No matter what happened with Jay, she was going to suggest they cancel their membership. She took three cleansing breaths as she processed how different things might be in just a few short hours. Jay could very well confess to being in love with another woman, or at the very least, he might admit to sleeping with another woman. Colleen told herself she could handle whatever it was he told her. She thought of what Johnny had written about her. "Courage," she said to herself.

Her boots clicked against the wooden stairs. Jay froze as

he watched her walk down the steps. "Who are you and what have you done with my wife?" Jay said.

Colleen brought her lips together, rubbing her gloss nervously. "I think I finally found her," she said with a weak smile.

The ride from the Adlers' house to Green Coast Cafe took fifteen minutes. Jay had been thoughtful to seek out a restaurant that served healthy organic food that was both gluten- and dairy-free. Jay put the car in park, turned the ignition and opened the door. Colleen sat still.

"Something wrong?" Jay asked.

Colleen kept her eyes straight ahead. She wasn't sure how to confront Jay. She never worked out the right words. She cleared her throat. "Did you sleep with Holly Brinkley?" she said. "If you did, I need to know. I need you to be honest. I can handle it."

Jay shut his door. He shifted his body toward Colleen. "What?" he said.

Colleen brought her eyes toward Jay. He guided her head all the way toward him. "What are you talking about?" His face looked as though it had been slapped. "I would never do that to you," Jay said, "I would never do that to us."

Tears filled Colleen's eyes. "I wouldn't blame you if you did," she said.

"Why would you think that?" Jay brought her hands up in his and kissed the tops of her fingers. "That has never happened with her or anyone else. You are my wife. You are the only one I want." He looked at her. "You have to believe that."

Colleen wanted to believe Jay's words. "But the picture

on Facebook. You drank champagne with her. The way you looked at her. What was that?"

"I don't know the picture you're referring to. I'm not on Facebook. The only evening I spent with Holly was at Alexis's Gallery party. Alexis introduced us because of Gabby and the work Holly's been doing with the Latino community. I wasn't even at the party for an hour," Jay said.

"Partying with Chad Chenick and beautiful women. Was Holly part of that?"

"Holly was not part of that or anything else. You know going out with my clients is part of my job. It's also a part I don't enjoy very much. I do what I need to do to keep clients happy but I have never been unfaithful to you. Never."

Colleen reached up and wiped the tears from his eyes. She kissed him. She savored the peppermint taste of his mouth and the enticing smell of his rosemary shampoo. She wanted him more at that moment than she had in a very long time.

Jay rested his forehead against Colleen's. "All I ever wanted since I was a kid was to have a family. Even before my dad died, we were never a family. It was always me, Eli and the nanny. I always envied what you had with your family. What my friends had with their families. You've given me a family. I would never do anything to risk what we have," Jay said.

Colleen, weak with relief, remained silent for a few seconds as she remained close to Jay. She felt ridiculous for allowing her obsession to go on for as long as it had. Why had she gotten so carried away? She should have just asked Jay right away. But if she'd done that, everything that she had accomplished over the past month would have been lost.

"I love you," Colleen said. "I'm starving. Let's go eat."

SEVENTEEN

"Colleen, is that really you?" Gertrude said. She brought her red-rimmed glasses up from the chain hanging around her neck and put them on top of her nose as she came out from behind the front desk. "I don't even recognize you!"

Colleen gave Gertrude a hug. "At times, I don't recognize myself."

Kory walked into the waiting area. "Look at you!" she said. "Someone went shopping."

"I barely recognize her," Gertrude said to Kory.

"This outfit is so you," Kory said. "Where did you find those boots? I absolutely love them. Are they handmade?"

"These are so old. I bought them in Texas right after Jay and I got engaged," Colleen said.

"They're gorgeous. So different from what you see around here. They look like they belong with my old teapot," Kory said.

Colleen laughed as she thought of her boots sitting high up on a shelf collecting dust because she didn't think they fit into her "perfect" world.

"I think it is safe to say that you have won the prize as quickest to transform in my program," Kory said. "How much have you lost?"

"Almost thirty pounds," Colleen said.

"I knew you could do it, but I have to admit that I didn't think you would do it so fast. You were pretty broken when we started working together four weeks ago. What do you think has been the biggest help?"

"Probably a tie between the detox and my meeting with Rachel," Colleen said. "They both freed me of the things I held on to that were holding me back. Embracing a healthier diet and breaking my habit of drinking so much wine every night made a huge difference in my weight. The messages from Johnny that Rachel was able to communicate to me helped me release the sadness I had been carrying around and helped me see the importance of having my family in my life."

"How was your trip?" Kory said.

"Outside of the fact that I arrived to find my dad in the hospital from a heart attack, it was great," Colleen said.

"Oh my goodness," Kory said. "Is he okay?"

"He just needs to slow down a little," Colleen said.

"Quite a weekend," Kory said.

"Last night Jay and I had a long talk. I never told you this, but I thought he was having an affair. Thankfully, he wasn't. But that was a big part of the reason I wanted to lose weight," Colleen said. "My insecurity brought me to you — you helped me take the steps I needed to take to learn the truth about myself and ultimately, the truth about my marriage." Colleen wiped her eyes with a tissue. "I don't know how I can ever thank you."

"You just did," Kory said.

"Over dinner last night, Jay and I decided that the girls and I are going to spend the summer in Brockville," Colleen said.

"He's going to drive down every Friday and take the month of July off as vacation."

"Your parents must be beside themselves," Kory said.

"I haven't told them yet. I'm going to call them this afternoon." They would be more excited than ever after what she and Jay had discussed at dinner. At least she hoped they would. Colleen forced herself to focus on Kory's face. Her thighs were trembling, not from fat, but with emotion.

"Today is your last day of the detox. How do you feel about that?" Kory said.

"Nervous. I'm scared of falling back into my old habits — scared I'm going to gain my weight back," Colleen said.

"You know what got you here. You can easily come back if you feel weight coming on. Let's plan biweekly maintenance sessions over the phone from the farm this summer. Slowly add a few things that you miss back into your diet — within reason. We can go through the things you miss and want to add back in," Kory said.

"I miss coffee. I ended up having a cup with my parents every morning while I was there," Colleen said.

"Coffee's fine. Just make sure you aren't becoming overly reliant on it. Don't add sugar to it and drink it black if you can. If you find yourself needing it every afternoon to get through the day, you need to pause and look at the other parts of your life and ask yourself: Are you getting enough quality sleep?" Kory said. "How's your nutrition?" she went on.

"I'm going to use Billy until the girls and I head to my parents. I'm not sure what it will be like eating my mom's food. I'm going to need some healthy recipes," Colleen said.

"The detox book I gave you at the beginning has a lot of

great recipes. I will put together a few more but remember healthy food doesn't have to be complicated. Salt, pepper and a drizzle of olive oil on a piece of meat and vegetables is all you need. You can grill it or roast in the oven," Kory said. "Keep up with the smoothies. Did you get a blender yet?"

"No, but I'll get one before Brockville. I'm not sure if I can get my mom and dad to drink them, but I'm going to try." Colleen laughed.

"How is the exercising going?" Kory said.

"I actually jogged today!" Colleen said.

"That's wonderful!" Kory said.

"My legs were wobbly, but I really enjoyed it," Colleen said.

"You're amazing, Colleen Adler. Let's celebrate all of this success and prepare you for your next adventure. How do you feel about another meditation?" Kory said.

COLLEEN SETTLED IN WITH A bottle of water on her front porch couch after her meeting with Kory. She wished she was able to deliver her news to her parents in person but she didn't want to wait that long. She dialed her parents' home phone. Normally, no one would be home at this time of the day but her dad was supposed to be taking it easy.

"What a surprise," John said, hearing Colleen's voice. "When are you guys coming down?"

"Remember when you said that technically, the farmhouse was already supposed to be mine?"

"That's how it's always gone in the past," he said. "Well, until your generation."

"I've decided I want to take over the house now," Colleen said.

"Everything okay between you and Jay?" John said.

"Things are great between us — better than they've ever been. I want to take over the responsibility of the house. I want to take over the ownership."

John was quiet for a few seconds. "Not sure I'm following you, honey."

"Starting now, I want take over all expenses of the house. I want you and mom to stay living there and take care of it," Colleen said.

"Um-hum," John said in the way he did when he was processing new information.

"There's a condition — you have to accept payment for looking after the house and for managing some work I want done."

"We can't accept payment from you," John said.

"It's the only way Jay and I will do it. There's another thing — you have to deal with me and the girls spending the entire summer there."

"What about Jay?" John said.

"He'll come on the weekends and will be there most of July — he's taking the month as vacation." If things go well, she hoped to leave the girls with her parents for a weekend or two so she could meet Jay in Chicago or New York. They hadn't had a romantic weekend alone together since the girls had been born.

"Honey, I'm not sure my heart can handle all of this," John said. He sounded like he was crying. "There's nothing I want more than you and your beautiful family here, but, honey, we can't accept payment from you."

"It's the only way," Colleen said. She would work on

getting her dad to rent their portion of the farm to Nate over the summer. Jay said he could easily put a rental agreement together for them. "I should have done it a long time ago," Colleen said.

He sat silent for a few minutes. "Honey, it's yours."

Colleen wanted to reach through the phone and give her dad a hug. "There's one last thing," Colleen said. "I want to build a swimming pool in the backyard."

"A pool?" John said. "Wait until I tell your mom."

COLLEEN PULLED UP IN FRONT of SS Beauty Bar and parked her car. She walked in to find another new young woman working the reception desk.

"I'm here to see Sandy," Colleen said.

Colleen took a seat and waited. She watched as the young women walked by checking their reflection in the mirrors surrounding the waiting area. Colleen sensed the girls' insecurities as she watched them. They were all so young and beautiful — no reason in the world to be insecure. Colleen no longer saw the girls' behavior as arrogant and aloof. Instead, she was sad for them. She felt a tug to tell them all about Kory.

"My God, you look wonderful!" Sandy said as she walked over. "I have you down for a keratin treatment today," she said as she began to organize her station.

"I want to do something different today," Colleen said.

Sandy stopped what she was doing and looked at Colleen.

"I want to cut my hair short," Colleen said.

"Are you sure? This gorgeous hair?" Sandy ran her fingers through Colleen's long hair.

"I want something that is easier to manage," Colleen said.

"I guess we can cut it shorter but first let's do the treatment," Sandy said.

"No treatment. I want to go back to curly," Colleen said.

"Really?" Sandy said. "You always hated it curly."

"That was before," Colleen said.

SHE WALKED OUT OF THE salon feeling as though she'd lost another thirty pounds. Her long hair was gone. Just as she saw in her dream, long strands of hair fell to her lap and onto the ground. Her chin-length curls bounce as she walked. She felt like dancing and laughing, just as her great-grandmother Mabel had.

The weather was too beautiful to go home. Colleen's energy led her down the sidewalk and into the cute boutique shops outside of SS Beauty Bar. Shopping with Jay and the girls had been so liberating. She wanted to buy a few more things for the summer ahead.

Colleen turned her head toward the sound of a car horn followed by clopping of high heels. Dinah, obviously too busy to walk the half a block to the crosswalk, stopped traffic as she jaywalked across the street. She looked as though she had just stepped off the spring runway in her white silk jumpsuit. Colleen had never seen Dinah wear such a low-cut top. The deep V-neck, adorned with fringe, revealed Dinah's most recent breast enhancement. Her once perfectly round tennis ball–sized breasts were now the size of softballs. They looked out of place on her small body. Dinah's sophistication vanished from Colleen's eyes.

"Dinah," Colleen said.

Turning around to see who called her name, Dinah

peeled away her oversized gold sunglasses. She didn't seem to recognize the person in front of her. "Oh, Colleen," she said, then paused to look Colleen up and down. "I thought you were with your parents." Her tone was accusatory and anything but pleasant. "You can imagine my disappointment on Mother's Day."

"I had a really nice time in Brockville, and my dad's doing much better," Colleen said, even though she knew Dinah didn't care.

"Did you bring those boots back with you? Your feet must be suffocating."

Colleen looked down at her boots before glancing to Dinah's feet. Multicolored glitter and crystal embellished flowers sat atop of Dinah's red-painted toes. "My feet are really comfortable," Colleen said as she brought her eyes up to Dinah.

"And what on earth have you done to your hair?" Dinah shook her head and rolled her eyes as she put her sunglasses back on. "Running late, got to go." She swung her floral-embroidered handbag over her shoulder and walked away.

Why a woman in her seventies would walk around in six-inch stilettos was a mystery to Colleen. She couldn't help but to laugh at why she ever let that woman bother her. She pointed her face up to the brilliant sunshine and took a deep breath into her heart, sending a prayer of forgiveness and gratitude. She had to forgive Dinah, just as Kory had taught her to forgive herself. She remembered one of the sayings that hung on the wall in Kory's office: *How people treat you is their karma; how you react is yours —— Wayne Dyer.*

EIGHTEEN

Saturday, May 25, 2011
Brockville, IL

Jay stopped in the gravel lane of Farm Five-Thirty-Five and pulled his iPhone from the pocket of his shorts. "Four-point-two-three miles," he said.

"I can't think of a better way to spend my time than walking out here across the land that's supported the past four generations of O'Briens," Colleen said.

"Our farm." Jay smiled and shook his head in wonder. He held Colleen's hand as they walked up the lane toward the house.

"What's Chloe doing?" Colleen said.

Chloe was on her bike pedaling as fast as her little legs would go. She careened from behind the handlebars heading straight toward them. Her hair, now chin length like Colleen's, blew away from her face to reveal an excited smile. Nelson and Cash trotted along behind her, curious where their new friend was leading them. Colleen's dad had gotten Mabel and Chloe each a new kitten. Chloe's kitten was having the ride of its life up in the little pink basket of her bicycle. As she got closer, Jay and Colleen couldn't help but laugh at her chosen ensemble of Hello Kitty pajama pants over her hot pink, polka-dot swimsuit.

"What's sticking out of her pants?" Jay said as Chloe got close.

"Mom, Dad, hurry! Grandpa said the pool temperature is eighty degrees. We can get in!" Chloe squealed before slowing down to turn her bike back the other direction toward the house. "Oh, and Grandma taught Mabel how to flip pancakes. We are having blueberry pancakes because it's Uncle Johnny's favorite. Mabel and I are going to help Grandma make a cake later so we can celebrate Uncle Johnny's birthday."

Jay and Colleen both stared at the protruding lumps in Chloe's pajama bottoms. "Honey, what's in your pockets?" Jay said.

"Eggs. Grandpa taught me how to get the eggs from the chickens in the coop," she said. "Bye!" She was off.

"My mom always said, there's no time for beauty and fashion on the farm," Colleen laughed.

Colleen sat on the porch swing and stared out at the field in front of her. The long, narrow green leaves on the rows of cornstalks swayed in the wind as their yellow tassels reached up high to receive the light from up above. The long winter provided dormancy for the soil, enabling it to give birth to another cycle of life. Colleen's dormancy was also over. She had planted her own seeds and nurtured them into life. She was rising up and shining through just like the plants in the distance. Abundant with gratitude, she was blooming into life.

ABOUT THE AUTHOR

Kristie Booker is the author of *Blooming Into Life*, a blogger and a Wellness Coach. She enjoys coaching and inspiring women through her writing as well as in person. Kristie lives in Chicago with her husband and two sons.

Visit her at www.kristiebooker.com or on Facebook.

Made in the USA
Lexington, KY
12 April 2018